Praise for
If Only in My Dreams

"[A] unique blend of romance, history, and fantasy. Thoroughly original and unpredictable, Markham's latest is a delight."   —*Booklist*

"The fantastic setup is balanced with convincing period details and strong characters, and the story's conclusion is unexpectedly real and refreshing. . . . A subtle, effective, and enjoyable entry into the growing field of time-travel romance."   —*Publishers Weekly*

"One of the most romantic love stories of the year; have the tissues near when you sit down to read *If Only in My Dreams*. . . . Fresh and original; an excellent time-travel that is unpredictable and thoroughly romantic . . . a perfect 10."   —Romance Designs

"[The] best book I have read in 2006, if not this century. . . . *If Only in My Dreams* takes place in 2006 and 1941. The transition between times is done smoothly. The characters come alive right from the first sentence. This is a book I would recommend to everyone."   —Romance Readers

"*If Only in My Dreams* requires a handful of Kleenex. The story is poignant and packed with a holiday feel that leaves lasting impressions with the reader. . . . Wendy Markham's writing is at her best. Easily, this is her best story to date."   —Roundtable Reviews

continued . . .

Also by Wendy Markham

If Only in My Dreams

The
Best Gift

Wendy Markham

A SIGNET ECLIPSE BOOK

SIGNET ECLIPSE
Published by New American Library, a division of
Penguin Group (USA) Inc., 375 Hudson Street,
New York, New York 10014, USA
Penguin Group (Canada), 90 Eglinton Avenue East, Suite 700, Toronto,
Ontario M4P 2Y3, Canada (a division of Pearson Penguin Canada Inc.)
Penguin Books Ltd., 80 Strand, London WC2R 0RL, England
Penguin Ireland, 25 St. Stephen's Green, Dublin 2,
Ireland (a division of Penguin Books Ltd.)
Penguin Group (Australia), 250 Camberwell Road, Camberwell, Victoria 3124,
Australia (a division of Pearson Australia Group Pty. Ltd.)
Penguin Books India Pvt. Ltd., 11 Community Centre, Panchsheel Park,
New Delhi - 110 017, India
Penguin Group (NZ), 67 Apollo Drive, Rosedale, North Shore 0632,
New Zealand (a division of Pearson New Zealand Ltd.)
Penguin Books (South Africa) (Pty.) Ltd., 24 Sturdee Avenue,
Rosebank, Johannesburg 2196, South Africa

Penguin Books Ltd., Registered Offices:
80 Strand, London WC2R 0RL, England

First published by Signet Eclipse, an imprint of New American Library,
a division of Penguin Group (USA) Inc.

First Printing, November 2009
10 9 8 7 6 5 4 3 2 1

Dedicated with love and gratitude
to my dear friend and third-grade teacher,
Janet Pizzolanti Foster,
who told an eight-year-old that she could write.
And to the two Lauras—
Cifelli and Blake Peterson—
thank you for making this happen . . . again!
And to my three patient guys: Mark,
Morgan, and Brody:
The book is done, and today is Mother's Day . . .
I'm ready to go celebrate now!

Prologue

New York City
October 2008

This isn't the first time Clara Becker has ridden the rickety old elevator to the fourth floor in the prewar Bronx apartment building, and she doesn't like to think that it might be the last.

But reality can't be ignored, and so she does her best to memorize the exquisite grillwork on the elevator door, and the echoing creak as it slides open, and the scent of pot roast that greets her in the corridor.

Always pot roast. Maybe one of the fourth-floor tenants actually cooks the same thing day in and day out. Or maybe it's simply a homey cooking smell that evokes the nostalgia of pot roast, family, and cozy rainy days indoors.

Today is a rainy day, all right—but she hasn't

spent much of it indoors. She ran errands all morning, then met her good friend and former makeup artist Jesus DeJesus in Tribeca for lunch.

"What's the occasion?" he had asked when she suggested an upscale bistro, her treat.

"No occasion. I just miss you," she had told him—not the entire truth. Yes, she did miss him; they hadn't seen each other nearly as often since she'd gotten married and ceased being a regularly employed actress.

But that was not the only reason she had wanted to have lunch. She was pretty sure, though, that if she'd said she had something to tell him, he'd have gotten the wrong idea. Aware that she'd been auditioning again lately, he might have assumed she'd landed a plum role in some film—or at least back in the soaps, where she'd spent her early career.

That couldn't have been farther from what she had to tell him—and when she had broken the real news, his reaction had been even more dramatic than she'd anticipated.

"Noooooo!" he had wailed. "How could you do this to me?"

She hadn't bothered to point out that it wasn't really about *him*. Jesus has a notorious flair for making *everything* about him. She used to find it an endearing quirk, but it had worn thin pretty quickly today.

"Can't you just be happy for me?" she had said, interrupting his ongoing lament.

"How can I be happy knowing this is going to be the final nail in the coffin of our friendship?"

Clara had been emotionally spent by the time she'd left the restaurant and hopped on the subway to the Bronx. She hopes Doris won't take the news as hard.

Reaching the door marked 4D, she knocks loudly with the heel of her palm, the way Doris taught her to do.

"Don't be shy—for God's sake, give it some good solid whacks," the old woman had told her on her first visit. "Otherwise I'll never hear you and you'll stand out here for days."

"Hold your horses—I'm here. I'm here," a familiar voice calls now from the other side of the door. When it flies open, Clara momentarily expects, as always, to find herself looking at an adolescent tomboy with red pigtails, freckles, and impish blue eyes.

The eyes are impish, all right, and the same deep shade of blue. But they're peering at her through a thick pair of bifocals. It's been decades since the freckles faded from a face now trenched with wrinkles and the red pigtails gave way to a snow-white updo.

Decades since this octogenarian was a precocious kid sister. Jed's kid sister.

"What a nice surprise!" She hugs Clara. "You poor thing, you're drenched. Don't you have an umbrella?"

"I do, but it's that sideways kind of rain that soaks you anyway." Clara tries to shake the droplets from her long brown hair, but wringing it out would probably be more effective.

"Oh, and I brought a little treat for you." She hands over a white paper shopping bag.

Doris peeks inside, then lets out a delighted squeal. "Licorice snaps! Aren't you a sweetheart. Thank you."

"You're welcome."

"You really shouldn't have. I know money is tight, and these aren't cheap." Like a little girl, Doris tears into the package and pops a couple of the bright-colored candies into her mouth. "Do you know that when I was a girl, these used to sell for two cents a box?"

Clara does know, because Doris has told her. Several times. Like most elderly people, she likes to reminisce and tends to repeat herself. But of course, Clara hangs on to every word because Doris's memories are particularly meaningful to her.

"They came in a red box back in the old days. I used to go to the movies with my brother Jed and he'd buy them for me."

Clara smiles. She knows that, too. But not because Doris ever told her.

Jed did.

Doris pries a piece of licorice from a tooth with her fingertip and smacks her lips.

"Everything changes in this world, but licorice snaps still taste the same. Only problem is, when I was young I didn't have to worry that they'd rip out my dentures." She offers Clara the box. "Here, have some."

"Oh, no thanks. I wouldn't want anything to happen to my dentures."

Doris, who always appreciates even the weakest quip, chuckles at that. "Come in, come in. Let's go sit on the couch and visit."

Watching her close the door and turn away, Clara says, "You really should slide the dead bolt and the chain, you know, Doris. This neighborhood isn't as safe as it used to be."

"Oh, ish kabibble. If anyone wants to come on in, they can just help themselves to anything they want—except my licorice snaps," she adds slyly, leading the way to the knickknack-cluttered living room.

The two large windows are spattered with raindrops, and there are several hummingbird feeders hanging outside. Doris collects everything related to hummingbirds—figurines, jewelry, even feeders, though she admits it would be unusual to see the tiny birds buzzing around her urban fire escape.

"Still, I never say never," she says, a favorite

phrase—about hummingbirds, and various other topics.

"You know, my kids finally gave up on trying to get me to move in with them."

"I don't think that would have been such a bad idea, though."

"It's a terrible idea. They're scattered all over the damned globe."

Well, not exactly. But Doris's family is pretty spread out—a daughter in Reno, a son in Boston, another who just retired to Florida.

"Then they wanted to talk me into one of those horrid places filled with old coots, but—"

"Assisted living," Clara cuts in, sitting beside her on the couch, "and they're actually kind of nice. My mother and stepfather are—"

"I'm sure other people do just fine, but me, I'm staying put. This is my home. I like it here."

"But—"

"Honey, if it works, don't fix it. That's what I say."

That *is* what she says—often. Along with "never say never," and countless other phrases Clara has come to consider Dorisisms.

"Like I told my kids, when I leave this place for the last time, it'll be in a body bag."

Clara cringes. "Doris, don't—"

"And my kids, when they're not harping on

me to move, they're telling me it's about time I started unloading some of this stuff." She waves a wrinkled hand around the room.

"Why?"

"I'm sure they think I'm going to kick the bucket any second now, and they'll be stuck having to come back here and clean it all out."

"Oh, Doris, I'm sure they don't—"

"Of course they do, and it doesn't bother me at all. I'd be thinking the same thing if I were them. That's how it was when my mother was getting up there in years." With a conspiratorial twinkle in her eye, she adds, "I made good and sure my brother Gilbert got stuck with cleaning out the old house—which I'm afraid didn't work out so well for you, my dear."

Doris is referring to the fact that Gilbert accidentally gave away to an antiques store a gift-wrapped package that had been stored in the attic since the early 1940s, intended as a Christmas gift from their brother Jed to his wartime sweetheart.

"Oh, it worked out in the end," she reminds Doris.

"So it did." With weathered fingertips, Doris pats Clara's left hand—the one that has worn a gold wedding band since her wedding last year. "And now you believe in magic. As you should."

Clara smiles, too. But it fades when she remembers why she came here today.

"Doris—this isn't just a social visit. I have to tell you something."

"Is it good news or bad?"

"That depends on how you look at it."

"Do I need something stronger than licorice snaps to hear it?"

Clara grins again—but it's bittersweet. She's going to miss Doris terribly.

"Do you remember how I told you that my husband lost his job at the investment firm?"

"Your husband and everyone else on Wall Street. Hard times."

It's impossible to tell by looking at Doris or her modest home that she once made a killing in the stock market. She prefers to live a low-key lifestyle, money or not, in the same rent-controlled apartment where she shared a long, happy marriage with her late husband.

"Are *you* okay?" Clara asks her now, caught off guard by the grim look on her face. "Financially, I mean."

"I had a lot of investments. You win some, you lose some." Doris shrugs. "Let's put it this way: I've got enough money to last a lifetime— as long as it's just whatever's left of this one. Tell me about your husband."

"He's been looking for something else, but it hasn't been easy. And I've been auditioning again, but once you've dropped out of sight for a while—well, that's not easy, either. Anyway, he finally found something decent, and they made him an offer last week—more money, even, than he was making, and he accepted, and it's a great opportunity . . ."

Doris claps her hands together. "Wonderful!"

". . . in California."

Doris raises a white eyebrow.

"He starts next week."

"You're moving away."

Clara nods. "The job is in the Bay area, and that's where he's from, so we'll have family there. . . ."

"That's important." Doris pats her hand. "And remember, you'll always have family here, too."

Clara swallows a lump in her throat. "It's going to be really hard to leave. I've lived here all my life."

"Good-byes are always hard. But you can't let that stop you. This is a wonderful opportunity for you and your husband to build a new life together. Smile when you look back, but don't be afraid to move on. You have to go live. Live for today, live for each other, live for yourself."

"You're the smartest woman I have ever known, Doris. I'm going to miss you."

"I'll miss you, too, my dear. But we'll see each other again, I'm sure."

"I'm sure," Clara echoes, but she isn't at all.

"I know what you're thinking."

She looks up in surprise to see Doris watching her closely, blue eyes sharper than ever.

"You're thinking exactly what my kids are thinking."

"Doris! Of course I'm not—"

"No, not about cleaning out all this crap I've accumulated over the years, but about my kicking the bucket. Come on, who are we kidding? I'm getting up there in years. I might not be around the next time you get back to New York for a visit."

"Don't say that."

"You listen to me, Clara. I'll be around. If not here—if not in this lifetime—I'll catch up with you sooner or later, right? Because I believe in magic, and so do you. Don't ever forget it."

Clara smiles through her tears. "I won't. I won't ever forget."

Chapter 1

San Florentina, California
Christmas Day 2009

Sitting cross-legged on the rug beside the lit Christmas tree on her favorite day of the year, Clara clutches the mug of untouched coffee her husband had insisted on preparing for her when she rolled out of bed forty-five minutes ago.

Drew shakes the gift-wrapped box. "Hey, it rattles."

She smiles. "No kidding."

He shakes it some more, watching her face for a clue. Clara glances away, feigning profound interest in a floating dust particle, afraid that if Drew looks into her eyes, he'll know.

She admires the living room, its mission woodwork, tall windows, leather furniture, warm-hued carpets, and draperies all bathed in the soft glow of twinkling white lights. They had moved into the house just in time for Clara to deck the halls.

Her gaze sweeps the massive boxwood wreath on the exposed brick above the fireplace. A pair of embroidered Christmas stockings is hanging from the wooden mantel, and a precious antique snow globe is nested on it amid potted poinsettias and her childhood collection of dark-haired angel figurines.

Beyond the snow globe's delicate curved glass is yet another brunette angel, one with a broken wing tip. If you wind the key on the globe's base, it plays "I'll Be Home for Christmas."

Drew found it in an antiques shop and gave it to her the Christmas they met, back in New York. Of course, he had no idea just how meaningful— or magical—it really was. Maybe someday she'll work up the nerve to tell him.

In any case, it's the best gift she ever received from her husband.

From anyone.

And now Drew is about to open one that's even better.

"You know, I really have no idea what this could be."

"Well, let's see. . . ." Carefully masking her expression, Clara dares to look his way again. "It can be something that rattles."

"No kidding. Like what?" He shakes it again, and she grins.

Right here, right now, on Christmas morning in the wonderland living room of their dream house, a bank of fog that looks almost like snow swirling beyond the wall of glass windows, Clara can't help but feel as if she finally has everything she's ever wanted.

No, she hasn't become a Hollywood superstar. She blew that chance when she got sick and dropped out of what would have been her first major film.

The Glenhaven Park Dozen, which opened last year, was nominated for a slew of Oscars, including Best Picture—and Best Actress for the newcomer who was recast in Clara's role.

That stung a little, because she *did* love acting, and she does miss it.

Just not enough to make all the necessary sacrifices that go with the territory.

Like spending months on location away from Drew.

Or giving up her privacy.

Or watching every morsel she puts into her mouth in an effort to stay starlet-thin. Having cancer taught her to love her body because it's strong and healthy now, even if she did go up a jeans size or two.

Maybe someday, she'll want to give her career another shot. But for now, things are perfect just as they are.

Almost . . . too perfect.

So perfect that if she allows herself to think about it, she might just worry that it could all go away tomorrow.

That's how it happens. One minute, you're living your too-good-to-be-true life, and the next minute, you're . . .

Well, *not*.

Please don't let it happen to me. To us.

"It sounds like a box of pebbles," Drew tells her.

"Why would I give you a box of pebbles?"

"To remind me of that weekend we spent at Pebble Beach last fall?"

"Um, no."

"That would have been a romantic gift."

"Trust me," she says, "this is much more romantic."

As romantic as being married to the love of her life, a kindhearted man with the warmest, most reassuring brown eyes she's ever seen. A man whose vow to stay with her in sickness and in health, for richer and for poorer, for better and for worse, has already been tested and held fast.

Her breast cancer, his losing his investment banking job in Manhattan and finding a new one that meant a cross-country move, building their dream house only to have Drew lose his new job, too, thanks to a tanking economy . . .

They've survived all of that, and then some. Life is good. After some financial struggles, Drew found another promising job. He started just last week. Clara has passed the three-year anniversary of her diagnosis, and remains cancer free.

"Everything looks great," her West Coast oncologist, Dr. Federman, remarked after the last round of routine tests in November, which again showed the all clear. He snapped his folder shut and smiled across his desk at her and Drew. "You two should go out and celebrate."

They promptly drove over to Napa and splurged on a romantic inn on a vineyard. A candlelit dinner, a bottle of good champagne, a wonderful feather bed . . .

When she later looked back, counting days on the calendar, and realized that was when it had happened, she wasn't really surprised. It had been a perfect night.

There's that word again. Perfect.

Stop being a worrywart. Life is good. Enjoy it.

Yes, here on a windswept cliff overlooking the Pacific Ocean, Clara is ready to put down roots, raise a family, grow old together with Drew.

"Something rattle-y and romantic. A box of diamonds?"

She rolls her eyes.

"Cap'n Crunch?"

"How is that romantic?"

"It's what we had for breakfast the first time you spent the night at my apartment. Don't tell me you forgot?"

"No, I remember, but, enough already! Just open the present and find out what it is!"

"All right, all right, I'm opening, I'm opening."

Uh-huh. Most people would tear into the paper. Not her husband.

Nope. He takes his time, deliberately—and maddeningly—slipping one fingertip beneath the seam to loosen the tape.

"Nice wrapping paper."

Clara nods and smiles through clenched teeth.

"Is this one of the rolls you bought from the little girl next door for that school fund-raiser? What's her name?"

"Amelia. Amelia Tucker," she adds, wondering whether he's trying to drive her crazy on purpose.

Can he possibly know what's inside and he's somehow . . . reluctant to open it?

Nah.

If he knew, he wouldn't be reluctant at all.

Anyway, after almost two years of marriage,

she knows that's just the way he is: always sa-
voring the moment.

And it's just the way she isn't. A native New
Yorker, she is, as Drew likes to say, in a perpetual state of hurry, scurry, and flurry.

It was all she could do not to coach him
along as he painstakingly opened all the other
presents she gave him, then meticulously folded
every shirt, sweater, and tie back into their
boxes and stacked them neatly under the tree,
along with her big splurge for him: the Filson
bag he's been coveting for years.

Clara, on the other hand, is surrounded by
crumpled paper and a heap of new treasures:
a decadent designer purse, the pair of ridicu-
lously expensive shearling slippers she paused
to admire every time they passed the window
display at Triangle Shoes down the street, a
couple of books, emerald earrings Drew sweetly
said match her eyes, and a bikini for their annual February trip to the Caribbean.

"Isn't it a little . . . skimpy?" she asked in
dismay, holding it up.

"Hell, yeah." He grinned. "And I can't wait
to see you in it on the beach."

Ha.

Little does he know.

"Are you going to open that," she asks now,
watching him put aside the wrapping paper

and shake the gift again, "or just play with the box?"

"Play with the box."

She sighs inwardly and pretends to take a sip from her mug as he reexamines the package, unaware that the mere smell of coffee makes her sick. So, lately, does the smell of Thai food, her favorite cuisine; it was all she could do not to vomit when Drew brought home a bagful of white cardboard carryout containers to surprise her the other night.

"I know you always like to save the best gift for last," he notes, "but that duffel bag was pretty damned good. How can you possibly top it?"

"You'll see." She offers her best mysterious smile.

"I have one more present for you, too, you know."

"You do?" Looking around, she doesn't see any more unopened gifts. "But you already got me so much, and—"

"Well, this time, I saved the best gift for last, just like you. I'll open yours, and then I'll give you mine."

"So it's not something I have to open?"

It's Drew's turn to offer a mysterious smile.

"Why do I feel like yours involves the bedroom?"

He laughs and reaches for her. "I didn't say that, but if you're in the mood for—"

"Drew! Just open the present!"

At last, he lifts the cover off the box and lifts out . . .

"A baby rattle?"

"Uh-huh." Tears rapidly fill her eyes and the puzzled look on his face disappears into a watery blur.

By the time she's blindly set aside her mug and wiped her eyes on the sleeve of her bathrobe, his clueless expression has been replaced by one of wonderment—and some tears of his own.

"Clara . . . ?"

She nods, her throat too clogged with emotion to say it aloud.

He grabs her, hugs her fiercely.

"We're going to have a baby?"

Recovering her voice, she sob/sings the word that's been joyfully pirouetting through her head since she got the news weeks ago: "Yes!"

Yes, yes, yes!

After months of trying, she, Clara McCallum Becker, is finally pregnant.

Dr. Svensen, her oncologist back in New York, had promised her that it would one day be possible. That the breast cancer treatment she'd endured three years ago wouldn't harm her reproductive organs.

But she wasn't so sure it was meant to be. Month after month, they tried. Month after month, she waited, prayed, hoped . . . to no avail.

And then, in November, in Napa, it happened.

She took a positive pregnancy test on the first Saturday in December, just before she and Drew went to see *The Nutcracker* in San Francisco. For her, the ballet is a lifelong holiday tradition—she was named after the little girl whose Christmas gifts come magically to life.

But this year, for the first time, she was too caught up in her own miraculous drama to focus on Tchaikovsky's.

Keeping the pregnancy secret from Drew was one of the hardest things she's ever had to do.

But it isn't the only secret she's ever kept from him.

At least this one is more believable, she thinks wryly as he releases her, grinning like the post-reformation Grinch.

Chances are he wouldn't be smiling like that if she told him her other secret.

"*Hey, Drew,*" she'd say casually, "*guess what? A few years ago, when I was filming* The Glenhaven Park Dozen, *I traveled back in time to December 1941 and fell in love with the real Jed*

Landry, one of the soldiers the movie was based on. Oh, yeah, and one other thing: the real Jed was killed in Normandy, but he was reincarnated. As you."

Uh-huh. Not going to happen.

In the grand scheme of things, it doesn't matter how he came to her. All that matters is that he's here.

Anyway, Drew would never believe the truth and frankly, if she hadn't lived through it, she wouldn't believe it, either.

As it is, her husband scarcely seems able to grasp the current miracle. He's patting her stomach like he's looking for evidence. But of course it's still flat—not flat like it was back when she lived on celery sticks and diet soda, but flat enough. The doctor said she probably won't start showing until after the first trimester.

"I can't . . . this is just . . ." He shakes his head in wonder. "When are you—I mean, *we*—due?"

"I'm seven weeks. Early summer."

"I'll be a daddy in early summer!"

She grins. "Yup. And I'll be a mommy."

"When did you find out?"

"A few weeks ago."

"*What?* You've known for that long and you didn't tell me? How did you manage that?"

"I'm just . . . good with secrets."

Maybe too good.

She wonders, as she has countless times in the past few years, whether she should tell him about the time travel and reincarnation after all.

But how can she ever say it out loud when hearing it in her own head makes her cringe?

Time travel.

Reincarnation.

You don't just drop those phrases into a casual conversation, even with your husband. You don't just shrug off traveling back to 1941 as if it were some everyday occurrence, something that could happen to anyone.

Why me? Why did it happen to me?

Clara wondered that very same thing when she found out about the breast cancer.

In the end, she realized that there was no rhyme or reason to any of it. All she could do was accept it and move on.

"So nobody else knows, right?"

Startled, she looks at Drew.

Oh.

They're talking about the baby.

"No! Of course not. Who would I tell before you?"

"I don't know . . . your mother?"

"You're joking, right?" The health-obsessed, fatalistic Jeanette Bradshaw will have a gazillion pregnancy worries to share with her daughter. Clara hasn't even been tempted to let her know yet about the baby. Thank God she lives on the opposite end of the continent, because she's the kind of mother who would take one look at Clara, pick up on her perpetual queasiness, and say, "You're sick. What's wrong?"

"When are we going to share the news with everyone?" Drew asks.

"I don't know. . . . Maybe we should wait until I'm through the first trimester. Until . . . you know . . . I'm past the miscarriage stage."

"Don't even say that word." Drew rubs her arm.

She's been telling herself not to even think it, either. But you can't ignore reality. Or statistics.

"I read that at least one in five pregnant women lost the baby in the first—"

"Our baby will be fine," Drew cuts in, as if that settles it, and shakes the plastic red rattle at her for emphasis.

Then, as if he suddenly remembered something, he goes absolutely still.

"What is it?"

"Uh-oh."

"What?"

"I forgot about your last present."

Relieved, she says, "No big deal."

"It might be." He gets to his feet. "Stay here."

"You don't want me to come with you?"

He shakes his head. So much for her bedroom suspicion.

"I'll go get it. And just so you know, if you don't want it because of . . . I can always . . . return it."

Mystified, she watches him head toward the back of the house. A few minutes ago, he said he'd saved the best gift for last. Why wouldn't she want it now that he knows she's pregnant?

Maybe it's another bikini. An even skimpier one. Or maybe . . . nonrefundable plane tickets to go on a trip around the baby's due date?

She hears the back door open, then close.

Okay, so he had to go outside to get it, whatever it is. Probably not plane tickets.

Clara waits.

Waits.

Waits for what seems like hours, until at last she hears the back door open again.

"I've got it," Drew calls. "Are you ready?"

"I'm ready."

"Close your eyes."

She does—then promptly opens them again at the sound of a strange, high-pitched squeal from the kitchen.

"Drew? Are you okay?"

"I'm fine. Are they closed?"

She shuts her eyes again. "Yup."

"Okay, here we come."

Wait . . . we?

"Merry Christmas, Clara. You can look now."

She opens her eyes to see her husband, wearing a red Santa hat—and clutching a Christmas stocking that contains a squirming black Lab puppy in a matching hat.

Chapter 2

For a week—ever since he decided to get Clara the puppy for Christmas—Drew tried to anticipate her reaction. Shocked delight? Shocked dismay? He wasn't sure which to expect.

Now that the moment is here, he sees on his wife's face a mixture of both delight and dismay—and shock. Definitely shock.

"What . . ." she begins, falters. "Who . . . ? Where . . . ?"

"He's all yours. I was worried we might not be able to . . . I mean, you wanted a baby so badly, and after everything you've gone through, I was afraid that . . ." He winces as the puppy puts its paws on his shoulder and licks his face. "Look, I know he's not a baby, but he's someone little for you to love and I thought he'd help you to heal if we couldn't have—"

Drew ducks as the dog knocks his Santa cap

off his head, then jerks its own cap off after it, and squirms his way out of the stocking, which also falls to the floor.

Laughing, Clara picks it up, along with the hats. "You are adorable."

"Me or the dog?"

"Both of you." She stands on tiptoes to plop Drew's cap back onto his head.

The puppy promptly snags the dangling white pom-pom and tugs the cap off again.

"Listen, Clara, if you don't want him now that we're going to have a baby after all—"

"Are you kidding?" She takes the little puppy from him and her face is instantly covered with wet doggie kisses. She hands Drew the stocking. "You should hang this up."

"So you want to keep him?"

"Definitely."

Relieved, he exhales for what feels like the first time since the news that he was going to be a dad took his breath away.

"Where did you get him?" Clara asks as the dog fervently laps her face.

"At a shelter. He's a purebred. I picked him up yesterday and he's been staying next door with the Tuckers."

"I thought you barely knew their name!"

"You're not the only actor around here."

"He's a purebred? Why would anyone give him up?"

"As I understand it, he belonged to a family on Nob Hill, and he, uh—apparently, he ate his mistress's mink coat," Drew says dryly, rubbing the puppy's head.

"He *ate* a mink coat?"

"Right. So she got rid of him."

Clara nuzzles the puppy's wet nose. "That's all right. You don't belong on Snob Hill. You belong here with us. Even if you do have the worst halitosis ever."

As if he understood and is offended, the puppy immediately wrenches himself out of her arms and scampers across the floor.

"What do you want to name him?" Drew asks, watching the ball of black fur dive into a pile of crumpled wrapping paper.

"I don't know—something Christmasy."

"Sugarplum? Since you've got that whole *Nutcracker* thing going on."

Clara grins and tilts her head. "Sugarplum . . . Sugarplum . . . I don't know. Does he look like a Sugarplum to you?"

As if on cue, the dog emerges from the wrapping paper with a red bow stuck to his head and skids across the floor.

"No. He looks like a Scamp or a Rascal to me."

As if to prove it, the puppy dives toward another heap of wrapping paper and grabs a piece in his mouth.

"Scamp and Rascal aren't Christmasy names, though," Clara points out.

"Nope," Drew agrees, absently watching him devour a chunk of paper, then admiring his wife's nicely rounded butt as she hurriedly bends over the dog.

Pondering the changes that will transform her body in the months ahead, Drew finds himself turned on and wonders whether they have time for a quick—

"Drew! Do you see what he's doing? Hey, dog, cut that out!" Clara tries to retrieve the soggy paper from his mouth. Too late.

"I can't believe he just ate paper while we were standing right here," she says helplessly.

At least Clara was on the ball enough to catch what the puppy was doing, unlike Drew, who had only one thing on his mind.

Which makes him wonder what kind of father he's going to be.

The kind who fantasizes about seducing his wife while their baby ingests household items that could be poisonous or choked on?

Thank God that Clara is the vigilant and responsible type.

"Is it dangerous to eat paper?" he asks her.

"How the heck would I know? Hopefully he'll vomit it back up."

Great. Just great.

He looks down at the dog, who seems perfectly fine. For now, anyway. Drew wonders about the incubation time for wrapping-paper-ink poison.

"How about Holly?"

Drew blinks.

"For a name," Clara reminds him. "Isn't that what we're talking about?"

No, at the moment, we're talking about how scary it is to have a puppy's life in our hands, and how much scarier it'll be when we have a baby to take care of, too.

Why did they think any of this was a good idea? Why weren't they content to leave well enough alone? Especially since well enough was pretty perfect . . .

"Drew?"

"What?"

"Holly?"

"Clara, he's a guy."

"Oh. Right. Noel?"

"That isn't a guy's name."

"It can be."

"No, it can't."

"Sure it can. In France, there's an actor named—"

"We're not in France," he reminds her, "and he's not an actor; he's a dog. A guy dog. How about Nick?"

"Nick?"

"As in Saint. That's Christmasy."

Clara shakes her head. "Too typical."

"Jingle? Snowflake?"

"Snowflake?" She eyes the wriggling black lab. "He's no Snowflake."

"Coal?"

"How is that Christmasy?"

"It's what Santa puts into your stocking if you're not good."

"Don't tell me that ever happened to you. I'm sure you were always a good little boy."

Drew raises an eyebrow. "Who knows? Maybe I have a secret past."

Something flickers in Clara's green eyes.

"What?" he asks, amused. "Don't tell me you really think—"

"Hey, we can always name him after a reindeer!" she cuts in. "How about Vixen?"

"Sounds like a hooker."

"Cupid?"

"Maybe for a Valentine's Day puppy . . ."

She runs through the rest of Santa's team, and Drew finds a reason to veto each one—then counters with a list of his own, which Clara systematically rules out.

"If we're having this much trouble naming a puppy," she says at last, looking frustrated, "how are we going to name a baby?"

"We should just pick a letter and stick with it for the dog and the baby, like my mother did."

"Your mother doesn't have a dog."

"No, but she named all of us using the same letter to keep things simple."

"If you ask me, it's more complicated. I could never keep your sisters straight when we first met."

"Debbie, Danielle, Doreen. Debbie is the one who—"

"I know them now!" she cuts in, grinning. "So if we did go with one letter to make our lives simpler according to you—"

"Or more complicated according to you—"

"Right. Which letter would we choose?"

"I don't know, but—" Drew interrupts himself with a curse and bolts toward the dog, who is gnawing the strap of his brand-new Filson bag. "No, puppy! No, no, no!" He examines the strap and curses again.

"Is it bad?"

"Teeth marks. Dammit." He looks at the puppy and waves the bag at him. "Does this look like a mink coat to you?"

The puppy seems to grin before bounding merrily away toward the heap of wrapping paper again.

"Drew?"

"Yeah?"

"I know you hardly ever curse, but . . . can you watch the language from now on?"

"Clara, he's a dog. He has no idea what I'm saying."

"No, I know, but you're going to be a daddy soon, and someday the baby will."

"You're right." He promptly drops to his knees and whispers to her stomach, "I'm sorry. I'll never say a bad word again. Okay?" He presses his ear against her belly button as if listening for a reply. "He says okay."

"He? So you think it's a boy?"

"Do you?"

"Sure. I can just see a little brown-eyed, brown-haired heartbreaker like his dad."

"Or maybe a little green-eyed, brunette femme fatale like her mom."

Seeing Clara suddenly swallow hard and reach for a chair back to steady herself, Drew immediately gets to his feet. "Are you okay?"

"Since you asked . . . this femme fatale is feeling *blech*."

"Your stomach?"

"Yup. It's almost like when I was going through the cancer treatments. But that was a scary, sad kind of sick and tired. This is . . ."

"What?"

"Joyful sick and tired."

He smiles and tilts his forehead against hers. "Only you would come up with 'joyful sick and tired.'"

"That's not all I'm going to come up with if I don't have breakfast, *now*. The doctor said that keeping something in my stomach will help with the morning sickness, even if the last thing I want to do is eat."

"Which doctor?"

"Handler. My ob-gyn." She heads for the kitchen, past more windows shrouded in fog, stopping along the way to plug in the electric candles sitting on the sill of each one.

"You went to the doctor without me?" Drew asks in dismay, on her heels like a puppy—and followed by the real puppy.

"I had to confirm the pregnancy with a blood test."

"Well, that was the last time, okay? From here on in, I'm with you every step of the way."

"Deal. I wouldn't want it any other way."

"Good. Because you're stuck with me at least until death do us part."

"At least?" she echoes, and he can't quite read the odd expression on her face.

"Well, of course I'm going to haunt you when I'm gone."

"Don't even kid around about that." She looks away, then exclaims, "Whoa, no you don't!" and reaches for the little Lab, about to scamper through the open door to the utility closet.

"So Dr. Handler didn't do a sonogram, did she?" Drew asks.

"She won't until the end of the first trimester." Clara closes the closet door. "Anyway, I wouldn't have wanted one without you there.

Everyone says it's an amazing experience to actually see the baby in the womb."

"Who's everyone?"

"Well, just my dad and Sharon. But you know how they are about their kids."

Yes, he knows. His father-in-law and his third wife have two young sons and positively dote on them.

Now, with a child of his own on the way, Drew comprehends for the first time just how difficult it must have been for his father-in-law not to live under the same roof with his little girl.

Then again, there were plenty of times, Clara told him, when he could have been there for her—like at her first Broadway opening—and wasn't. The man made his choices. He had to live with them.

Too bad Clara did, too.

Thank God that's not going to happen to me. To us.

He reaches out and gives his wife a hug. "Hey. I really, really, love you. You know that?"

"I really, really do. And I'm really, really going to throw up all over you if I don't eat something, like, now."

He releases her and she hurriedly grabs a box of crackers from the cupboard.

"Here, sit down." He pulls out a stool at the long granite-topped breakfast bar and she sits, crunching into a saltine. "I'll fix you a big healthy breakfast. What do you want? Eggs?"

"Eggs? Gawd, no." She makes a face.

"No, not *worms*," he deadpans. "Eggs."

She mimes gagging.

"You love eggs."

"Not lately, I don't. I have this awful aversion to them right now. Please don't say the word again, okay?"

"Eggs?"

"Not funny."

"You really don't want me to say it?"

"Not for the next nine months. Or until the morning sickness passes. It's supposed to, by the end of the first trimester."

"How do you know?"

"I read it in *What to Expect When You're Expecting*. It's a great book—you should read it, too."

"Where is it?"

"Hidden in the bottom of my pajama drawer upstairs."

"So that's where you keep stuff you don't want me to see?"

"Darn it. Now I'll have to find a new place to stash all my deep, dark secrets." She grins, still looking pretty green around the gills.

"So in, what? Another month, you're home free?"

"Maybe not home free, but no more morning

sickness. And no more worrying that something's going to go wrong with the pregnancy."

Drew touches her hand. "Hey, everything will be fine. I promise."

"You can't promise that. You don't know."

"Sure I do," he assures her, just as he always has.

Through all the long months of cancer treatment, he was by her side, promising her that she was going to be okay. That's what you do when you love someone. You reassure them, get them through the hard times, refuse to consider anything but the best-case scenario.

That's his role as a husband, as far as he's concerned. To convey strength—no matter how vulnerable he's feeling.

"This is our happy beginning. Let's just enjoy every minute, okay?"

"Okay," she promises in return, and the shadows in her eyes are gone . . . for now, anyway.

Chapter 3

The big, airy kitchen is Clara's favorite room in the house.

About the same square footage as her entire Manhattan apartment, it's decorated for the season with festive boughs of greenery and, of course, electric candles in all the windows.

After all those years of city living, there are no close-set neighboring houses to crowd them. Beyond the wide pane of glass above the stainless-steel sink and cherry cabinets hangs a hummingbird feeder Doris sent them as a housewarming gift.

Every time Clara looks at it, she thinks longingly of her old friend back east. She and Doris keep in touch with occasional phone calls, but it isn't the same. Doris is increasingly hard of hearing, and anyway, the time zone difference makes it difficult, given Doris's early-to-bed, early-to-rise habit. It's usually evening whenever Clara thinks of calling her, and she knows Doris will have been long asleep by then back in New York.

Oh, well. They did exchange Christmas cards, and Clara sent Doris a much-appreciated gift: an entire carton of licorice snaps.

Doris wrote in her own card that she has a gift for Clara, too—but it's a surprise, and it won't arrive until after the holidays. "It should turn up on your doorstep sometime just after New Year's," she wrote, "so keep an eye out."

"You know," Clara tells Drew now, still looking at the hummingbird feeder, "someday, we might actually see a hummingbird out there."

"Maybe," he agrees, glancing at the window. "But even if we don't, the view is still pretty great."

That, it is. Beyond the wall of glass lies a magnificent vista: the sea, and towering evergreens, and the sky—on rare clear days, anyway.

Clara fully expected to find the chilly, foggy, unpredictable northern California weather distasteful, but to her surprise, she's actually enjoyed it . . . so far, anyway.

She does miss her family—including Doris—and her friends and a good old-fashioned East Coast white Christmas. Not that it always snowed over the holidays in New York. In fact, most years, it didn't.

True, the little shops that line the main street of picturesque San Florentina can't hold a candle to the store windows on Manhattan's Fifth Avenue. The light-strung pines on the town square are nothing compared to the majestic one at Rockefeller Center. And the local church choir's holiday concert is no match for the Radio City Rockettes.

Okay, so maybe she *is* a little homesick today. *But you* are *home. Here, with Drew.*

She watches Drew reach for the orange prescription bottle she insists he keep out on the windowsill above the sink, where he's sure to see it and remember to take it every day. In theory, anyway.

"It's just cholesterol medication," he reminds her, whenever she scolds him for managing to forget. "It's not life or death."

That's debatable. High cholesterol runs in Drew's family. His grandfather dropped dead of a heart attack in his forties, and his father, in increasingly fragile health, has suffered two.

"That's not going to happen to me," Drew promised Clara. "Look at me. Don't I look healthy?"

Sure he does. No one would ever suspect anything could be physically wrong with a man who oozes vitality.

Just as no one would ever guess that she's a cancer survivor.

You just never know.

Seeing her watching him remove a pill from the bottle, he asks, "What?"

"Aren't you due for a refill on that prescription?"

He peers into the bottle. "Nope. Plenty left."

"If you were taking it every day, you'd be out by now."

"I take it almost every day, and I feel fine. I felt fine before the doctor put me on it, and I feel fine whenever I forget to take it. There's nothing wrong with me."

"But you and I both know that most disease is hereditary," she cautions him.

No kidding. Her own maternal grandmother had died young of breast cancer—a fact that was never far from Clara's mind when she herself was undergoing treatment.

"Mental illness is also hereditary, and you don't think I'm going to start riding around town on an imaginary motorcycle like my crazy aunt Stella, do you?"

She has to laugh at that, having met his great-aunt Stella, a harmless flake who frequently inhabits his parents' guest room and goes through life making *vrrrm, vrrrm* noises and wearing a biker helmet.

Drew swallows a pill and returns the bottle

to its spot on the sill, then rummages through the cupboards.

The puppy wriggles in Clara's arms. "Okay, okay, down you go."

"And stay out of trouble," Drew warns, then asks Clara, "How does French toast sound?"

"Great."

"You do know there are eggs in French toast."

"Just don't talk about it, please."

Drew—a man who knows his way around a kitchen—pulls the big rectangular cast-iron griddle from a cupboard and sets it on the range. Whistling "Deck the Halls," he plops a generous slab of butter on it and turns up the flame.

"It's kind of strange, don't you think?" Clara asks, chin in hand, watching him.

"What is?"

"Spending Christmas Day alone together, just the two of us, without our families."

"It's kind of awesome—that's what it is. I had enough of my family last night to last me for a while."

They spent Christmas Eve at Drew's parents' annual open house.

Clara adores her in-laws. Drew's background is the polar opposite of her own, the kind of life she sometimes dreamed of as a New York City kid and the only child of divorced parents.

Her in-laws are indisputably madly in love

after forty-odd years of marriage and continue to reside in the large Pacific Heights home where Drew grew up. His three sisters are all happily wed with seven kids among them, and the older two who live out of town are visiting over the holidays. His sister Doreen and the rest of his extended family, including his ninety-five-year-old grandma, all live in the Bay area.

Every Becker get-together is brimming with laughter and music and food, populated by countless relatives and friends of all ages.

"We said we wanted a nice, relaxing Christmas Day after all that chaos, remember?" Drew pushes the butter around the griddle with a spatula.

"I know."

"You don't sound convinced now. What's wrong? Missing your family?"

Clara's parents and their respective spouses are on the opposite side of the country. And she and Drew haven't lived in San Florentina long enough to have made close friends here yet. Still . . .

He turns down the flame, abandons the spatula, and comes over to put his arms around her. "Just think . . . this is the last Christmas when it'll be just the two of us. Next year, Santa will come."

"The baby will be only six months old."

"You don't think he'll still believe in Santa?"

She laughs at that.

He kisses her forehead. "Sure he will. I do."

"Speaking of the baby . . . I was thinking about the nursery."

"What nursery?"

"The one we're going to set up in the corner room across the hall from ours. I've been looking at paint samples and—"

"Paint samples? Already? We've got plenty of time to—"

"No, I know, but I want everything to be ready when the baby comes. I was thinking we could do the walls in a pale yellow with white accents, and the furniture could be white, too—kind of antique-looking but not real antiques because old cribs can be dangerous, you know?"

"I don't, but I'll take your word for it."

"Just, whatever you do, don't mention to my father and Sharon that we're setting up the nursery before the baby comes, because they're superstitious about that."

"Why?"

"I don't know, they think it can summon the evil eye or something."

"God forbid we summon the evil eye," Drew says lightly. "Listen, I know the clock is ticking but I'm still trying to absorb all of this baby stuff, so do you think we can put off decorating the nursery until tomorrow, at least?"

"Party pooper."

"Who, me?" He returns to the stove. "So do you still want to go to a movie this afternoon?"

"What about him?" Clara indicates the puppy, now suspiciously sniffing around the doormat.

"He'll be fine. He came with a crate. It's next door at the Tuckers', along with all his other stuff."

"We're going to lock him in a *crate*?"

"Not a crate crate. A dog crate."

"I know, but . . . that seems mean."

"Clara, that's what people do when they have to leave puppies alone in the house. Or downstairs at night."

"We're going to lock him in a crate every night?"

"Not in a bad way." Drew sees her expression and sighs. "Where do you want him to sleep? In our bed with us?"

"No, of course not. But maybe on the rug or something."

Drew is shaking his head before she even finishes her sentence. "I don't think we should even get into the habit of letting him come upstairs."

"Why not?"

"We have a baby on the way."

"And . . . ?"

"And . . . you know." Drew gives her a look. "He . . . eats things."

Clara bursts out laughing.

"Oh, sure, you think it's funny now. But this dog is a loose cannon. We can't have him wandering around the house."

"Whatever. He'll live down here. But I'm going to make him a cozy bed. I don't want him to feel like he's in prison every night."

Cracking eggs into a bowl, Drew drops a shell onto the floor and stoops to pick it up. "That's fine, but just—hey! No! *No!*"

The puppy scampers away with the eggshell in his mouth. Amused, Clara watches Drew chase after him and attempt to pry his teeth apart.

"What the h—" he catches himself, "what the *dickens* do you think you're doing, you crazy dog?"

"Drew . . . Dickens!"

"You're kidding, right?" Drew protests from the floor as he wrestles with the puppy. "I can't tease you about haunting you when I'm dead, I can't curse, I can't say 'eggs,' and now I can't even say—"

"No, I meant that's it! That's a great name for him. Dickens. It even starts with a *D*—he'll fit in perfectly with your side of the family."

"I thought you said you wanted something Christmasy."

"Who wrote *A Christmas Carol* . . . ?"

Drew grins. "Perfect. Dickens, it is. Did you hear that, pal? Your name is Dickens."

The puppy wags its tail.

"He likes it," Clara decides. "Come here, Dickens."

He obediently trots over to her. As she reaches down to pet him, he grabs her slipper from her foot and dashes into a corner with it.

With an exasperated sigh, Drew starts after him.

"It's okay, let him go. You just got me that beautiful new pair for Christmas."

"Well, you'd better hide them before he decides to have them for lunch."

Dickens drops the slipper abruptly and looks up, head cocked, as if listening.

"What is it, boy?" Drew asks.

The dog looks at the door and barks sharply.

"You want out?"

"Maybe he's offended that we're talking about him and he wants to make a break for it," Clara tells Drew.

The dog barks again, then paces, stops, and whines at them.

"Aw, what's wrong, puppy?" Clara asks.

"He probably has to go out. I'll take him." Drew crosses to the back door and opens it, grabbing his jacket from a hook. "Let's go."

Dickens promptly makes a beeline for the opposite side of the room.

"Hey, come back here. I thought you had to go out. Here, boy. Come on."

The dog ignores the command, parking himself in the doorway to the dining room and whining again.

"Dickens! Here. Here, boy!"

Nothing.

With an exasperated shake of his head, Drew closes the door. "You think maybe we need to enroll him in obedience school?"

"Yeah, and I hate to say it but I'm thinking the crate isn't a bad idea after all, if we do go out later."

"Good. I'm guessing there's something playing down at Regal that we want to see."

"Mikey's new movie opens today."

Mikey, as in Michael Marshall, Clara's old friend and onetime costar, who also happens to be Hollywood's hottest heartthrob. He's one of the few people from her acting days with whom she still keeps in touch.

Another is Jesus DeJesus, who, come to think of it, has called twice this week and left messages. She has yet to find time to call him back.

But I will, she promises herself with a twinge of guilt. *And I'll have to be sure not to slip about being pregnant.*

There was a time when she confided in Jesus— and Mikey, too—about everything.

Well, almost everything. She never told them about her time travel experience.

When Drew first came along and became her main confidant, Jesus was worried their friendship would suffer. She promised him it wouldn't—even after she moved to the West Coast, leaving him behind in New York.

But when was the last time you talked to him?

Okay, it's been a while, but she's been busy lately, preoccupied with the pregnancy and the move and Christmas. She'll definitely give Jesus a call back before the day is over.

Drew goes back to cracking eggs into a bowl. "Let's go see Michael's movie, then. It's the gladiator one, right?"

"Yes, and I'm sure it'll be jammed. We should go early. I'll check the movie times."

"Don't worry about it. We have all the time in the world."

She quirks an eyebrow at him.

"What?"

"You always say that. 'We have all the time in the world.'"

"So? We do. Especially today. We can just relax, play it by ear."

"You know I hate to play things by ear."

"Oh, that's right. Ms. Hurry-Scurry-Flurry likes a solid plan."

"You know it. Hand me my purse, will you, please?" She gestures at it, hanging on a hook beside the door. "I've got the movie phone number programmed into my cell phone."

"And your cell phone is in your purse?" he asks, handing it over.

"Yup."

"Sure about that?"

She peeks inside. "Nope."

Drew nods smugly. "Didn't think so. You know what I should have gotten you for Christmas? One of those voice-activated locator things for your phone so you wouldn't keep losing it."

"I've never *lost* it," she points out. "I've just . . . *misplaced* it a few times. And anyway, I don't need a locator on it. All I have to do is call it and listen for the ring."

"That would work really well . . . if you ever remembered to charge the battery."

"Good point." Clara sighs and stands.

"I didn't mean you should do it now."

"I'm just going to go grab the newspaper. The movie schedule is in there, and God only knows where my cell phone is."

"No, you sit here and rest, and I'll go get the paper."

"Um, it's sitting out on the doorstep," she points out dryly. "It's not like I have to hike all the way down the hillside into town."

"I know, sweetie, but I want you to take it easy."

"I know, sweetie, but I want to get away from watching you crack all those disgusting eggs."

"Fine. Just . . . be careful."

"Be careful? Walking to the front door?"

"You've got precious cargo in there." He gives her stomach a gentle pat as she passes.

Dickens, still crouched in the doorway, barks at her.

"What is it, boy? You look out of sorts."

"You don't know him well enough to say that," Drew points out. "I'm starting to wonder if he's got serious issues."

"It's okay, I love you even if you are nuttier than a fruitcake."

Drew frowns.

"Hey, I meant the dog, not you," Clara says.

"No, I just . . . that just reminded me of something."

"What did?"

"Fruitcake." He shrugs. "I don't know what."

Fruitcake.

It reminds Clara of something, too. Of some-*one*.

Old Minnie Bouvier, Jed Landry's Glenhaven Park neighbor, went out one snowy December night in 1941 to buy ground cloves for her annual batch of holiday fruitcakes, and never came home again.

Clara was there when Minnie was fatally struck by Arnold Wilkens's Packard as he rushed his laboring wife Maisie to the hospital. Minnie Bouvier died there right around the time Maisie gave birth to her baby boy, Denton. The same Denton Wilkens who would later direct Clara in *The Glenhaven Park Dozen*.

She's long since realized that there are no coincidences in her life.

Drew looks lost in thought.

"I wonder what fruitcake reminds you of," she says slowly, watching him carefully as he looks up, startled.

"What?"

"Fruitcake," she repeats, wondering if there's any chance . . .

Drew shrugs and turns away from her, back to the stove. "It reminds me that it's Christmas, and you're hungry, and I'm making breakfast for you."

Clara nods. Of course there's no chance he could possibly remember Minnie Bouvier. Or Arnold, or Maisie, or any of the others.

Those memories belong to another person, another lifetime.

Then again . . .

Sometimes, a person can have a flash of inexplicable memory that might really be a glimpse into their own past . . . as somebody else.

She read that once in a book about reincarnation, a topic that had interested her long before Jed—and Drew—came along.

She always liked to hope that her grandfather, who had lost his wife, her grandmother, at a young age to breast cancer, would get a second chance with his soul mate. That the two of them might be reborn as babies who would grow up, find each other, and fall in love all over again.

Now she definitely believes it—and not just for her grandparents.

Humming "Deck the Halls" in unison with Drew's resumed whistling, she steps around Dickens, who barks at her.

"What is it? You want to come with me so you can eat the newspaper?"

Another bark.

"Oh, you want to go to the movies, too?"

He barks again and she pats his head.

"I know, but you can't. You're not that into gladiators, anyway, are you?"

Another bark.

"Maybe you are. Sorry, I can't help you there. You'll be spending your afternoon in a very nice crate, though."

He continues to bark as Clara makes her way to the front door. She reaches the hall just as the subway rumbles by, shaking the whole apartment.

Wait a minute . . .

This isn't her apartment. It's a house.

She's not in New York City anymore. She's in northern California.

There's no subway here.

The only thing that would make the ground rumble and shake in northern California is . . .

"Earthquake!" Drew interrupts his whistling to announce from the kitchen.

"I know. I feel it." She reaches for the wall to brace herself as the room rattles and rolls around her, and Dickens barks wildly.

She's been through a couple of temblors since the move—tiny ones, Drew assured her, and they were brief. Still, she was unnerved.

"Drew?" she calls, hearing glass breaking in the kitchen as a couple of books slide off a table a few feet from where she stands.

That's never happened before.

"Get into a doorway! I'm coming! Dickens, get over here, you crazy dog!"

More breaking glass, and she hears him curse.

"Hey, watch the language!" she reminds him as she moves toward the nearest doorway, holding the wall, reminding herself that this is no big deal in northern California. She'll get used to it.

The light fixture above her head flickers and sways.

"Holy crap!" Drew's voice—always so reassuring—is hoarse.

He's scared. Oh God. Drew, the native Californian, her big, strong husband, who just minutes ago promised her that everything would be fine, is scared.

Now the whole world is violently shaking. Windows rattle, cabinet doors swing open, dishes fall and shatter. Pottery and lamps topple from shelves and tabletops, breaking on the hardwoods and tile. With a tinkling of lights and ornaments and a heavy thump, the Christmas tree goes over in the living room.

"Clara! The doorway!" Drew hollers from the next room, sounding frantic.

"I know!"

She's almost there, but it's like walking on a trampoline. Terrified, she moves along the wall, calling for Drew, and then . . .

Chapter 4

Clara opens her eyes.

Morning.

Dim gray light falls through the big glass window beside the bed.

Christmas Day, she remembers.

"Hey, Drew." She turns her head toward him. "I just had the scariest dream. There was an earthquake, and—Drew?"

His side of the sprawling California king bed is empty.

Not just empty.

Made.

The decorative pillow, in its sham, is still in place, and the covers are pulled all the way up.

That's odd.

Why would he make half the bed with her in it?

"Drew?"

Clara sits up quickly.

Too quickly.

"Whoa," she mutters, swept by dizziness and a tide of nausea.

Her stomach . . .

Morning sickness.

Right. She's pregnant.

Funny how she manages to forget sometimes.

But every time she does, and then remembers, it's like a happy little surprise party in her head . . .

Surprise! You're pregnant!

Yay!

She reaches down to pat her stomach.

Surprise . . .

You're showing!

Wow!

She read that her belly might seem to "pop" overnight, but she hadn't realized it would be this pronounced. Running her fingertips over the firm, rounded ball beneath her ribs, she's shocked at how big she is. She can't wait to show—

Wait a minute. Drew doesn't know yet, remember?

You just dreamed that you told him . . .

And that he gave you a puppy . . .

And then you dreamed the earthquake.

Yes, and thank God that part was just a dream. A nightmare, really.

Anyway, Drew wasn't supposed to find out about the baby until later this morning when she gives him the Christmas present containing the rattle. But unless she can cover up with her robe, he's going to take one look at her and figure it out.

Sitting up, she feels another wave of nausea. Oh, ick.

I can't wait till the first trimester is over.

Swinging her legs over the side of the bed, she notices that the electric candle on the windowsill beside the bed is missing.

That's odd.

She looks at the other windows.

Where are all her candles?

It doesn't make sense. They were here when she fell asleep, the bedroom bathed in their soft white glow.

"Drew?" she calls. "Did you move the candles?"

No reply.

She glances at the clock on the nightstand to see what time it is—just past seven—and notices a box of saltines resting beside it.

What is that doing here?

The ground is reassuringly steady beneath her feet as she stands, and her lower back aches.

Again, she looks at the box of saltines.

Okay, this really makes no sense. . . .

Unless she sleepwalked her way down to the kitchen to get it in the middle of the night.

She's never done anything like that before, but according to *What to Expect,* pregnancy can cause all kinds of strange symptoms. She'll have to check to see if sleepwalking is one of them.

Her robe is hanging on the bedpost. She reaches for it, hoping it will cover her belly.

Wait a minute . . .

This isn't her robe.

Her robe is white terry cloth.

This one is red velour.

Somewhere in the back of her mind, a sense of uneasiness takes hold.

Am I losing my mind?

No. You're just pregnant.

Pregnancy causes forgetfulness. The book said so.

Okay, so she must have bought a new robe, or maybe she got one as a gift at Drew's family's open house last night, and she forgot.

Unsettled, she pulls it on and glances down at her stomach.

What the . . . ?

She's *huge.*

She looks like she's seven or eight months pregnant, at least.

Not two.

Maybe I should call the doctor, she decides as she starts to turn toward the door.

She stops short, nearly running into a chair.

What is that doing there?

The furniture is rearranged.

Not only that, but the bedroom is filled with stacked cardboard cartons.

It wasn't like this last night. What in the world is going on?

"Oh my God . . . Drew! Drew!"

Frightened, she hurries into the hall and down the stairs, clinging to the banister. Her center of gravity seems to be off.

"Drew?"

At the foot of the stairs, she's greeted by a shocking sight:

More boxes.

But . . . they finished unpacking everything before Thanksgiving.

Christmas presents, she tells herself. *They must be Christmas presents from Drew.*

Only they're not wrapped, and the boxes aren't gift boxes, they're cardboard cartons. Moving cartons. And there are no Christmas decorations, and there is no Christmas tree, and no sign of her husband.

I'm losing my mind.

"Drew!"

The house is silent.

Dark.

Empty.

She can feel it.

Still, she searches, calling his name, crying.

"Where are you? Drew! *Drew!*"

Boxes fill every room. Nothing but boxes; no books on the shelves, no snow globe on the mantel, no pots or pans or dishes in the cupboards.

There's furniture, but it's all moved around, and there are a few pieces she's never seen before.

And her candles . . . her electric candles . . .

They're gone, with the tree and the other decorations.

Dear God, what is going on?

Maybe the earthquake wasn't the nightmare.

Maybe this is.

Wake up, Clara.

You have to wake up now.

"Drew!" she shrieks, propelling her bulky frame toward the front door.

She throws it open.

Damp fog swirls before her.

"Drew!" She doesn't care what time it is, doesn't care who hears her.

She needs her husband.

Glancing wildly around, she sees that there's only one car in the driveway: her own.

Drew is obviously not here.

"Drew!" she calls anyway. "Drew!"

Something catches her eye. She looks down to see the morning paper lying on the mat.

The headline reads CEREMONIES TO MARK THIRD ANNIVERSARY OF CATASTROPHIC QUAKE.

Slowly, Clara picks up the newspaper, then hears a rustling in the shrubbery.

"Drew?" Poised, listening, she waits for a human response.

Nothing.

"Drew?"

This time, something . . . but it isn't human.

In a blur of fur, a black bear cub launches from the shrubbery, heading straight for her. Before she can react, the creature has snatched the newspaper from her hand, blown past her and into the house. Horrified, Clara turns to see it skid to a stop in the front hall.

It drops the paper on the floor. Then it barks, and shakes off the damp with a jangling collar, and she realizes that it isn't a bear cub after all.

It's a black dog.

A Lab, just like the one Drew gave her in her dream . . . only this is no puppy. It's fully grown, and it's wagging its tail at her, and it's in her house and looking for all the world as though it belongs here.

Shaken, she turns away from the dog, wondering if perhaps its owner is about to emerge from the fog, too.

"Hello? Is anyone there?"

Silence.

Clara shrugs.

What now?

After a moment, she walks over and reaches gingerly for the paper. The dog bats at her hand with a fat paw, but more playfully than maliciously. Still, she drops the paper.

He noses at it, then tears into one of the sections—sports, she realizes, spotting a 49ers headline hanging from his jaw.

Dogs like paper, she recalls. At least, the puppy she dreamed about liked paper. This, though, is no puppy. This is a full-grown dog whose strong teeth are shredding the sports section.

Cautiously, she retrieves the rest of the paper, and glances again at the front-page headline.

CEREMONIES TO MARK THIRD ANNIVERSARY
OF CATASTROPHIC QUAKE

Must have been the one in Thailand that caused that deadly tsunami. . . . That happened a few years back, around Christmas, didn't it?

She scans the lead paragraph.

Across the region this holiday weekend, residents will commemorate the deadliest earthquake ever to hit the Bay area.

The Bay area?

The quake, which measured 8.3 on the Richter scale and caused massive—

Dazed, her heart racing, she forces herself to look away from the article, up at the dateline.

December 25, 2012.

"Oh no . . . Oh God, not again."

Pressing a fist to her trembling mouth, swaying as though she's about to faint, Clara realizes she didn't dream it—it really happened.

Three years ago.

Chapter 5

As the ground sways violently beneath Drew's feet and car alarms begin to wail out in the driveway, he's swept by a violent vision.

A glimpse of gray shoreline riddled with smoke and fire. Deafening chaos erupting all around him; gunfire and urgent commands and the anguished screams of dying men. He's in the water, and his mouth is filled with the salty, metallic taste of fear, or seawater, or blood. . . .

Drew has been here before, countless times, in reoccurring nightmares and odd, fleeting, waking-hour recollections of scenes from an old war movie he must have seen once a long, long time ago.

"Drew!"

At the sound of Clara's voice calling for him, he opens his eyes to find that the shaking has stopped as suddenly as it began.

He can hear sirens in the distance, mingling with the wail of the car alarms still going off in the driveway. It's an eerie sound, and one that has accompanied every earthquake he's ever experienced.

"Drew!"

"Clara! Where are you?"

"I'm in here!"

He frantically picks his way through a litter of toppled housewares and broken glass to his wife's side. She's crouched in the doorway between the foyer and the living room, surrounded by pottery shards and fallen furniture, looking shell-shocked but physically unharmed.

"Are you okay?" He helps her to her feet.

She leans into him, trembling. "I think so. I'm just . . . I don't know, for a minute I thought I was . . . God, that was so scary."

"Quakes always are, but—"

"Quakes?" Her expression is blank.

The sirens Drew can hear outside the house seem to sound inside his head as well, as though warning him that something is terribly wrong with his wife. Clara is looking at him as though she has no idea what he's talking about.

"Did you get hit on the head?" he asks, gently running his fingers over her hair. He doesn't feel a bump or any open cuts, which is a good sign.

Then he remembers—it could be far worse than a bump on the head. She's pregnant.

"Is the baby okay?" he asks, trying not to sound as frantic as he suddenly feels inside.

"Baby?" she echoes, so cluelessly that he's certain she must have a concussion, or worse.

"Clara—"

"Oh God. The baby." She touches her stomach with a trembling hand.

"Do you have any pain there, or any . . . anything?"

"No . . ."

"So you think the baby is okay?"

"I guess so. I mean . . . how do I know for sure?"

He cups his fingers reassuringly over hers.

"*I* know," he tells her. "It's okay."

She nods and looks around as if she's disoriented. "Drew, it was horrible. It was Christmas, and I couldn't find you, and—"

"I was in the kitchen when the quake started, and you were going to get the paper—"

"The paper . . . There was a headline"—she shudders—"about the quake. It was catastrophic."

Vaguely confused, he tells her, "It was bad, but not catastrophic, I don't think."

"No, it said so in the paper."

"Clara . . . honey, I think you must have gotten hit on the head or something." Again, he touches her scalp. "Does this hurt?"

"No."

She's lying, he realizes, because she squeezes her eyes closed, almost in a wince.

"Do you think I might have blacked out or something, though? Because I had this . . . I don't know, this dream or something, that I was here, in this house, and it was Christmas, but you weren't here, and there was this huge dog, and—"

"We need to get you to the ER," Drew tells her.

Her eyes snap open.

"I'm fine, but the dog—"

"You just said you blacked out."

"No, I . . . I don't know, maybe I was just scared. I had this flash of—I guess I was just imagining things, you know?"

Does he know? No one knows better than he does about strange flashes of imaginations.

"But the dog," she repeats, looking around.

"Dog?"

"The puppy," she says impatiently. "Where's the puppy?"

Puppy?

It takes Drew a few seconds to remember the new puppy and realize she's not hallucinating again, and another few seconds to recall the new puppy's name.

"Dickens!" he calls tentatively, and is rewarded with a faint bark from somewhere in the back of the house. Moments later, a furry black cannonball launches into the room, yapping excitedly.

Drew scoops him up and the dog licks his face.

"And you knew that earthquake was coming, didn't you? That's why you were acting so weird. You even went into the doorway. You're the smartest dog ever."

"And the luckiest." Clara shakes her head at the shambles surrounding them. "Thank God nothing fell on him—or us, for that matter."

"Are you sure you're not hurt anywhere?"

"Positive." She looks more like herself now. "But those car alarms are going to give me a headache."

He sets the puppy on its feet and looks around for a set of car keys to go turn them off.

"That really wasn't catastrophic?"

Struck by something in her voice, he turns to see her hand still pressed protectively over her stomach, a worried look in her eyes.

"I don't think so, but it was scary."

Clara nods in silence

"Hey," Drew says, "it's okay. We're together. We survived. We always do, right?"

She smiles faintly at him. "You're right. We always do."

Chapter 6

As Drew steps out the front door, car keys in hand, Clara releases the breath she's been holding since . . .

Well, since 2012, she thinks wryly—but only for a split second, before wry gives way, once again, to sheer disbelief.

And yet, why wouldn't she believe she just slipped, for a few terrifying moments, into the future? Didn't she spend days at a time in the past and not only live to tell about it, but fall in love?

Twice for that matter. In love with Jed in 1941, and in love with his modern-day counterpart who, of course, has no idea that his wife tends to zip back and forth in time.

But I almost gave it away just now.

Outside, one car alarm and then the other fall abruptly silent, leaving only the distant whine of sirens. Any second now, Drew will be back and she'll have to go back to pretending everything is as okay as it can be in the aftermath of a visit to the future . . . let alone a quake that was, indeed, catastrophic. At least, according to the 2012 newspaper.

Maybe she should tell Drew what really happened. He was so worried about her just now.

And she always knew, deep down, that she'd tell him the truth one day. Either because she wanted to, or because she had to.

But neither is the case right now, Clara reminds herself. *You don't want to, and you don't have to.*

Drew seemed to buy that she was just shaken up from the earthquake. In fact . . .

Did she hit her head and imagine the whole thing?

She reaches up to probe around beneath her hair, searching for a tender spot, finding none.

Come on, who are you kidding? You didn't imagine it. It really happened.

"Clara?" Drew is back, crunching over broken glass beside the front door. "The cars are okay, and I took a quick walk around the house to check the foundation. No damage that I can see."

"Good."

"Why don't you go sit down for a minute?"

he asks, and she looks up to see him watching her with an expression of sweet concern.

"I'm fine. We have to clean this up."

"I'll do it."

"So will I."

"Sit down for five minutes."

"Sit down? Are you kidding? Look at this mess."

He takes her arm and gestures with the other hand at the couch in the next room. "Sit down. Rest. Do it for me."

"Drew—"

"Then do it for the baby."

She clamps her mouth shut and allows him to lead her to the couch. Shaking her head, she sits and leans her head back, not wanting to admit, even to herself, that she really might need a time-out.

"I'm going to go find the shop vac. I'll be back. Maybe you can take a little nap."

She nods wearily, eyes closed. Maybe she can.

Chapter 7

Opening her eyes, Clara finds herself in Drew's recliner.

She could have sworn she'd been resting on the couch.

"Drew?" she calls, noticing that the sirens have stopped and so, for that matter, has the hum of the shop vac that lulled her to sleep.

She wonders, for a moment, how long she's been napping. Then she sees the tower of cardboard boxes. And the rolled newspaper in her hand. One with a familiar headline and a 2012 dateline.

Leaping up from the chair, she paces past the boxes, more boxes, more boxes . . . all the way to the kitchen.

"It'll be all right. You can get through this. You can get through anything, remember?" Clara mutters to herself.

Hearing a jangling sound, she turns to see the big black dog behind her.

"Dickens?" she asks tentatively.

He tilts his head and barks.

"So is that a yes or a no?"

Another cryptic bark. Then he plops on the floor with a yawn and luxuriously rolls over, belly up.

"Make yourself at home, why don't you." She surveys him. "*Are* you at home? Are you Dickens?"

He stretches and rolls back onto his feet.

"Okay, great. You're not talking. Whatever." For all she knows, she let a stray into the house.

She notices that he seems to have something other than a fat wet tongue and sharp teeth in his mouth.

What is he chewing on? A wet rag?

Paper, she realizes. *What's left of the paper, anyway.*

He drops a soggy, pulpy, ink-smeared shred at her feet.

Clara nods with recognition.

"Dickens. Definitely."

She might have only known him for a matter of minutes on that Christmas morning three years ago, but he clearly belongs here—which means she does, too.

Clara is too relieved to worry about what the

paper might once have been—for all she knows, a lottery check for a million dollars.

"Where's Drew, boy?" she asks, stooping to pet him.

The dog stops chewing, flashing an expectant look at the door, then at her.

What does that mean? That Drew will be back any second?

Maybe it doesn't mean anything.

"I wish you could talk," she tells Dickens. "Because I have a feeling you know what's going on here, don't you?"

He gives her such an astute look that she half expects him to reply in English. But that only happens in dreams, she reminds herself, or in movies. Not in real life.

Then again . . . this is *her* real life. Is a conversing canine really that much more far-fetched than zipping back and forth through time?

The dog has clearly lost interest in her, having gone back to devouring the remaining paper with gusto.

So here she is.

In the future.

How does she get back?

"I've done it before," she reminds herself—and Dickens, in case he's listening. "I can do it again."

She frowns.

"Who am I kidding?"

One can only do something *again* if one has done it *before*.

Unfortunately, she hasn't.

Time travel, yes. She's never gone forward, though. She's just visited the past. On more than one occasion. But it hasn't happened since that December day three years—

Six years ago.

Dear God, this is 2012. She's a regular Marty McFly, minus wild-eyed Doc Brown and the handy DeLorean.

Last time, all she had to do to get back to the present was hop the vintage train that had carried her back to 1941 in the first place.

This time, there is no obvious portal, like the train. What is she supposed to do, wait around for another major earthquake?

She looks again at the newspaper headline and despair washes over her.

The future isn't like the past.

With the past, at least, you know what's coming. Good or bad—at least you know.

Not so with the future. The future is scary. Terrifying.

And not only is Clara clueless about what lies ahead—and, for that matter, about what's going on right now, on Christmas morning in an empty house—but she has no idea what happened in the three years she just skipped. There was the earthquake, and then . . .

What?

Was she swallowed by some kind of a time-warp fault in the earth?

Is this an alternate universe? Or has she dropped in on her own future?

"Drew!" she shouts, trying not to panic. "Where are you? Drew!"

Silence, other than a jingling of the dog's collar.

Dickens is watching her warily, as if to say, *Do not freak out. You cannot freak out.*

"You're right," she tells the dog. "It's not good for the baby."

She touches her pregnant stomach.

"It's okay. It's going to be okay."

Maybe it's not, but . . .

It turned out just fine last time she slipped through a time warp, right?

And at least this one has landed her in her own house. Although it doesn't look like her house, and it doesn't feel like her house—not with all these moving boxes, and no sign of Drew.

Christmas Day.

Why isn't he here?

Why are they moving?

This was supposed to be their dream house. They were going to live happily ever after here, put down roots, start a family.

Obviously, they have—started, and contin-ued. Clara pats her stomach, where baby number two is obviously safely past the first—and maybe even the second—trimester.

But where is her other child? Her firstborn? He or she would be a toddler by now. Shouldn't the house be filled with toys, sippy cups, little shoes . . . whatever else it is that toddlers need?

Clara's gaze falls on a stack of boxes.

Okay, so maybe all that stuff is packed away for the move.

But why are we moving?

And anyway . . . would every last thing really be boxed up? a little voice nags. *Shouldn't there be something that isn't packed yet?*

Frowning, she crosses over to the fridge, yanks the door open.

The shelves are pretty bare.

Organic salad greens, bottled water, mangoes, goat cheese, leftover pad Thai . . .

Clara gapes at the unfamiliar take-out container. Then, heart pounding, she slams the fridge shut as if she's just seen a disembodied head on the glass shelf.

Why is the pad Thai in a plastic Tupperware-looking thing? Where's the old-fashioned cardboard container they use at her favorite local place? Why isn't anything familiar?

Shouldn't there be milk? String cheese? Yogurt or Go-GURT or whatever it is that little kids eat . . . ?

If this is her fridge, her house, her future . . .

Then where's her child? Where's Drew?

Why is there no sign of either of them?

Why is she alone on Christmas morning?

Maybe Drew took our child out somewhere, and they'll be back any second now. . . .

Out . . .

On Christmas morning?

Where would they have gone without her?

Okay, think things through. Be logical.

Fact: Drew is obviously around here some-where—or at least he was a few months ago—because she's pregnant.

Logic. Good.

Fact: they're obviously out of milk.

Strong possibility: Dickens just ate the grocery list.

She glances over at the dog, who now trots across the floor with someone's red jacket—probably her red jacket—in his teeth.

"Where's Drew?" she asks the dog. "Did he go out to the store?"

But wouldn't he go alone?

Is anything even open?

Clara paces across the kitchen again, trailed by Dickens.

"What's the matter, boy? Are you hungry? Probably. I mean, you're eating a coat. Then again, you like to eat coats. That's how you got here in the first place, right?"

With a sigh, she goes through the cupboards—

mostly bare—and finds some Alpo and a plastic dog bowl. Opening the can, she says, "Trust me; you're going to love this. Or—who knows? Maybe you only eat outerwear."

But Dickens dives into the food the second she puts it on the floor.

"Good. At least you're normal. Sort of."

Clara starts pacing again and finds herself standing in front of . . .

"The phone!"

How did she miss the obvious?

Unlike Clara, who's always misplacing her cell phone, Drew never leaves the house without his.

She snatches up the receiver and dials his number.

The line rings.

She watches Dickens chowing down as she waits for Drew to pick up. Of course he's going to provide a perfectly reasonable explanation; one that will make her slap her head and wonder how she could have thought . . .

No way. You're not even going there, she commands her brain as the phone rings again . . . and again . . .

Then a click.

But it isn't Drew's voice that greets her; it's a disembodied operator.

"The number you are trying to reach has been

disconnected. Please check the number and try your call again."

Her heart sinking, thoughts racing, Clara tosses the receiver onto a chair.

It doesn't make sense. Drew would never leave her alone, and pregnant, on Christmas.

Not the Drew she knew three years ago, anyway.

Nor would they ever willingly move out of this house, which is exactly what they—or at least she—seem to be doing.

That means there are only two logical possibilities, both as unimaginable as they are horrific.

Either Drew changed, and their marriage somehow crashed and burned, the way her parents' marriage did . . .

Or something terrible happened to him.

Chapter 8

A good fifteen minutes later, as composed as she can be under the circumstances, Clara makes her way upstairs to the master bedroom.

Hand shaking, she opens the doors to the walk-in closet.

Empty.

But not just Drew's side. Hers, too.

Racing to his tall bureau, she pulls out drawer after drawer. They're all empty as well.

So is her own dresser. But sitting on top of it is an open suitcase that contains a stack of folded items—all of them, at a glance, unfamiliar. Clara picks up an enormous-looking blouse, oversized high-waisted panties, and a pair of jeans with a stretchy fabric panel across the hips. Maternity clothes. Cute. Well, not really. But she feels a flutter of excitement looking down again at her large, rounded stomach—followed by a twinge of worry.

Drew.

For God's sake, where are you?

She turns and looks again at the mountain of stacked boxes. The rest of her clothes, and Drew's, must be in them, along with everything else that once occupied the bedroom drawers and closet shelves.

What about the suitcase?

The 1941 Samsonite Streamlite, filled with period clothing, has long held a place of honor among her possessions. Drew believes it once belonged to Clara's late grandmother—a rare and necessary lie.

In reality, it was originally a prop from *The Glenhaven Park Dozen*, and when Clara found herself propelled back to the forties, the suitcase went with her. The contents came in handy while she was there.

She left it all behind on her last visit, believing she'd never see it again. Then Doris—Jed's long-ago kid sister—showed up on her doorstep with the suitcase and a letter Jed had written to Clara almost sixty-five years earlier.

The letter.

Every once in a while, she takes it out and rereads it, marveling at the familiar slant of the handwriting. Truly, it could pass for Drew's.

Don't wait for me, Jed wrote on that long-ago day, knowing it would be years before the letter reached her. *Just look for me.*

She did. And she found him.

Clara just hopes that the yellowed pages are still zipped into the lining of the suitcase—and that the suitcase is in one of these boxes.

There's only one way to find out.

Clara tiptoes to reach for a carton on top of the stack and starts to lift it. She immediately thinks better of it when her lower belly suddenly seems to twitch and harden painfully.

"Whoa!" She puts the box back on the stack and presses a hand against her stomach. Beneath the rock-like surface, she senses the baby's movements. Frightened, she asks, "Did I hurt you?"

After a few seconds, the tension subsides. Clara sinks onto the bed, relieved.

"That was really, really stupid," she mutters to herself.

Then she looks up helplessly at the tall stack of boxes and remembers something.

Irony of ironies, she and Drew first connected over a pile of moving cartons just like this one. It was November fifteenth, a little over three—make that six—years ago. A date that will live on in infamy for Clara and Drew, not unlike December 7, 1941—which they also experienced firsthand. But of course, Drew has no memory of that.

The day they met—in this lifetime—he was unloading a U-Haul in front of her Manhattan brownstone building, having just rented the apartment below hers. On her way in, she held the door for him. Looking into his eyes for the first time, she felt a flash of recognition that was, for a split second, mirrored in his own expression.

That didn't seem surprising at the time. She was an actress; she'd been on the soaps and by that time had even had some bit parts in movies. People often recognized her on the street or subway—particularly die-hard *One Life to Live* fans who addressed her by her character's name.

But Drew had never heard of Arabella Saffron, let alone Clara McCallum. Nor had he ever seen her in a movie.

She had never seen him before, either—not as Drew Becker, anyway. At that point, she had yet to even meet Jed Landry.

Now, of course, she understands exactly why two total strangers might have the sense that they'd already met.

Because we had. In another place, another time.

The last words Jed Landry ever said to her were, "Look for me, Clara . . . because I'm going to find you. I promise."

He did.

And he will again, she promises herself, the tower of boxes blurred by tears. She wipes at her eyes with the sleeve of her robe.

He's out there somewhere. She just has to get to him.

She takes a deep breath to steady herself.

First things first. In her condition, she clearly can't go around climbing or lifting anything heavy. But her legs are presumably working just fine. Jaw set, she stands and strides to the adjoining bathroom.

The granite counter surrounding the double sinks—typically littered with an array of his-and-her toiletries—is, at a glance, unusually bare.

There's her Secret solid, her favorite moisturizer, her green mouthwash, and mint toothpaste.

But there is no sign of Drew's shaving cream, his hairbrush, his Old Spice deodorant, his cinnamon toothpaste.

Maybe he switched brands and he's using mine?

Drew? No. No way. Her husband is a creature of habit. He uses Close-Up. Always has, always will.

She forces herself to look at the built-in toothbrush holder above the sink, knowing, before her eyes settle on it, what she'll find.

There's only one toothbrush.

Drew wouldn't go out for milk toting a case full of toiletries.

That doesn't mean he isn't off traveling somewhere, though. Maybe he's on a business trip. . . .

On Christmas Day?

Okay, a ski trip, then. An avid skier, Drew's been wanting her to learn. She planned on it, but even if she had learned, in her current condition, she obviously can't join him on the slopes, so . . .

So he'd go away without me for the holidays?

Never, never, never.

Panic threatens to take hold, but she resists.

There has to be a logical explanation. She just isn't seeing it because she's in unfamiliar territory.

She catches sight of her reflection in the mirror above the sink.

Make that disconcertingly *familiar* unfamiliar territory.

At least she doesn't look much different than she did three years ago, other than a fuller face and figure from the pregnancy. There's not a hint of gray in her long brown hair—*unless I color it now?*

Struck by another thought, she pulls at the neckline of her pajama top and peers inside. There's the old scar from her bout with cancer, but it's the only one. Her breasts remain reassuringly intact.

So I really am a survivor.

A smile plays at her lips as she leaves the bathroom.

At least, once she's returned to the past—or rather, the present—she won't have to live in fear that the cancer is looming just ahead, regardless of the oncologist's reassurances.

Her remission was for real. She'll be able to breathe easier when she gets back.

If you get back.

Of course you will. You've done it before. . . . You can do it again.

And this time, she promises herself, *you're going to tell Drew the whole story. This is too much to deal with on your own, and anyway, he deserves to know, even if it does freak him out.*

Clara heads into the hall. After hesitating for a moment, she opens the door opposite the master bedroom.

Just this morning—just three years ago—she'd told Drew of her plans for converting the large corner room to a nursery.

Peering in now, she sees that the walls are indeed a soft yellow. But the room is completely empty. No crib or changing table, no boxes filled with a child's belongings to be moved to wherever they're going to live next . . .

That's all right. It doesn't mean anything. They have another baby on the way, so they probably moved their toddler down the hall to make room here for the new sibling.

And then, for some reason, we decided to leave our dream house. Why? Where are we going? Are we leaving California?

When she opens the next door, she finds a stark white room with a whole wall of built-in bookshelves, all of them empty. They weren't there three years ago. Nor were the desk, rolling chair, file cabinets, and disassembled computer equipment. There are boxes, too—dozens of them, most, at a glance, marked BOOKS or FILES. Clearly, this is—*was?*—a home office.

Why here? What happened to the one downstairs, off the living room?

Clara turns away. There's only one potential bedroom door left in the upstairs hall.

She opens it warily, fervently hoping to find signs that a two-year-old resides within.

Please, please, please . . .

"No." Clara backs away, unsettled by the sight of another room with plain white walls— this one, like the nursery, completely hollow.

Slamming the door closed and leaning against it, she forces herself to consider the facts: only the master bedroom contains a bed. Therefore, it seems as though only two people live here.

Or one, Clara reluctantly admits to herself, remembering the single toothbrush in the master bath.

Nerves rapidly fraying, she notices that the door to the hall bathroom is ajar. She glances in and notes that there's not a single sign of use. No waste paper basket, no towel on the towel bar or bath mat at the tub.

"It's okay," she says aloud, striding toward the stairs. "It doesn't mean anything. We're moving out anyway."

Dickens meets her at the foot of the stairs with an anxious-sounding bark.

"What's going on, boy?" She reaches down to pat him—then, remembering the home office, glances into the living room.

"What the . . . ?"

Going into the room for a closer look, trailed by Dickens, she realizes that the door to the glassed-in home office is . . . gone.

The spot is now just a wall with a window. Peering through it, Clara sees that a bed of shrubbery and dense groundcover fills the footprint where the office once sat.

She looks abruptly at the dog, who seems to be waiting expectantly beside her.

"I know. This is crazy, right? Who knows— maybe *I'm* crazy. You know what we need to do? We need to call someone who can tell us where Drew is. I'll do the talking."

Dickens wags his tail eagerly, as if to say, *Great idea. But who are we going to call?*

The answer is a no-brainer. There's only one person in the world who would understand how she could wake up in the future.

Doris.

Clara looks around for a phone, but the living room cordless seems to be packed away. She heads for the kitchen, picks up the phone there, begins dialing—then stops short, Doris's voice echoing in her head.

Come on, who are we kidding? I'm getting up there in years. Chances are, I might not be around the next time you get back to New York for a visit.

Three—no, more than four—years have gone by since that rainy day Clara said good-bye to her old friend back in New York.

What if . . .

No. Come on. Don't be morbid.

She finishes dialing. The phone rings—just once. And it isn't Doris's voice that answers; it's a robotic recording.

"The number you are trying to reach has been disconnected. Please check the number and try again."

Shaken, Clara hangs up.

Maybe Doris is in a nursing home somewhere.

I'm staying put. When I leave this place for the last time, it'll be in a body bag.

Clara pushes the thought from her head. Now is not the time to lose her composure. And there are plenty of other people she can call.

Her parents, Drew's parents . . .

But none of her loved ones will have gotten any younger, either.

Chances are her parents and Drew's are fine, but if they're not and there's been a loss . . .

She doesn't want to know about it. Not now, while she's in the midst of trying to figure out why Drew isn't with her on Christmas and why, heaven help her, there's no sign of their child.

A lump of emotion clogs her throat.

No. Don't go there.

Clara forces it back down as she hurries toward the kitchen, trailed by the dog. She grabs the phone and dials the first number that pops into her head: Mike's.

It rings only once before an unfamiliar female voice answers. Not unusual. Mike rarely answers his own phone, and lately, he tends to be surrounded by an entourage—lately, as in three years ago.

"Hi . . . who is this?" Clara asks.

"This is Tim," the voice says, and cracks—clueing her into the fact that it belongs not to a woman, but to an adolescent boy. "Who's this?"

"I was looking for Mike . . ."

"Mike Cadley?"

Who? "No, Mike Marshall."

There's a pause.

Then Tim says, "Good one, Jessica. Ha-ha. What're you going to do next, call up asking for Brad Pitt or some other random old guy?"

Huh?

Before Clara can get past her speechlessness over hearing Brad Pitt and Mike Marshall lumped together as random old guys, Tim goes on, "My parents are getting pissed that the phone keeps ringing. Dude, you've got to stop calling me with all these stupid pranks."

Ah, at least some things haven't changed: adolescent boys still call everyone—including adolescent girls—"dude."

Tim hangs up without further ado.

Poor Jessica.

Poor Mike.

And poor me.

Clara should have realized she'd never get a hold of him, considering that he's forced to change his number every time the paparazzi or his fans manage to track it down. And regardless of what may or may not have gone on in his career in the past three years, it's not like she can just dial information and ask for his new contact information.

She runs through a mental list of confidants. Besides Drew's family, there's no one in California she feels close to. She hasn't been here long enough to make friends yet.

Back in New York, there's Karen Vinton, her therapist . . .

Former therapist. She hadn't spoken to Karen since the move. She can hardly call her now, out of the blue, on Christmas no less—with a dilemma like this.

Dickens, she sees, is watching her as if wondering what her next move will be.

"You know what they say," she tells the dog with a shrug. "When in doubt, call on Jesus."

Again she dials from memory.

This time, the phone rings quite a few times on the other end before someone answers with a shouted "Hola!" over a noisy background of chatter and music.

Relief courses through her at the sound of a familiar voice at last. He's her best friend. He'll know what to do.

"Jesus, it's Clara."

"Who?"

At least, he *was* a friend in the now that occurred three years ago.

"Clara Becker . . . I mean, Clara McCallum," she amends, wondering whether they've somehow drifted apart now that they're living on opposite coasts, despite her vow not to let that happen.

"Wait a minute; hang on." On his end, Jesus shouts something in Spanish. She hears laughter, then the chatter and music seem to fade a bit.

Jesus is back on the line, saying, "That's better. Now *who* is this?"

"It's Clara."

"Clairol! *Feliz Navidad!*" He sounds pleasantly surprised, and she's thrilled to hear her old nickname.

She opens her mouth to say—something, she has no idea what, because how do you tell someone you've just popped in from the past?

But before she can speak, Jesus goes on, "Sorry about that before, I've got a houseful of *loco* family and friends and I couldn't hear a damned thing. I had to go into a closet with the phone, and you know me—I haven't been closeted in years."

He laughs—a little too hard—at his own joke. Same old Jesus. Thank goodness. Clara laughs, too, feeling a ripple of giddy pleasure at the realization that she's no longer entirely alone in this strange world.

"So, tell me," Jesus says, "where are you?"

"I'm . . . home." *I think. For now, anyway.* She glances uneasily at the stack of moving boxes.

"No, I mean, where's home these days? Are you still out in California?"

Her heart sinks.

"Yeah, we . . . we are. How about you?" she forces herself to ask in return, as if this is just a friendly holiday catch-up call between old friends. Or former friends, depressing as the notion may be.

"Me? I'm in New York—where else? When I'm not on location, anyway."

There's a sudden burst of noise on his end, and a voice asks him something in Spanish.

"Will you wait a minute?" Jesus replies in English. "Can't you see I'm on the phone here?"

"Hey, Jesus, let me let you go," Clara tells him. "We can talk another time. You're in the middle of a party and I . . . I've got stuff to do, too."

Like freak out.

"Listen up, Clairol, I'm really glad you called. It's been way too long. Let's talk again soon. I want to hear all about your life now."

Yeah, you're not the only one.

She hangs up the phone with a promise to call again, and looks down at Dickens, now lying at her feet.

"So, that was a total bust," she tells him. "No more phone calls. Not yet, anyway. Okay?"

Hearing a loud canine snore, she leans in and sees that the dog is sound asleep.

"Great. I'm glad someone can relax around here."

Shaking her head, Clara is about to hang up the phone again when she notices the Caller ID window and remembers something.

There should be a log of all incoming calls . . .

Yes! There is.

Triumphant, she scrolls through the list, looking for familiar numbers.

There aren't many—though she does spot quite a few calls from her mother, thank goodness. Apparently, Jeanette is alive and well and still living in her Florida assisted living apartment.

I could call her . . . but what would I say?

And what if she tells me something I don't want to hear?

I'm not ready for that.

She scrolls through the rest of the numbers, searching for calls from Drew's office or his cell phone—even knowing it's been disconnected.

Nothing.

There's a chance that one of the unfamiliar numbers could be his.

She randomly dials one that appears several times.

"You have reached the law offices of Fitzgerald and Walters. Please leave a message and we will return your call on the next business day."

Clara hangs up quickly, unsettled. Why would lawyers be calling here? And more than once?

The only time she and Drew ever used an attorney was for their real estate closing. . . .

Wait a minute—they're obviously in the process of moving again. That must be why Fitzgerald and Walters has been in touch so frequently.

But people use lawyers to handle other matters, too.

Divorces.

Wills.

Stop that! Don't be ridiculous!

She hurriedly leaves the phone behind, wandering through the house in search of more encouraging clues.

In the dining room, she randomly chooses a box on the dining room floor and rips open the tape. Inside, there's a mound of crumpled newspaper that obviously protects fragile contents.

She unwraps a yellow plate. Another plate. Another.

The bold, Mexican-style pottery look is unfamiliar. Her taste, it seems, has changed over the past few years. She always favored more delicate designs, softer colors, vintage styles— even before she dropped in on the 1940s.

Shoving the box of plates aside, she wonders whether she should open another. But the dining room is full of housewares, unlikely to yield anything of interest.

In the living room, she realizes that she's physically and emotionally exhausted. She plops down on the couch and leans her head back, absorbing the silence.

Any second now, she tells herself, *the front door is going to open and Drew is going to walk through it.*

Just wait. You'll see.

She does wait.

And wait.

And wait, until the silence threatens to smother her last hope.

But she refuses to let that happen, clinging fiercely to a shred of optimism, reminding herself that the man she loves already found his way back to her once before despite impossible odds.

They've already breached the great chasm of war and illness and time and even death itself.

There's no way he's lost to her now.

They were meant to be together.

Maybe he's not here yet, but he's coming.

I honestly believe that, with all my heart.

Hearing a jingling of dog tags, Clara looks up to see Dickens.

"Well, look who's up. Did you have a nice nap?"

In lieu of a reply, the dog lunges at the couch and snags a throw pillow in his teeth.

"Hey! What are you doing, you crazy dog?" Clara manages to wrestle it away from him, only to have him make a grab for the television remote on the cushion beside her.

"That is not a snack!" Clara rescues the television remote before he can swipe it.

Impulsively, she aims it at the large flat-screen TV across the room. With any luck, it hasn't been disconnected yet for the move.

She just needs a connection to the world beyond her doorstep; some sense that she hasn't stepped into some postapocalyptic scenario where she's the last person alive on earth.

The news footage that greets her as the television screen comes into focus is anything but reassuring.

As the camera pans a rubble-strewn landscape, a female reporter is in the midst of a terse voice-over. ". . . and total devastation where the quake's epicenter was located, about twenty miles northwest of the Bay area."

Clara stares.

San Florentina is about twenty miles northwest of the Bay area . . . but there's nothing remotely recognizable about the images on screen.

"At 8.7 on the Richter scale, the massive quake was preceded by a series of what would later prove to be strong foreshocks beginning on Christmas morning, 2009, causing widespread damage throughout the region."

Foreshock? That violent shaking was a freaking *foreshock*?

"No way," Clara tells Dickens, shaking her head.

The television camera shifts to a man-on-the-street interview.

A reporter holds a microphone toward a man standing against the backdrop of a construction site. Clara leans forward, recognizing him. His face is gaunt and more wrinkled, and his jet-black hair has gone gray, but she's positive that's

Paolo Martino. Since she's been pregnant she's become quite a regular at Scoops, his ice-cream shop on Main Street. The good-natured proprietor always gives her extra whipped cream and two cherries—one for good luck, as he always likes to say.

"You know, living here, we were always bracing ourselves for the Big One. Then, with all the damage on Christmas Day, I guess we just thought that was it. But that was nothing compared to what was coming a few days later. It was such a beautiful, sunny day, everything was fine, and then—boom."

Paolo's ominous words resonate with Clara, and her thoughts whirl back to the terrifying quake she experienced. That was nothing? Dear God.

"I lost everything—my home, my business, my car," Paolo somberly tells the reporter. "But I'm one of the lucky ones. All of that could be replaced. A lot of people I know here, they lost . . . you know. A lot worse. I'm alive, and I have my family."

Dread creeps over Clara as Paolo pauses to bow his head, wipe at his eyes.

"I understand that like many people in San Florentina, you've spent the last three years recovering from injuries you suffered in the quake," the reporter goes on, "and now you're finally rebuilding your home and business."

"That's right. We'll be open in time for spring." Paolo's smile doesn't quite reach his eyes.

The camera cuts back to the newsroom, where the anchors are seated before a graphic that reads THREE YEARS LATER: REMEMBERING THE BIG ONE.

"We'll be coming to you live throughout the day as we cover ceremonies throughout the Bay area to commemorate the catastrophic quake of 2009. And now, we turn to brighter things: the weather forecast. Today's heavy coastal fog will continue into tomorrow as—"

Clara changes the station abruptly.

She doesn't care about the weather forecast. She needs more information about what, exactly, went on around here three years ago. It's as if her entire life as she knew it was swallowed by the notorious San Andreas Fault.

But she's not going to let herself think the worst—that something happened to Drew in that earthquake. No, because she saw him right afterward and he was fine. And anyway, he's obviously around, because she's pregnant *now*, three years later.

What if it isn't his baby?

The thought of that is unimaginable. Laughable, almost. She can't possibly fathom any circumstances where she would be living here, in their house, and carrying another man's child.

But you're moving out.

So? People move all the time.

And anyway, the bottom line is that if Drew weren't out there somewhere, she would sense it. . . .

Wouldn't you?

Of course.

She would know, in her heart, if he were never coming home.

Then again . . .

Would you?

She spent all that time with Jed in 1941 knowing all along that he was going to go off and get himself killed in the war. She's certain she'd have felt it even if she hadn't known it for a fact; that she would have sensed, in her heart, that his days—their days—were numbered. With Jed, there was such an aura of urgency, an acute awareness that they didn't have forever.

Ah, but you were wrong about that, weren't you?

And this is different.

This is the future.

If Drew were no longer alive, she'd feel it. It's that simple. There would be an emptiness in her heart, instead of hope.

After channel surfing past several commercials, a home shopping program, a travel documentary, and *A Christmas Story*, she lands on CNN.

For a moment, seeing the familiar backdrop

of rubble and devastation, she believes she's found what she's looking for.

But this coverage has nothing to do with earthquakes.

It's all about a horrific foreign war, one that hasn't even begun to flare up in the present—or rather, the past. And then there's a report on a promising medical breakthrough, and a recent assassination, and peace talks in the Middle East that appear to be much further along these days. . . .

Good news, bad news.

But no old news about a California earth-quake.

Weary, Clara closes her eyes.

Maybe this is all just a really bad dream.

Chapter 9

Drew is in the front hall, vacuuming broken glass, when Dickens races in from the next room, barking at the front door.

"No. Careful, puppy, you're going to get hurt." Drew frowns and turns off the shop vac, then scoops the dog into his arms.

More barking.

"Shhh, you're going to wake Clara." He peeks into the living room to see his wife still sitting on the couch, sound asleep.

The puppy squirms as Drew carries him into the kitchen. "Sorry, fella, but it's just for a little while," he tells Dickens, wrestling him into his crate.

Returning to the front hall, he's about to turn on the shop vac again when he hears a pounding at the front door, and realizes somebody's there. No wonder the dog was barking.

Drew hurries to answer the knock, wondering who's here, and hoping whoever it is will have some information about the quake. Both the TV and Internet are down and the phone lines are jammed.

He kicks aside a shard of broken glass and opens the door to see his neighbor, Jeff Tucker, and his daughter Amelia, a chubby strawberry blonde with glasses, braces, and an abundance of freckles.

"Everybody all right here?" Jeff asks. He's wearing what Clara likes to call the local uniform: a Columbia fleece jacket, jeans, boots, and a baseball cap. Oakland A's. Drew is a San Francisco Giants fan, himself.

"We're fine," he tells Jeff. "Just some damage around the house. How about you?"

"Same thing. That was a pretty good shake."

"Is the puppy okay?" Amelia asks anxiously, looking past Drew's shoulder into the house, where the barking goes on at full volume. "He sounds upset."

"Oh, he's fine. Just loud."

"Maybe he doesn't like hearing all those sirens."

"Maybe," Drew agrees, noticing that the far-off sirens continue to wail ominously. "Or maybe he's just hungry or something."

"Well, I don't see how he could be," Amanda

pipes up, "because this morning at our house, he ate—"

"She's been real worried about the dog," Jeff interrupts his daughter. "Got pretty attached to him since you dropped him by yesterday."

"My mom said it was a good thing he wasn't staying, though."

Uh-oh.

"Did she, now?" Drew asks, wondering whether Nancy Tucker happens to have a mink coat.

"Yes, because you'll never believe what he—"

"Amelia," Jeff says quickly, "no need to get into all that."

Uh-oh is right.

"All what?" Drew asks reluctantly.

"Nothing," Jeff assures him, "it was fine. We were glad to keep him for you. Amelia and her brothers had a great time playing with him, and he was no trouble at all."

"Except when he—"

Seeing the warning glance Jeff shoots his daughter, Drew asks himself whether he honestly wants to know what kind of trouble Dickens caused during his brief stay at the neighbors' house.

Not really, he decides guiltily. *Not with everything else that's gone on today.*

"Well . . . thanks again for keeping him," he

tells Jeff, adding, to Amelia, "And you can come over and visit him anytime you want."

"I can? Thanks! I think a puppy would be the best present ever," she adds wistfully. "Was your wife surprised?"

"Very. Want to come in and say hello to her and Dickens? That's what we named him."

"Oh, that's so cute!" Amelia looks at her father. "Can I go see him, Dad?"

"Only for a minute."

"So any idea how strong the quake was or where it was centered?" Drew asks Jeff.

"Not a clue, but my guess is a good four or five, and pretty close by."

"I figured the same thing. Oh, leave your shoes on," Drew tells Amelia, seeing that she's about to remove her sneakers. "There's still some broken glass on the floor. I'm trying to get it all, but . . ."

"Are you sure? They're totally muddy."

"Positive," he tells her, and he can tell she's thinking she'd never get away with that at home.

Drew has only met Nancy Tucker a couple of times, but that was enough to realize she's a meticulous housekeeper. Maybe that's why, according to her daughter, she wasn't exactly disappointed when he picked up the dog this morning. Maybe Dickens got mud on her floor.

Or worse.

As Amelia dashes off toward the kitchen, Jeff

tells Drew, "We really just wanted to make sure you were okay over here. Phones are jammed up or I would've called."

"I know, I can't even get a call out on my cell," Drew replies, closing the door behind them. "Can I make you a cup of coffee, or—"

"No, really, we've got to get back home pretty quickly. Nancy's got her hands full with the boys, and she's probably cursing me out right about now." He rolls his eyes.

"Well, I'm glad you came by. We're feeling pretty cut off from the rest of the world. Well, I am, anyway."

"Where's Clara?"

"She's actually taking a nap. She—"

"Is it okay if I got him out of the crate?" Amelia interrupts from the kitchen doorway, and Drew looks up to see her holding the puppy like a doll. Or a baby.

Maybe Amelia can babysit for our child someday, Drew finds himself thinking, and then . . .

Wow.

We're going to have a baby.

Every time the realization strikes him anew, butterflies launch in his stomach.

"Amelia! What would make you let him out of his crate?" Jeff scolds.

"No, it's okay," Drew assures them. "He doesn't like it in there very much."

"I know. When my mom—"

"Amelia, go put him back where you found him," her father cuts her off.

"I will. In two seconds. He wanted to see me, didn't you, Dickens?" Amelia adds in a cheerful and affectionate falsetto.

Dickens yelps happily.

"Drew!" Clara calls from the next room, and he bolts.

She's sitting straight up, rubbing her eyes, looking utterly bewildered.

"Are you feeling okay?" Drew asks, crossing over to the couch.

"I just . . . was I sleeping?"

"Yep."

"Merry Christmas, Clara," Jeff comments behind them, and Jeff sees Drew stepping around this morning's discarded wrapping paper and stacks of gifts that now mix with items displaced from the quake.

Clara looks up in surprise. "Oh, I didn't even see you there. Hi, Jed."

"It's Jeff," their neighbor corrects her.

"Oh, I'm sorry," Clara says. "I meant Jeff, not Jed."

Jed . . .

Drew experiences a flash of—well, it would be considered a memory if it had actually happened to him, but he's quite certain he's never ridden in the rumble seat of an old-fashioned car.

Yet for an instant, he sees himself doing just that. Well, he doesn't see *himself* doing it, per se.

It's more as if he's inside someone else's head, looking out at the car and a couple of unfamiliar boys in the front seat and a blur of someone waving from the sidewalk.

He hears a blast of an *ah-ooh-gah* car horn, and a female voice calling, "Hi, Jed!" and he turns to look, and he notes that he's driving down what looks like an old-fashioned Main Street USA, but for some reason it feels incredibly familiar.

No, wait, it's . . .

It *is* familiar—but not because he's ever been there. He's pretty sure the street his brain just conjured up is the small town set that was used for last year's blockbuster *The Glenhaven Park Dozen*. Clara was filming the movie when they met, before she was diagnosed with cancer and had to drop out of the cast.

And the name Jed—that's familiar, too. Jed was the hero's name in the movie, based on a group of real-life small-town soldiers who died together in the war.

The film's director, Denton Wilkens, invited Clara to the Hollywood premiere of *The Glenhaven Park Dozen*. Drew accompanied her, a heady experience—and not just because of the red carpet and flashbulbs and frenzied female fans screaming for Clara's friend Mike, who was starring in the film.

When they sat in the darkened theater and the celluloid world took over, Drew found himself utterly lost in another era—and an extraordinary sense of déjà vu.

Of course it made sense that Drew would identify with Michael Marshall's character, Jed Landry, considering that he was the on-screen love interest of Violet, whom Clara had originally been cast to play.

Besides, Denton Wilkens is famous for making hauntingly realistic period films with meticulous attention to detail. Plenty of people get lost in his films.

But for Drew, it all seemed so . . . real.

"How did you like it?" he remembers Clara asking anxiously as they exited the theater.

"It was amazing. I felt like I was living it," he admitted, and for a moment, judging by a fleeting expression in her eyes, he felt almost as if she knew that there was more to it than that.

But their relationship was new and vulnerable, and he wasn't about to tell her that he was haunted by bizarre dreams—even when he was awake.

Even now, he can't tell her that he has these little episodes in which he'll imagine himself as someone else, and it's so real he can taste and smell and hear it all.

In fact, sometimes it's his own five senses that seem to trigger the false flashbacks in the first place. He'll catch a sniff of something wafting in the air, like cigarette smoke or snow or roast chicken. . . .

Or he'll hear snatches of oldies music or a conversational turn of phrase, or even just a word, like *fruitcake*. . . .

Earlier, the moment Clara said the word, he was reminded of an old lady lying in a snowy street, bleeding. But of course that had nothing to do with fruitcake, and he's never witnessed anything like that scene in real life, thank God. He doesn't know where the image came from, or why it was triggered by that particular word, or what any of it might mean. . . .

Other than that you're nuttier than a fruitcake yourself, bub.

Drew has always privately laughed—or at least shrugged—off the vivid dreams and nightmares, the flashes of scenes that seem straight out of a vintage movie or someone else's life.

But it isn't just about imagining himself as someone else.

It's about having his emotions kick into overdrive without warning, and for no good reason.

Like, the other day, he was watching TV—one of those Hallmark commercials where the world is all Currier and Ives, with music and sleigh bells and children on sleds and whirling white flakes coming down—and there was a passing shot of a red mitten lying in the snow.

All at once, Drew was overwhelmed with a strange, intense, and entirely inexplicable sense of longing. Tears actually sprang to his eyes, and he was glad Clara had dozed off beside him on the couch because there he was, a grown man, crying over a mitten and a Hallmark commercial.

And then there are the voices. The ones he hears in his head once in a while.

They don't say anything specific, or, God forbid, tell him to do anything, as they do in all those news accounts of psychotic people who commit crimes.

It's more like he's overhearing bits and pieces of conversations other people are having—sometimes, they're talking around him, and sometimes, they're talking directly to him. But not *him*, because he never has any idea what, or even whom, they're talking about.

Once, clear as day, he heard a female voice shriek, "*Doris! Did you cut up my girdle to make a slingshot?*"

He doesn't even know anyone named Doris. Clara once did—she had an elderly pal by that name back in New York. But it's not as though Drew ever met her.

The name Doris . . . girdles . . .

Where on earth did that stuff even come from?

And then, just recently, heading out into a rainy day, he suddenly heard a male voice saying, "*Don't forget to wear your galoshes, son.*"

Galoshes? He had no idea what those even were, exactly, until he looked it up and found that they're thin rubber shoes that slip over your regular shoes to protect them from inclement weather. They were popular in the days when men went around wearing suits and hats everywhere.

The days of girdles and galoshes, rumble seats and swing music . . .

Lately, these strange little incidents are striking Drew so often that he's starting to wonder if maybe he really is . . .

Well, bat-shit crazy.

Like Aunt Stella.

His father always reminds everyone that she wasn't always an imaginary biker chick.

"She used to be normal just like the rest of us," he likes to say, and then he'll make some joke about the rest of them not being all that normal, either.

"What happened to her, Dad?" Drew and his sisters have all asked from time to time, and that's when his mother always gave his father a warning look, and Dad changed the subject.

When he was younger, Drew never gave Aunt Stella's problems much thought.

But now that strange things are happening to him with more and more frequency . . .

Well, for all Drew knows, his aunt's fateful slide off the deep end started with hallucinations just like his.

Yes, and the next thing he knows, he'll be wearing a crash helmet for no reason and Clara will have left him for someone else. Someone *sane.*

"Drew?" Clara's voice intrudes and he blinks, seeing both her and Jeff Tucker watching him as though they're waiting for him to say something.

"What?"

"I said, do *you* feel okay? You keep asking about me, but now you're the one who seems a little . . ."

"I'm fine," he says quickly. "Why?"

"You just had this look on your face like . . ."

Like I was imagining myself as someone else— apparently Jed Landry, the movie hero—riding around in a rumble seat?

Ha.

He's never told anyone, and he isn't about to start now.

"I'm fine," he assures his wife, hoping that it's true.

Chapter 10

The Tuckers are long gone, Dickens is unwillingly back in his crate, and Drew has, after a couple of detours, resumed his vacuuming.

In the living room, Clara picks through the scattered Christmas ornaments, hanging those that are undamaged on the upright-again tree.

Miraculously, only a handful of fragile decorations were lost, and none had any particular sentimental value.

Even more miraculously, her snow globe, while perched precariously close to the edge of the mantel, also made it through the earthquake in one piece.

Clara pushed it all the way back against the wall, but she isn't going to leave it there. No, she's going to pack it away in bubble wrap and foam peanuts and whatever else she can find to cushion it from what lies ahead.

The Big One.

Every time she allows herself to think about it, she's struck by icy foreboding—and a terrible sense of déjà vu.

Clara hangs a striped porcelain candy cane on the tree, lost in thought.

This is just like being back in 1941 and knowing not only that Pearl Harbor was going to be bombed any second, but that Jed Landry was going to enlist and go off to die in the war, and there was nothing she could do to stop any of it from happening.

She bends to pluck a Swarovski ornament from the rug and turns it around and around, making sure the delicate piece is intact.

Experience—and her old physics teacher Mr. Kershaw—taught her that you can't change what's already happened in the past. He told Clara it would violate the law of quantum mechanics that says that what you do in the present is an inevitable product of the past.

But this isn't the past—it's the present.

It's only the past when she's in the future.

Fingers trembling, Clara carefully places the crystal star on a high branch.

Really, she needs to talk to Mr. Kershaw right away. She hasn't spoken to him since she left New York, but they did exchange Christmas cards and she knows just where to find him.

But do I really want to hear what he's going to say if I start asking questions about what is and isn't scientifically possible?

Yes. And even if she can't save the rest of the world—or their town, or their house—she can at least make sure she and Drew are in a safe, distant place when the devastating 8.7 quake strikes. . . .

When, exactly?

Paolo said it hit on a sunny day, and that it happened "a few" days after the Christmas foreshock. How many is a few?

Two days? Three?

Why didn't she pay more attention to the timing when she was watching the news in 2012?

She was too horrified by Paolo's account of the staggering losses in San Florentina, too preoccupied with figuring out where Drew was, and their baby, too frightened that they, too, might have been casualties.

But everything is all right again . . . for now. She's back in the present, back in her life, with Drew in the next room and their baby on the way.

She touches her stomach, unnerved by how flat it is again. She'd actually gotten used to her big belly in the short time she'd spent in the future. Now, you'd never know she was pregnant just to look at her.

"Hey."

She looks up to see Drew in the doorway. "Oh . . . hey."

"You're not having stomach pains, are you?"

"No. Not at all."

"But you've got to be hungry again, right?"

Hungry?

She hasn't thought about it in a while, but suddenly she's ravenous.

"I could definitely eat."

"So could I." He holds out his hand.

She takes it. "I'll finish the tree later."

"It looks great. I can't believe it fell over and the ornaments didn't even shatter."

"A few did."

"But nothing precious."

"No, nothing precious," she agrees.

As they head to the kitchen, she glances over her shoulder to see the snow globe reassuringly intact on the mantel.

The little angel has made it through a lot over the years, with only a broken wing tip to show for it.

But the worst, Clara knows, is yet to come.

Chapter 11

Morning.

Again.

Clara opens her eyes and her gaze falls on a box of saltines sitting on the nightstand beside the alarm clock.

For a moment, she stares at it, wondering why she finds the sight vaguely disturbing. Then the room beyond—and her thoughts—come into focus and she sits up quickly.

Too quickly.

Acrid bile chokes her throat and she gulps it back, sinking against the pillow again. Morning sickness.

Too nauseated to move for fear of throwing up, she notes that the clock reads 6:11. *Morning or evening?* she wonders, disoriented. It's impossible to tell from the murky light falling through the glass panes across from the bed, punctuated by the glow of an electric candle.

A candle?

She reaches out and pats the mattress beside her, searching for the warm weight of her husband. But the bed is empty. She can feel it even before she turns her head, battling nausea, and confirms the fact.

Thoughts scrambled, she replays everything she can possibly recall of what happened . . . yesterday? Three years ago? When?

Is she in the future or the present? Hell, for all she knows, she's in the past, living various Christmas days over and over like a wayward anti-Scrooge.

Only one way to find out what's going on. She sits up again, gingerly this time.

Okay, so far, so good. She swings her legs over the edge of the bed. A little queasy, but nothing she can't—

Oh, barf.

She vaults from the bed toward the bathroom and makes it just in time.

"Whoa . . . are you okay?"

Kneeling on the floor, clinging miserably to the toilet bowl, Clara looks up to see Drew standing over her with shaving cream covering half his face.

"Drew!" she gasps. "You're here!"

"So are you . . . and you know I love you, but you've got some . . ." He gestures at her face.

Oh, ick.

He helps her to her feet, grabs a washcloth, runs it under hot water, wrings it out, and gives it to her.

She wipes her mouth, fighting the urge to throw herself into his arms.

"What's the date today?" she asks casually, drying her face on the towel he hands her.

He raises an eyebrow. "Uh, the twenty-sixth?"

"December twenty-sixth." She says the month just to be sure, not wanting it to sound like a question.

Drew nods slowly. "Day after Christmas."

"I know!"

"For a second there, you sounded a little . . . confused."

"I guess that earthquake yesterday really scrambled my brains," she tells him quickly— then wonders whether that was such a good idea. "Um . . . there *was* an earthquake yesterday, right?

"You're kidding, right?"

"There *wasn't* an earthquake yesterday?"

Now Drew looks really concerned. "Are you okay?"

"I'm totally fine. I just wondered if maybe I dreamed it," she tells him because, of course, there was an earthquake, and anyone in her right mind would remember it . . . even if it was just a foreshock.

"You don't look fine. Are you still queasy?"

"No—yes—Hey, where are you going?" she asks as he heads toward the bedroom.

"To get the crackers. I put them on the night-stand for you when I came up to bed last night, because it said in that pregnancy book that it might help the morning sickness if you eat something before you even get up. Didn't you see them?"

"Yes, I did, and that was sweet of you, but I don't need crackers. I just need for us to be to-gether. Come here. Can we do that? Can we just be together? Please?"

"Sure we can." He gives her a quick squeeze, then starts away again. "I'm just going to go down into town, like we said, and pick up the papers and see how much damage there is from the quake, and then—"

"*Noooo!*" she wails, following him.

Drew, obviously taken aback by her drama queen response, doesn't seem to know what to say for a moment.

When he turns to rest a soothing hand on her shoulder, his brown eyes are laced with con-cern. "What's wrong?"

"It could be dangerous. You shouldn't go. Please don't go down there."

"Why not?"

"Because . . . I don't want to be alone here."

"But last night you said you wanted to stay home this morning and rest. Did you forget?"

"No, it's . . ."

She shakes her head, realizing she does remember that. She remembers yesterday: assessing the damage from the quake, and trying to put the house back together with Dickens underfoot, and the Tuckers stopping over . . .

Yet she also remembers a different yesterday: a house filled with moving boxes, and an oversized Dickens, and no Drew . . .

She remembers two yesterdays.

She lived two yesterdays—only one hasn't happened yet, and—

"Clara?"

"What? I mean, yes, I guess I did forget I said that," she lies, sinking down on the edge of the bed.

But that's not why I'm upset.

"Mommy brain," Drew informs her with a knowing nod. "I read all about it. You know, you were right. That book is really interesting. Did you know that in a few weeks, the height of the fundus will be—"

"I have no idea what a fundus even is," Clara cuts in shrilly.

Doesn't he know the world as they know it is about to be shattered?

Of course he doesn't know. You're the only one who knows, just like before, in 1941.

"The fundus," Drew says calmly, turning toward the closet, "is the top of the uterus and they measure it to—"

"Drew . . . we need to get out of here!"

Poised in the closet doorway, he turns back to look at her. *"What?"*

"Please. Let's just . . . let's get on a plane. We'll go to New York, or to Florida, or . . ."

"Clara."

"Please. Please just listen to me. We have to go away for at least a few days, or a week."

"We will. We're going to the Caribbean in Feb—"

"No, *now!*"

"Now? Today?"

"It's a Saturday," she says. "What else do we have to do?"

"Finish putting our house back together before I have to be at work at five o'clock Monday morning before the market opens in New York. And, anyway, even if we did want to get away, we can't just pick up and go anymore. We have the dog now."

"He can come, too."

He shakes his head. "We just got him, he's barely trained, and after the way he howled and kept us up last night, you really think he'd be good company on a road trip? Or a cross-country plane trip?"

She shrugs miserably. "I just . . . I just really feel like we need to go somewhere. Anywhere."

"But why?"

Tell him!

Tell him the truth!

He's your husband. If anyone can possibly understand, he will.

But then, she had told Jed, in the end. And while he'd listened patiently, and hadn't laughed or called her crazy, he hadn't believed her, either. He'd thought she was delusional from her bump on the head.

Jed was Jed, though. They might have been soul mates, but they had just met.

Drew is Drew. They're married; they've known each other for years.

Still . . .

When you get right down to it, Jed is Drew, and Drew is Jed and, anyway, no one in his right mind—even if he loves her—is going to believe that she's been zipping back and forth through time.

She sees that Drew is once again staring at her with concern—or is it mild alarm?

He's probably wondering how he got stuck with a wife who has barf breath and doesn't even know what day it is. Who wouldn't be?

Then, all at once, his expression changes, as if the light has suddenly dawned.

"I know what this is about."

"You . . . you do?"

He nods and opens his arms. "Come here."

Folded in Drew's reassuring embrace, Clara struggles to calm her frantic thoughts.

"You're freaking out about all the changes that are coming," Drew tells her. "I read that it happens to everyone at some point during her pregnancy. It's normal to feel trapped when you realize there's no turning back. But this is what we've always wanted. You have to remember that, okay?"

She pulls back bleakly and looks up at him, nodding.

"And I'm going to be with you every step of the way. I promise."

You shouldn't make promises you can't be sure you'll be able to keep, she wants to tell him. *Some things are beyond your control.*

But she doesn't dare say it. Not here and now. Not until she knows for sure whether there's a chance she can change something that has yet to happen.

Mr. Kershaw. I have to talk to him right away.

Chapter 12

"Are you sure you don't want to come with me?" Drew asks Clara, hesitating in the doorway with his car keys in hand.

"No, I'll stay here. I wish you would, too."

"I just want to see it for myself. I know we've only lived here for a few months but I feel like it's home."

"So do I, but . . ." She toys with the sash of her white terry-cloth robe. "Just please tell me again that you're going to be super careful down there."

"I'm going to be super careful down there."

"And you won't go near any buildings with cracked foundations."

"No cracked foundations."

"And there might be downed live wires—"

"I'll only step on the downed dead ones."

"I'm serious."

"So am I."

"Then why are you smiling?"

"Because if you're this worried about me, I can just imagine how you're going to be every time our kid walks out the door."

She shakes her head, smiling faintly, though her green eyes remain troubled. "I can't help it. I love you. I just want to make sure you come home safely."

Struck by the unexpected quaver in her voice, he leans back in to give her a tight hug.

"That's all anyone ever wants, isn't it?" he tells her. "We just want the people we love to come home safely every time they leave us."

Releasing her, he could swear he sees tears in her eyes.

"Clara—are you crying?"

"No." She wipes a telltale trickle from her cheek, admitting, "Yes. I don't even know why. It's probably just hormones."

Probably. He sat up late last night reading the book from her drawer, and learned all about the havoc a pregnancy can wreak on a woman's body and soul.

Suddenly reluctant to leave her in this fragile state, he says, "I don't have to go into town if you don't want to be left a—"

"No! No, you should go. You should definitely go. I'll be fine. Just be careful."

"I will. Hey, don't forget to charge your cell

phone just in case." Yesterday, hers had only one battery bar—typical—and the battery had gone dead by last night.

"Just in case what?"

"In case there's a problem with the regular phones again. They might be working on the lines if there's been damage and—"

"I promise I'll find it and charge it."

"You don't even know where it is?" He sighs.

"I'll find it. Go. I love you."

She all but pushes him out the door and closes it behind him.

Drew shakes his head, then shrugs and heads to the car.

If this morning has been any indication, they're in for a real roller-coaster ride between now and next summer.

But you've always liked roller coasters, he reminds himself, knowing he wouldn't trade this experience for anything.

He tunes the car radio to the local station, KSFL, hoping for a news update. Instead, he hears an annoying commercial punctuated by sleigh bells, a ho-ho-hoing Santa, and a helium-inhaling elf voice-over.

The drive into town takes about ten minutes along a winding coastal road dotted with yellow signs warning of S curves. Driving through the fog, Drew glimpses the usual landmarks: majestic stands of old-growth redwoods, the jutting Harriman overlook high above the sea, a pebbly stretch of beach where fat seals lounge atop boulders like bloated tourists on poolside chaises.

Most of the houses that dot the highway are obscured from view by fog and evergreen foliage, so there's no way to gauge the destruction.

At last, a series of commercials on the car radio finally give way to the news.

"The quake registered more than five on the Richter scale," an announcer states. "It caused widespread damage and some injuries, but fortunately no casualties have been reported."

Thank God for that, Drew thinks, guiding the car along a steep decline. *It could have been worse. Much worse.*

Still, as the road slopes into the final hairpin leading into town, he braces himself. Both the Internet and television news—both of which were up and running again by late yesterday afternoon—featured sobering camera footage and countless photographs taken in the hilly area east of San Florentina.

"Some older houses suffered significant structural harm," the radio report continues, "but most newer construction appears to have been spared due to revised building codes in recent years."

Drew is all too familiar with those codes. The first time he and Clara met with Reese Janson, the architect who designed their home, they asked him if it could be made "earthquake proof."

"Earthquake resistant, yes," Reese replied. "But there's no such thing as earthquake proof."

He went on to caution them that a two-story home would be more vulnerable than a single story.

But Clara had grown up in a small apartment and longed for a "real" house with a stairway leading up to bedrooms. And Drew's childhood home, a tall Victorian, had withstood the Great 1906 San Francisco Earthquake, along with another century's worth of seismic activity.

In the end, they opted not to change their plans, and the architect promised to make their home as stable as possible.

Maybe Drew should give Reese Janson a call to let him know he did a great job of it.

Driving into the center of town, he's heartened to see that all appears normal, with the exception of orange cones marking some gaping pavement cracks, and teams of workmen hammering plywood over shattered plate-glass windows at a couple of businesses.

Drew parks in a diagonal spot alongside the town square, near a trio of tall pines strung with cheerful Christmas lights. Stepping out of the car, he hears evidence of repairs: the whir of a buzz saw amid steady hammering.

As he walks along the sidewalk toward the

row of shops, the buzz saw stops abruptly and music reaches his ears.

Christmas carols have been piped over the town's PA system to entertain Main Street shoppers throughout the season—yet another quaint touch that charmed Drew and Clara when they first visited just over a year ago.

Bing Crosby is singing about a white Christmas, and Drew is instantly carried back to another time and place.

This time, thank goodness, it really is a memory—and one of his favorites: his first date with Clara.

It was on Christmas Eve, three years ago. He took her to *The Nutcracker* ballet in New York.

She seemed a little detached at first, and his heart sank. He'd only seen her a few times, but it was enough to know he was interested.

More than interested, really.

The moment they first met, it was as if something clicked into place. He experienced an immediate connection to her and he now knows that she felt the same way. But she hid it pretty well. He found out why after the ballet that night.

It turned out that she had recently heard a woman's voice filtering from his apartment out into the hall as she passed his door, and immediately jumped to the wrong conclusion.

When he explained that he'd been watching

the old movie *White Christmas* on the night in question, and the female voice she'd heard had belonged to Rosemary Clooney, Clara was adorably embarrassed.

He kissed her on the cheek when he left her at her door that night, fighting the strange instinct to grab her in a passionate embrace as if they were already lovers. Not that he'd never been physically attracted to a beautiful woman before. But what he felt toward Clara seemed as powerfully emotional as it was physical, and that made no sense. He barely knew her.

On Christmas morning, while he was out walking on the Lower East Side, he came across the vintage snow globe in a store cluttered with castoffs. It seemed familiar to him when he first saw it—maybe because he'd seen a similar one somewhere in his life, or maybe because the dark-haired angel reminded him of Clara.

On an impulse, he bought it for her. Then—on an even more brazen impulse—he decided to stop by and give it to her right then.

As he handed over the gift-wrapped package, he was suddenly sure it was a bad idea and that she'd wonder why on earth he was presenting her someone's old junk.

But—miracle of miracles—she seemed overjoyed.

Well, she is an actress, he remembers thinking at the time, watching her rapt expression as she gazed at the snow globe, listening to the tinkling rendition of "I'll Be Home for Christmas."

But he soon realized that her reaction was genuine. She really did love the gift, and she really was touched by his gesture. She invited him to share Christmas Day with her family—and, basically, they haven't been apart since.

Remembering how anxious she was when he left the house today, he instinctively quickens his pace.

Don't worry, he tells her silently. *I was home for Christmas and I'll be home the day after, too . . . and the day after . . . and the day after. . . .*

I'll be there, like I promised.

Drew stops short.

I'll be there, like I promised. . . .

He isn't just thinking the phrase; he can actually *see* the words—can see himself painstakingly writing them on a piece of paper, using a fountain pen.

He closes his eyes.

It's part of a letter, written on stationery, and it begins *Dearest Clara . . .*

He's positive he's never written to his wife before, other than e-mail. In fact, he's also positive that he hasn't handwritten a letter in years—probably not since his mother used to stand over him making him write thank-you notes for birthday presents.

But if he ever *did* write a letter to anyone—

even Clara—he probably wouldn't start it with an old-fashioned sentiment like *Dearest*.

"Drew!"

He looks up to see a familiar face—though it takes him a minute to place it.

Steve Mifflin, from the men's basketball league that plays on Sunday mornings in the high school gym. Drew joined after they moved in, figuring it would be good for his health—and for meeting the locals.

He's just stepping out of Scoops, the ice-cream parlor, carrying a white paper bag.

"Hey, how's it going, Steve? Everything okay at your place?"

"Could be better. A piece of sculpture fell on my daughter Heather's foot."

"Oh no." Drew hasn't known him for long, but he's already well aware that Steve's three girls are the center of his world. "Is it broken?"

"No, but she's hurting. I came out to pick up some more Advil for her—and a big rocky-road hot-fudge sundae. Ice cream always helps, right?"

"Yeah, and not just little girls. Maybe I'll bring my wife some ice cream, too. She talks about this place." And now he knows why she's been coming here so often. Ice-cream cravings.

"Is she all right?"

"Not hurt in the quake or anything like that. Just . . ."

Pregnant.

Suddenly he's dying to say tell someone. *Anyone*, even a random acquaintance on the street.

But Clara made it clear she doesn't want to tell anyone yet because she's worried something is going to go wrong with the pregnancy.

Maybe they should rethink that plan. They've been through enough. Nothing's going to go wrong now, and the sooner they can start sharing their joy, the better.

"Well, I've got to get home," Steve tells him, car keys in hand. "Guess I'll see you tomorrow morning at the gym?"

"I'll be there."

There it is again—*I'll be there.*

Why does he feel like he's seen that before, in writing, in his own hand?

You haven't.

So stop dwelling on it. It's just one of those things.

As he steps into the ice-cream parlor, a bell attached to the door jingles pleasantly.

Whoa—where did that come from?

An old-fashioned soda fountain counter lined with round chrome-sided stools seems to have replaced the glass-fronted serving case along one wall.

But in the blink of an eye—literally—it's gone, and the case, filled with tubs of ice cream, is back where it belongs.

Frowning, Drew looks around at the white-washed walls, chalkboard menu, and several wrought-iron tables and chairs—all of them empty on this chilly December day.

The owner, a middle-aged man named Paolo, comes in from the back room, cell phone against his ear. "No, I have another customer. . . . Yes, really . . . I'll call you back in a few minutes. . . . Yes . . . Yes . . . I have to go, Diana, good-bye."

He hangs up and shakes his head at Drew. "My wife. You'd think we haven't seen each other in years, she has so much to say to me. It's been—maybe—a few hours."

Seeing the twinkle in the man's eye, Drew pushes the strange soda fountain hallucination out of his head and smiles back at him. "What are you, newlyweds?"

"Newlyweds! That's a good one. No, we've been married for twenty-three years." Paolo points to the gold band on Drew's left ring finger. "You?"

"Almost two."

"Years? Now who's the newlywed? Listen, I'll tell you a little secret. The first year or two, you're still getting to know each other. There are still some surprises. Good ones. Bad ones, too. You clash a little . . . or a lot."

"Sure."

"But if you can still wake up every morning now, look at the same woman, and say you're happy, you'll be happy forever, because it gets better and better."

Not for everyone, though. Plenty of people split up well into a marriage. Like Clara's parents.

"Trust me." Paolo wags a finger at him. "I'm right."

Drew, who gets the feeling this isn't the first time Paolo has uttered that particular phrase, says, "I hope you are."

"Always. Ask my wife. Do you have any kids yet?"

Again, Drew is tempted to spill the glad tidings to a virtual stranger. He's never going to last another five weeks with this secret.

"Uh, no kids yet."

"Good. Don't rush."

Terrific.

"Why not?" Drew asks, undaunted. "We love kids."

"Who doesn't? Kids are great. But they change everything. Diana and I, we have five. But we waited a couple of years before we had them. We made sure we had plenty of time to just enjoy being together. *Capisce?*"

"*Capisce.*"

That's the thing about small towns, Drew thinks, amused, watching the man pile scoops of French vanilla into a plastic bowl for Clara's sundae.

You come in to buy an ice cream, you wind up with a stranger telling you his life story.

But that's Paolo's story . . . not Drew's.

He and Clara are more than ready to have a baby now. They'll still have plenty of time to enjoy being together.

All the time in the world.

Chapter 13

Clara always had a good rapport with her high school physics teacher, despite the fact that she wasn't exactly his star pupil. Far from it.

Still, she was surprised to find that he actually remembered her when she first contacted him three years ago. She figured it was because she had become, as he put it, "a big movie star now."

But later, she realized it was because they were meant to reconnect later in life, bonding not just over a mutual interest in time travel, but over cancer, of all things. Years ago, Mr. Kershaw's only child, Bianca, had overcome impossible odds to survive a childhood brain tumor. After Clara's own diagnosis, he was a tremendous source of support and comfort, never doubting that she could—and would—beat the disease.

Now, as she dials his telephone number, she wonders if she'll even find him at home in his rent-controlled Upper West Side apartment. Retired and long-divorced, he usually spends the holidays with his daughter and her family.

But he answers the phone with a cheery "Hello?"

"Mr. Kershaw, it's Clara."

"Clara! I was just worrying about you. I saw on the news last night that there had been a big quake out there yesterday. Is everything all right?"

"We're fine. I mean, it was scary, but, you know, we survived."

This one, anyway.

"You're living right there along the San Andreas Fault, aren't you?"

"I sure am."

"A precarious place to settle, to say the least."

"I know. But my husband grew up near here and . . . well, I guess I wasn't really all that worried about earthquakes until now."

"I've never experienced a quake before, and I've always been fascinated, given my field of study. What was it like?"

"One minute, you're standing on solid ground, and the next, without warning, it's been pulled out from under you, and there's nothing sturdy to grab on to."

"That sounds terrifying."

"It is." She hesitates, wishing she could voice her true fear. Then she asks, "What if yesterday was only a foreshock?"

There's a pause on the other end of the line. "I have to admit that based on my research into whether strength heterogeneities along the fault influence rupture growth, it would seem that the paleoseismological—"

"Hey, did you forget who you're talking to?" Clara cuts in, amused despite her malaise.

He chuckles. "I'm sorry."

Grabbing a pen and paper, she says, "Hetero—what?"

"Heterogeneities—you'll recall, an element of earthquake physics. We did cover the topic back when you were in my class."

Jotting down notes, she murmurs, "I'm sure we covered a lot of things that have slipped my mind over the years." *Or at the time they were being discussed in the first place.*

"Suffice to say that according to an August 1984 report in the *Bulletin of the Seismological Society of America*, forty-four percent of the strike-slip earthquakes in the San Andreas system were preceded by immediate foreshocks defined as having occurred within three days and ten kilometers of the main shock; thus, following the Bayes' theorem, the conditional probability of—"

"Mr. Kershaw?" she interrupts, scribbling away. "Plain English?"

"Sorry. Let's see . . . unfortunately, the field of earthquake physics has not progressed as dramatically as many other sciences over the last few decades. The only way to determine whether a seismic disturbance is the main shock or a foreshock of a larger event is in retrospect."

Yeah, tell me about it.

"Speaking of retrospect . . ." She shifts gears. "Do you remember when you helped me to research time travel a few years back?"

"Of course. Whatever became of that role?"

"Well, I thought it had pretty much . . . fallen through. But now it looks like it's popped up again."

"Really! I didn't realize you'd gone back to work. I thought you were content to be away from all that."

"I was." *I still am.* "But, you know, things change. And I guess I need a—sort of a refresher course."

"Glad to help. Next time you're in New York, perhaps we can get together and—"

"Uh, actually, can I just ask you a few questions right now, over the phone?"

"Ask away."

"You told me that there was more scientific evidence that time travel to the future is more possible than to the past, right?"

"Not in so many words. What I believe I said was that based on the fact that our perception of time is relative to our motion, we might theoretically be able to speed—"

"But there was a famous physicist, wasn't there, who time traveled to the future? A woman named Caroll?"

"Ah, yes. Carroll Alley. A man, by the way. And he didn't travel to the future, per se. He synchronized two atomic clocks, put one on a plane, and flew it for several hours. When it landed, it was behind the one on the ground, meaning that time had slowed for it. It had, effectively, traveled to the future."

"You also said that if it were possible to travel back to the past, you couldn't change what had already happened, because that would violate the law of quantum mechanics, right?"

"Clara, I'm impressed. Clearly, you haven't forgotten everything."

No. She hasn't. She hasn't forgotten the law that says that what you do in the present is an inevitable product of the past.

"What about the future?" she asks Mr. Kershaw. "Can you go forward to the future, see something that's going to happen, and then return to the past—I mean, the present—and change it so that it won't happen after all?"

He's silent.

"If you visit the future, then the present becomes the past, right?" She doesn't wait for a response. "And then, when you get back, what you do in the past—meaning the present—will impact what happens in the future."

"I'm not sure I follow."

"Let's say that I visit the future and I see that a friend is going to—um, break his arm by slipping on an icy sidewalk. Couldn't I then go back to my own time and make sure that my friend doesn't leave the house on the day I know it's going to happen? That doesn't violate the law of quantum mechanics."

"I don't think—"

"I mean, you can't change the past because it's already happened. But the future hasn't happened yet."

"It has," Mr. Kershaw says simply, "if you've glimpsed it."

"What do you mean?"

"If you arrive in the future, then every event that transpired to create that world—every event leading up to the moment of your arrival—has already happened, correct?"

"I don't know."

Patiently, he elaborates, "Every moment between the moment you left the present behind and the moment you arrived in the so-called future would be, in effect, a part of the past."

Clara tries to wrap her brain around that—

and decides that she doesn't want to. Not if it means accepting that a future without Drew is her destiny.

"Do you see what I'm saying?" Mr. Kershaw asks.

"I'm not sure."

"For that matter, I'm not sure that I'm the one who should be saying it. What you're really asking, my dear, is whether our fate is predetermined. Perhaps that's a question for a philosopher or a theologian rather than a physicist. And maybe there is no real answer."

"Maybe not," she murmurs.

"I'm afraid I haven't helped much with your research this time, have I?"

"No, you've . . . you've helped a lot."

She thanks him and forces herself to make a few minutes' worth of small talk before hanging up.

She's going to do whatever she can to prevent the preordained future from coming to pass, regardless of what science dictates or what she learned the last time through her own experience. After all . . .

Never say never.

The voice in her head is Doris's, and she smiles faintly, remembering.

She ventured back to 1941 and fell in love with Jed despite knowing he was going to die and that there was nothing she could do to keep from losing him. And it turned out she hadn't lost him at all. Not the essence of him. Not his heart and his soul.

If something happens to the man she has come to love as Drew Becker, he'll find his way back to her again somehow, someday. Maybe not in this lifetime, and maybe she'll have no recollection of any of this, but they're soul mates, and they belong together.

That certainty will simply have to be enough to sustain her through whatever lies ahead.

Chapter 14

Three walls of the home office off the living room are almost entirely made of glass. Maybe that's why it won't exist three years from now. Maybe all that glass shattered in the Big One.

Maybe?

This room wouldn't stand a chance in an 8.7 magnitude quake.

It's amazing to think that the house survived it, but somehow, it did.

And if the house held up, then the people in it should have survived as well.

Clara had, and Dickens, too. They must have been home—or in an equally insulated spot—when it hit.

What about Drew?

But Clara doesn't want to dwell on ominous possibilities at the moment; nor does she want to gaze out at the scenic evergreen hillside.

Seated at the desk, with Dickens snoozing at her feet, she's reading about wormholes and paradoxes—again.

It's been a few years since she initially delved into the topic of time travel on the Internet. These days, there are even more Web sites devoted entirely to the subject.

Some are of a scientific bent, others decidedly new age. One site even collects an advance payment from people who wish to be transported to the future using technology presumed to be available by then. Moments after you pay your fare, someone from the future purportedly picks you up and whisks you forward in time.

Stranger things have happened, Clara supposes.

To me, anyway.

Hearing gravel crunching outside, she glances out the wall of windows to see Drew's car pulling into the driveway.

"See, Dickens?" She looks down at the dog, suddenly awake with perked-up ears. "He promised he'd come back to us, and here he is."

Much sooner than she expected him, in fact.

She quickly closes out the screen she'd been reading on the computer, fighting the impulse to run out and greet Drew passionately. Dickens does no such thing, racing to the next room, barking wildly.

When Clara reaches the door, Dickens is bounding up and down as Drew holds a white paper bag out of his reach amid futile pleas of "Down, boy! Down!"

Clara shakes her head, grinning. "Whatcha got there, honey?"

"A hot fudge sundae for you. If Lebron James here doesn't snatch it out of my hand first."

"Ice cream!" It's Clara's turn to grab for the bag. "What made you think of doing that?"

"I put two and two together and figured you were craving it. Here"—he hands her the bag—"but it's probably melted by now."

"Ask me if I care." She wraps her arms around his neck. "You're the best."

"Yeah, well . . ." He leans in to kiss her. "I love you."

Clara presses against him, suddenly craving more than ice cream. He smells so good, so familiar: like cold fresh air and woodsy soap and home. She buries her face in his shoulder, remembering how empty the house felt—how empty she felt—without him.

"Thank God you're back, Drew."

He pulls back to look at her. "I was barely gone half an hour."

"It felt like forever."

And forever without him is something she never wants to face again.

She kisses him, pressing herself against the hard length of his body, just as she has hundreds of times in the past.

The past . . .

The future . . .

None of it really matters, does it?

All that matters is the present, here with him. Because really, that's all you ever have, anyway.

"Hey, you're pretty randy for the middle of the day," Drew murmurs against her mouth. "How about if we—"

Something slams into them both, nearly knocking them off their feet.

Dickens—and he's snagged the brass ring, dangling the white bag of ice cream from his jaw as he trots away toward the kitchen.

"Hey, get back here!" Drew hollers, starting after him.

Clara grabs his sleeve. "It was probably melted, anyway. Let him have it."

"But I got it for you."

"I know. You can do something else for me instead." She laces her fingers around his neck. "Upstairs. Okay?"

He grins down at her. "Okay. Let's hurry before you-know-who decides three's company."

They take the steps two at a time, holding hands, Drew in the lead. In the bedroom, he kicks the door closed, then, as an apparent after-thought, locks it.

Seeing her questioning look, he says, "Just in case."

"In case . . . what?"

"In case that crazy dog knows how to turn a doorknob."

Clara pulls him down onto the bed. "Is this what it's going to be like from now on, with a dog and a baby? Sneaking around, locked doors? Aren't we ever going to feel like we're alone together in our own house?"

"Probably not."

"Hey, you were supposed to say 'of course we are.'"

"Then—of course we are." He nuzzles her neck.

"You don't sound convinced."

"Can we talk about this later?"

"You're the one who's always so reassuring and confident about everything." Clara nudges him away, propping herself up on her elbows. "I feel like you're thinking things are going to be different now."

"Things *are* going to be different. They're already different. But I told you—we don't have to keep the dog."

"I *want* to keep the dog. It's not about the dog. And I want to have a baby. I just want everything to stay the same, too." She swallows a lump in her throat, knowing she sounds ridiculous.

Drew sighs and rolls over onto his back, elbows and face pointed at the ceiling.

"Are you mad?"

"Mad? No! I just need a minute to . . . you know. Shift gears."

She rests her head on his shoulder, her fingers lightly pianoing his chest. This is nuts.

Here she is, worrying about the uncertainties that lie ahead instead of living in the moment.

Didn't she learn anything the last time, with Jed?

Didn't she resolve, after talking to Mr. Kershaw, to stop dwelling on what might happen, and to have faith that no matter what, she and Drew will find a way to be together?

"Clara?"

"Yeah?"

"I'm thinking it would be a lot easier for me to shift gears if you weren't touching me like that."

She removes her hand—then, after a moment, slips it under his shirt, saying, "Or, you could not shift gears after all."

"I thought you wanted to talk."

"I thought I did, too. But you know what? You were right. Everything's going to be great."

"Did I say that? Brilliant. You should definitely listen to me." He wraps his arms around her and rolls her over.

Laughing, she tugs his shirt up over his shoulders and gladly tosses it—along with her nagging worries—aside.

Chapter 15

Drew is dreaming about snow—a beautiful, heavy snowfall—and he's walking through it with Clara. She's wearing her favorite red mittens and red, red lipstick—the kind she never wears. And then there's a dog—he can't see it through the swirling curtain of white but he can hear barking.

"Drew! Drew!"

Startled awake, he opens his eyes. Clara is hovering over him, her frantic expression illuminated in the glow from the electric candles in the window. And somewhere downstairs, a dog—*their* dog—is barking.

"What—"

Clara clutches his arm, hard. "It's an earthquake!"

Instinctively, he pushes her back down and

dives on top of her, shielding her body with his own as the bed shakes, the windows rattle.

"This is bad, isn't it." It isn't a question. Clara sounds like she's on the verge of tears.

That isn't like his wife. She never once cried over her cancer, not in front of him, anyway. She's always been strong, no matter what fate hurtles in her direction.

But she's pregnant now. Emotional. Vulnerable. Frightened.

"It's just an aftershock," he tells her, stroking her hair. "It's not bad—and, anyway, I think it's over."

The tremors have already subsided—but not the ones wracking her body. Holding her close, he can feel her heart racing.

"Hey," he whispers, staying right where he is, protecting her, "relax. We're okay."

Downstairs, Dickens has stopped barking. Drew can hear the distant sound of his collar jingling and his feet clicking across the hardwood floor as he presumably returns to his oversized cushion in the living room to settle in again.

"Goes with the territory, living here," he tells Clara. "You'll get used to it."

No reply.

"Clara?"

"Yeah?"

Tension still radiates from her limbs.

"You're not saying anything."

"I . . . I don't know what to say. Other than that I'm scared out of my mind."

"I guess the big one on Christmas really threw you off your game, huh?"

"That wasn't the Big One!"

"I didn't mean—"

"No, you said the Big One, and everyone is always talking about the Big One, and it's still coming, Drew. These are all foreshocks. We have to get out of here." She pushes him off her and sits up.

"You're panicking. Calm down."

"I can't help it."

He holds both her trembling shoulders, rests his chin on one. "Talk to me." Silence.

"It isn't like you to be so freaked out. I think your hormones must be—"

"You're right," she cuts in abruptly. "It's my hormones. I know it is. I'm a mess. So can't you just humor me, Drew? Can't we just go away? Just until New Year's? Please?"

"I'd love to, but you know I have to work. We talked about this. It's a new job. I can't just not show up because I felt like taking off for a few days."

Not that *he* even feels like taking off.

They're home at last, settling into their new house over the holidays—and Clara has a crazy whim to fly the coop *now*? It makes no sense whatsoever.

"How about if we go back to that inn in Napa for New Year's Eve?" He suggests. "We can leave as soon as I get out of work, and we'll even stay through the weekend, if you want."

She shakes her head.

"What about tomorrow? I mean, today? We'll go down and visit my parents, do some shopping, have lunch, whatever you want. . . ."

"I don't know. . . ."

"Come on. It'll cheer you up. Let's do it."

"Can we stay down there till dark?"

That's an odd way for her to phrase it. "Sure. We can have dinner somewhere, if you want."

"What about the dog?"

"He'll be fine. Okay?"

"Okay," she says in a small voice.

"Good."

In the darkness, he hears a sniffle. Oh no.

"Don't cry, sweetie. Please don't cry. We have everything we ever wanted. You shouldn't be crying—unless they're happy tears. Are they?"

She makes a choking sound that Drew hopes is a laugh—but he doubts it.

He looks at the digital clock and sighs. "It's three a.m. Come on; let's try to go back to sleep. Everything will look a lot brighter in the morning. It always does."

Chapter 16

Clara fell asleep with Drew's optimism ringing in her head. But the moment she awakens to find the room bathed in gloomy daylight, she realizes that he was wrong.

Things are not looking brighter this morning at all.

Things are looking very . . . 2012.

Stacks of boxes alongside the bed. No candles in the window. And, she senses, no Drew.

She shouts his name into the empty house anyway.

Somewhere on the first floor, Dickens barks.

"Here, boy," Clara calls, sitting up and swinging her legs over the side of the bed. She waits for the dog to bound into the room.

"Hey, Dickens, where are you?"

He whines a little, still at the foot of the stairs.

The light dawns. "Oh—you're not allowed up here, are you?"

Another whine from the apparently reformed scofflaw.

"Hey, Dickens! I'm giving you permission to break the rules. Come here!" Clara puts two fingers between her lips and whistles.

Not one to let any grass grow under his feet, the dog scampers up the steps and skids into the room.

Wow, he's huge.

"Hey, you grew up." Clara pats his head. "And I just . . . grew."

Just when she got used to her flat stomach, it's burgeoning again. Cumbersome, perhaps, but it's definitely more exciting to be able to see the evidence of the new life growing inside her.

If only Drew were here to share it with her.

"We have to go find out what's what, okay, Dickens?"

He yawns agreeably, exhaling dog breath in her face. She feels a little nauseated as she stands—but not too bad.

"Good. That's a good sign," she tells the dog.

He looks at her, apparently thinking, *Yeah? How so?*

"It's easier to think positive thoughts when your head isn't in the toilet—though I can only speak for myself."

She pulls on her robe and belts it loosely

over her rounded-again belly, where a sudden thumping sensation gives her pause.

Whoa! The baby is kicking.

Smiling in delight, Clara stands absolutely still, her hand resting against her womb.

"Hey, little one," she calls softly. "I can't wait to meet you."

And I know your Daddy can't, either, she adds silently, *wherever he is.*

In the bathroom, Clara checks to see whether Drew's toothbrush and shaver have miraculously reappeared beside the sink.

"Just because they're gone," she tells Dickens, "doesn't mean the worst."

Dickens looks at her, then casually slurps from the toilet bowl.

"Hey!" Clara grabs his collar. "What did I just tell you about putting your head in—"

She breaks off, looking at the silver dog tag resting against her hand.

An address is engraved on it—and it's not this one.

"Okay . . . so why does this say you live at 9 Sequoia Way?"

Dickens tries to squirm out of her grasp.

Remembering how he dive-bombed his way in the door yesterday—was it yesterday?—she wonders whether perhaps he is a stray after all. A stray, and an opportunist.

"Did you wander in off the street?" she asks,

releasing his collar. "Is your owner out looking for you? Or am I your owner? Is this where we're moving? Are you Dickens, or not?"

He sure looks like the puppy she knew three years ago. Acts like him, too, she notes, grabbing him as he aims his head for the toilet bowl again.

And he did stay put at the bottom of the stairs when she first called him, as if he knew the rules of the house.

Knew them—and followed them.

"Maybe you're *not* you," Clara tells him. "I guess there's only one way to find out."

A half hour later, wearing an oversized sweater and pair of maternity jeans that looked like they'd be more comfortable than they are, Clara opens the front door and spots a newspaper lying on the step.

Stooping with some effort, thanks to her belly, she retrieves it and glances at the date.

Wednesday, December 26, 2012.

It's a weekday.

Maybe Drew already left for work. The market opens early on the East Coast.

Maybe, maybe, please, God, maybe.

She tosses the paper through the open door to the house for later. No time to look at it now. She's a woman on a mission.

With Dickens beside her, she locks the front door and heads across the driveway to the unfamiliar car. Climbing into the driver's seat, she notices that it smells brand-new. The dog settles himself in the passenger's seat with the air of someone who knows the drill. Either he's Dickens, or he's an imposter making himself right at home.

"I guess we're about to find out," she tells him, and starts the car with a set of keys she found in a purse that also contained her wallet.

Not the wallet she had three years ago, but a similar one. It contains the usual credit cards, some cash, and her familiar California driver's license, not yet expired.

No cell phone—but that's not necessarily unusual. She's never been very good at keeping track of it. She did dial the number to see if she could hear it ringing somewhere in the house, but was met with silence on this end and an automated voice message on the other: *The person you are trying to reach is not available. Please leave a message.*

She opted not to, considering that the person she was trying to reach was herself.

Now, she enters the Sequoia Way address into the sleek GPS device on the dashboard. It would have taken a few minutes for the destination to pop up on the 2009 GPS, but it appears instantaneously on this one.

"Technology marches on," Clara informs Dickens, who presumably couldn't care less. He's just gazing out the window, looking for all the world as though he's out for a leisurely Sunday drive.

After consulting the map and noting that Sequoia Way appears to be a winding street on the northeast end of San Florentina, Clara shifts the car into gear and heads down the driveway onto the main road.

"I just hope we don't find out that you're someone else's dog," she tells Dickens, "because I kind of like having you around, you know?"

She glances over at him and is gratified to see that he does, indeed, seem to know.

Maybe, she thinks hopefully as she begins the drive toward town, *the dog tag is brand-new and 9 Sequoia Way is about to become the Beckers' new address.*

A boxwood Christmas wreath is affixed to the mailbox at the foot of the neighboring driveway. Through a bank of fog and evergreens, Clara catches a reassuring glimpse of the Tucker home intact on the hillside above.

For a split second, she considers stopping there. Surely her next-door neighbors would be aware of the current status of the Becker family—and probably even the reason they're moving out of their dream house.

Then again, what if the Tuckers aren't even living there anymore? A lot can happen in three years. They could have moved away.

And even if they're still here, Clara barely knows them in the present/past. Is she really going to knock on their door and ask them where her husband and child are? Is she really prepared to hear a potentially disturbing answer from virtual strangers?

As she winds her way along the narrow two-lane highway high above the sea, she notes that everything looks pretty much the same as it did three years ago. Everything she can see, anyway, amid the billowing early morning mist. Which isn't much more than trees, boulders, and blue-gray water.

Still, she's reassured by the familiarity of her surroundings. . . .

Until she rounds the final curve in the road and suddenly nothing is familiar. Nothing at all.

A traffic light appears out of nowhere, glowing red in the fog. Clara slams on the brakes. The through street has become a dead end, blocked by a massive construction zone beyond plywood and chain-link fencing.

She consults the GPS and turns right. San Florentina's main artery has apparently been rerouted around a maze of excavations, new foundations, and half-built structures. The once-charming town square is cluttered with trucks and bulldozers; orange signs, barrels, Dumpsters; stacks of planking and pipe and cinder blocks.

Dazed, Clara takes in the foreign landscape as she drives, passing vacant lots where buildings used to be and buildings where there were open spaces. Unpaved streets trail off to nowhere like phantom limbs.

Gone are the gazebo and fountain, the diagonal parking spots, the storefronts with awnings and hand-painted signs. The sturdy brick library and the local savings and loan have vanished, replaced by a rutted parking lot.

Clara pulls into a space there and turns off the car, shaken.

She should have known.

She *did* know: San Florentina was demolished in the earthquake. She heard all about it, even saw the evidence on the news.

Yet the harsh reality still hit her like a wrecking ball, and it takes her a few moments to regain her composure.

When she does, she looks over at Dickens, up on all fours in the seat beside her.

"Come on," she tells him, opening the door. "I'm not ready to go to Sequoia Way just yet."

Dickens obligingly hops out after her, then lifts his hind leg and pees on the tire.

"Oh, for the love of . . ." Clara shakes her head and reaches back into the backseat for the leash she found at the house.

About to close the car door, she's struck by a sudden realization.

The backseat is empty.

The leash is there, but . . . that's all.

There's no child car seat in the back, and there should be.

Relax, maybe it's in Drew's car.

But shouldn't there be one in her own car as well? Surely they have two car seats.

They're expensive. Maybe we're too strapped for cash.

So strapped they can't even afford a second car seat?

The car smells new. We probably just haven't gotten a new seat for it yet.

That makes sense, right?

Of course it does.

Clinging stubbornly to that possibility, Clara pushes the matter from her mind and locks the car. Then she fastens the leash around the dog's collar, and they set off toward what used to be Main Street.

For all she knows, it's still Main Street, minus the pavement, the traffic, the window-shoppers, and many of the buildings. The nearly block-long brick edifice that once housed a number of businesses, including Triangle Shoe store where Drew just bought her new slippers, has vanished altogether.

Instead of piped-in Christmas Carols, the air hums with the music of buzz saws, the staccato beat of hammers, the rumble of bulldozers, and the steady, high-pitched beeping of trucks moving in reverse.

Dickens stops and sniffs around the sidewalk every couple of yards, and he occasionally lifts his hind leg to nonchalantly christen a lamppost, a tree, the quintessential fire hydrant.

"I'm supposed to be the one with the bladder problems," she informs him as he does his business on a parking meter. "You're not even pregnant."

Then again . . .

She glances down to make sure this dog really isn't a female Dickens impersonator.

Nope. He's all male, all right.

Hearing the sharp staccato burst of a whistle being blown, she turns to see a uniformed cop on the opposite side of the street.

The stout officer, who sports a brush cut and a blond mustache, is clearly in the process of writing a parking ticket for a double-parked Jeep. But he's looking directly at her, silver whistle between his lips, and her heart sinks.

Uh-oh.

Maybe this isn't Dickens after all, and his true owner has reported him missing, and she's about to be arrested for dog-napping.

"Ma'am, are you aware that your dog just violated the California penal code?"

So dogs aren't allowed to urinate on the street in 2012?

Terrific. Dickens has been violating the penal—
or pee-nal, ha!—code all over town. Okay, well
it's no big deal. Now she knows.

"I'm sorry, Officer," she calls back.

She tugs Dickens's leash, but now the cop
has slapped the ticket under the Jeep's windshield wiper and is heading right for them.

"I'm afraid I'm going to have to haul you
both off to the slammer."

The slammer? Cops actually talk that way?

On the heels of that incredulous thought,
Clara recovers the presence of mind to wonder
if he's really going to arrest her.

And Dickens? Can a dog actually be arrested, too?

Isn't the slammer a little drastic for peeing on
a hydrant?

"I'm . . . I, uh, I'm sorry," she stammers again.
"Really, I didn't—"

"Aw, save it for the judge!"

Speechless at his attitude, she gapes at him,
feeling as though she's stumbled into a cross
between an old movie set and a futuristic mili-
tant society.

He bursts out laughing. "Hey, you should've
stuck with acting, Clara. You're pretty good."
He gives her a hug, then pets the dog's head.
"Dickens, you've got one heck of a tiny bladder
for such a gigantic beast."

Clara . . .

Dickens . . .

He knows us!

And we're not going to jail!

"Did you have a good Christmas?" he asks her.

"Yes," she manages to respond, thoughts whirling with all the questions she longs to ask him—if she could just figure out how to begin.

"Been feeling okay?" he asks, gesturing at her stomach.

So he knows she's pregnant.

Big deal. Anyone looking at her would know that.

But what else does he know?

"I'm fine," she assures him, floundering for the right way to ask him about Drew. "I just—you know—I'm looking for—"

Before she can say her husband's name, she hears a shout.

"Aw, jeez, Bobby!"

They both turn to see the Jeep's owner, apparently, waving the ticket in dismay.

"I was only there for five minutes," the twenty-something guy tells the cop.

"I watched the car for at least fifteen before I wrote you up."

"What? No way, Bobby!"

The officer—Bobby, apparently—glances at Clara. "Sorry. Duty calls. Have a good one."

"You, too," she calls after him as he crosses the street to the disgruntled driver.

For a moment, she watches the exchange, wondering whether she should wait until they're finished.

She decides against it. Telling him she's looking for her husband might not be the best idea. The policeman will probably want to know how long he's been missing, and then what?

She can hardly tell him it's been three years since his exact whereabouts were certain.

Maybe for now, she'll just take a stroll along the street, try to come up with something better in case she runs into her cop friend again.

"Come on, Dickens. Let's go. And try not to violate any more penal codes, even if they are fake."

She rounds a corner and is relieved to see that the few shops that are still standing—or perhaps, standing again—seem to be back in business. Among them is Scoops, where a magic-marker-on-poster board sign in the window bears just one promising word: OPEN.

But when she reaches the door, she finds it locked.

"It's a little early in the morning for ice cream, don't you think?" a voice behind her asks.

She turns to see a woman about her own age smiling at her. She's tall and slender, very pretty even without a stitch of makeup and her brown hair pulled back in a rubber band.

Does she know me, like the cop did? Clara wonders. *Or is she just a chatty passerby?*

"It's, um, never too early for ice cream when you're pregnant," she improvises, and gives her protruding belly a pat.

"You can say that again," the woman replies as if she knows from personal experience.

Clara darts a glance at her midsection through her open jacket. Her snug-fitting white T-shirt is tucked into her jeans, and her belly is absolutely flat. She's definitely not a fellow pregnant person—unless she's in her first trimester.

"You know, every time I see you walking around pregnant, I want to cry with sheer happiness," the woman tells Clara.

"You, uh . . . you do?"

"Absolutely." Sure enough, her gray eyes are looking a little . . . moist.

"Well, that's so . . . ."

Weird is what it is. Totally weird.

"So, when are you due, exactly?" the woman asks Clara.

Ha. I wish I knew.

"Not soon enough," she replies evasively.

"Do you guys have names picked out?"

You guys . . .

As in Clara and Drew.

She must know us.

Or maybe not. Maybe she's a total stranger who's merely assuming Clara is half of a couple. A total, nutty stranger who goes around crying over random pregnant women.

"We're still . . . you know. Working on names."

"I know how that goes. Harry and I had an awful time."

Harry.

If she were a stranger, she probably would have said *my husband* instead.

Then again, you never know.

She might be one of those chatty people who simply talks about her own life and everyone who's part of it in an overly familiar way.

Clara looks at the pretty brunette, trying to gauge whether that's the case.

It's impossible to tell—and, judging by the expectant expression on her face, it's Clara's turn to speak.

"So what name did you come up with?" she hears herself ask.

The woman gives her a strange look. Either that was too nosy a question for a stranger to ask, or Clara should have known the answer.

The latter is obviously true, judging by the woman's tone and arched brows when she replies, "Um . . . Prudence?"

"Oh, Prudence! Right! I remember."

"You should. You're the one who came up with it."

Huh? Since when do I name other people's babies? Especially Prudence.

"I'll never forget what you said, Clara, the day I told you that ever since the *Mayflower*, every firstborn daughter in my family has been named Prudence, but I was going to break the streak."

"What did I say?"

"Don't tell me you forgot!"

"No, I just . . . I like to hear about my own cleverness." Yeah. Talk about lame.

But the woman smiles.

"Who doesn't?" she asks pleasantly. "What you said was, 'Honey, if it works, don't fix it.'"

Clara smiles wistfully, thinking of Doris—then feels a sharp tug on the leash in her other hand.

She looks down just in time to see Dickens lurch into a full-blown frenzy, focused on something down the block. Clara sees that it's a squirrel-sized, red-sweater-clad dog on a leash held by an elderly woman who just stepped out of the coffee shop.

Barking wildly, Dickens pulls on the leash, dragging Clara along the sidewalk toward the little dog and away from Prudence's mother.

Uncertain whether to be relieved or dismayed, Clara calls over her shoulder, "See you later!"

The reply is drowned out by her dog, now snarling.

"Dickens, cut it out!"

Up ahead, the tiny dog nonchalantly browses a patch of grass at the base of a tree, but the old lady looks panic-stricken.

"Don't worry," Clara calls to her. "I've got him."

No, she doesn't. Dickens is closing in on the pair, with Clara helplessly in tow.

The old lady frantically tugs her own dog's leash in the opposite direction. "Gerald! Gerald! It's *him* again!"

Gerald looks up, sees Dickens, and lets out a high-pitched yelp.

"Dickens! Stop this right now!" Arms outstretched alongside her gigantic belly, Clara holds the leash with both hands as Dickens ignores the command, pretty much dragging her along by her heels.

"Oh no! Oh no!" Gerald's owner wails. "Run, Gerald! Run!"

"It's okay, ma'am! Really, he's loud but he's harmless."

Yeah, right. Judging by the way Dickens is salivating, he's planning to devour the little dog, sweater and all.

The old lady scuttles her terrorized pet back toward the coffee shop as fast as her thick-soled shoes can carry her. Just as Dickens is about to pounce, she and the dog disappear through the door and it bangs closed behind them.

Clara sees them behind the glass, trembling at the close call.

"I'm so sorry!" she mouths.

The old lady makes the sign of the cross.

Clara looks down at Dickens, who appears not the least bit apologetic.

"Obviously, we know them—or at least, *they* know *you*," Clara tells him as she leads him away. "But somehow I doubt we're going to get anything out of this connection."

She sighs, wondering if she should forget the plan, get back into the car, and go home.

Maybe Drew will be there by now, and everything will be back to normal.

But maybe he won't, and maybe it won't. Maybe her "normal" is gone forever.

Oh, please. Will you stop?

You've been through a lot worse than this, for Pete's sake. Don't let some old lady and her ridiculous dog break your spirit.

Drew is out there somewhere.

He'll find his way back to you.

You just have to have faith.

"Come on, Dickens. We might as well go see if we can find Sequoia Way."

Chapter 17

"This is definitely our lucky day," Drew tells Clara as he sets the emergency brake and turns off the engine.

Not only did they manage to zip over the Golden Gate Bridge with minimal traffic, but the fog lifted as they reached the Bay area, giving way to crisp late morning sunshine. Even better, there's actually a curbside parking spot on the steep street right alongside his parents' home.

"I just hope it stays lucky," Clara replies cryptically, and he looks at her in surprise.

"Why wouldn't it?"

She offers a smile, but it's forced. "I was just kidding."

No, she wasn't.

"What's up with you today?"

"Nothing," she says quickly—too quickly. "Why?"

"You seem like you're on edge."

Yes, and he realizes she's been pretty quiet ever since he woke up to find her in the living room, curled up on the couch and watching the Weather Channel. She informed him—not that he'd asked—that it was going to be a cloudy, foggy day, but that tomorrow will be sunny and beautiful.

"I'm tired, that's all," she tells him now. "We were up all night. *I* was, anyway. I don't know how you went right back to sleep after that earthquake."

"It was just an aftershock." He opens the car door. "And it's not good for you to lose sleep now that you're resting for two."

"I know, but I couldn't help it." She yawns. "I promise I'll take a nap for two later. How's that?"

"Good plan."

Drew climbs out of the car. By the time he reaches the passenger side, his wife is already out on the sidewalk. She looks smaller than usual somehow, huddled into a thick tweed coat with a red scarf swaddled around her neck against the chill.

"You're supposed to let me be a gentleman," he scolds her. "Especially now that you're . . ."

"What? Getting out of the car for two?"

"Exactly." He locks the car with a double-chirp of the keys and drapes an arm around her shoulder.

Together, they head toward the three-story Queen Anne Victorian.

Like the others on the block, its sloping foundation is diagonal, aligned with the street's steep grade. It's a classic San Francisco painted lady, butter-colored with dark green, sage, and ocher trim.

When Drew was growing up, it was festooned in shades of rose and mauve. It wasn't easy being the boy who lived in the pink gingerbread house with three larger-than-life older sisters, crazy Aunt Stella, and a doting mother who once approached him on the Little League field when he was on deck, swinging, and dabbed at his face with a spit-dampened lace hankie.

Somehow, when he was about thirteen, Drew convinced his father that his life would be a lot easier if they painted the house a more manly hue. Somehow, his father convinced his mother to go along with it. Somehow, his mother convinced the two of them that pastel yellow was more manly.

And somehow, Drew survived despite it all.

That reminds him—Clara wants to paint the

baby's room pastel yellow. Maybe he'll try to talk her into navy. Or hunter green. Or even plain old white.

Together, they approach the tall front steps.

"Are we sure," Drew asks, "that we don't want to tell my family the news?"

"We're positive."

"Maybe it would be nice to share it with everyone while my sisters are still in town."

"I know, but . . . what if something goes wrong?"

"It won't."

"What if—"

"Hey. Cut it out. What-ifs are toxic. We're going to be fine."

She pauses on the top step, looking up at him wearing a worried expression. "Do you honestly believe that with all your heart?"

"I honestly do. And so do you, deep down inside."

"I do? How do you know?"

He pulls her close. "Because you're talking about us. And things always work out for us, because they have to."

"Why?"

Because that's what I keep promising you, and if you believe it, it might come true.

Aloud, he tells her simply, "That's just the way we roll."

She smiles faintly. "That's your answer?"

"Makes sense to me."

"The scary thing is that it makes sense to me, too," she tells him. "But I'm not ready to share our news with anyone just yet, okay? I'd like to keep it our secret just for a while longer."

He kisses her forehead. "That's fine with me. My sisters would just be all over you and want to tell you all about their delivery room adventures and my mother would start pestering you about when she can babysit, and they'd all drive us crazy from now until the baby comes."

"Yeah, but that's what families are for. You're so lucky you grew up here, surrounded by all that chaos and stability and love."

"Our baby will grow up the same way . . . hopefully with a little less chaos." He reaches for the doorknob and opens it for her. "Come on, let's go in."

They step into the front hall, where they're immediately sideswiped by a scooter. It's one of his nephews—he can't tell which, because the boy is wearing a helmet, and because his sisters have a whole cluster of kids who are all between the ages of four and seven and roughly the same size and build.

"Hey, Aunt Clara! Hey, Uncle Drew!"

"Hi, Kevin." She plants a kiss on his helmet as he zooms past hollering, *"Grandma, Aunt Clara and Uncle Drew are here!"*

"Are you sure that was Kevin?" Drew asks

Clara, taking off his coat and opening the front hall closet only to find it jammed.

"I'm positive it's Kevin. You're not?"

"Sometimes those guys all look alike." He takes her jacket and, after a glance at the overflowing coat tree beside the door, opts to drape them both over a holly-festooned newel post.

"You're kidding, right?"

"Not really."

"But they're your nephews. Please tell me you can tell them apart."

"When they're not wearing helmets. Otherwise, it's easy to mistake them for each other. Or Aunt Stella."

She grins at that. "Well, it was hard enough for me to tell your sisters apart when I first met them, and they weren't even wearing helmets."

"You always say that, but I don't get why it was so confusing. It's not like they even look alike."

"It's all those *D* names, remember?"

"Yeah, but then I taught you the trick to keep them straight. . . . My sister Debbie acts like a debutante, my sister Dani was the tomboy and refused to answer to anyone who called her Danielle, and my sister Doris is the a*dor*able one." Seeing Clara's eyes widen, he asks, "What? What's wrong?"

"Your sister *Doreen*."

"Right. She's the adorable one."

"You said 'my sister Doris.'"

My sister Doris . . . ?

A girl with freckles and red pigtails flashes before his mind's eye.

Not Doreen. She's a fair-skinned blonde.

"Doris! Did you cut my girdle up to make a slingshot?"

"Drew?"

He blinks. "Yeah, I meant Doreen. Slip of the tongue."

"Look at you two, empty-handed."

Drew looks up to see his brother-in-law Rick coming down the stairs carrying a portable folding crib, a pink Hello Kitty suitcase, a tub of Lincoln Logs, and a camera bag.

"Running away from home?" Drew asks him dryly, going over to hold the door open for him.

"No, but I might consider it once we *get* home, after an eight-hour drive with three over-tired kids in a compact car loaded down with all the crap we came with, and another heap of stuff they got for Christmas."

"Need some help?" Clara asks.

"Nah, this is the last load. We're going to get on the road right after we eat. Just enjoy travel-ing light while it lasts, guys, because once you start having kids, your arms will always be full of stuff, and your car will be full of stuff, and your house will be full of stuff—and trust me, none of it will even be yours."

With that, he walks out the door, and Clara and Drew look at each other.

Before they can say a word, his mother pops in from the kitchen.

"Drew! Clara! What a great surprise!"

Wearing faded jeans and a pair of fashionable-framed glasses perched low on her nose, ash-blond Sandy Becker looks twenty years younger than she actually is. Between her family, her hobbies, and her volunteer work in several civic organizations, her life has always been a whirlwind of activity—and that's just the way she likes it.

Her three daughters are contentedly following in her footsteps. Meanwhile, Drew's father, a corporate accountant, has a more laid-back, quiet demeanor. Like father, like son.

"What brings you two into town today? I thought you were planning to spend a quiet weekend."

"We were. But then Clara apparently decided she hadn't gotten her fill of chaos the other night, so we're back for more."

"You came to the right place." His mother hugs her. "I hope you're hungry, because you're just in time for breakfast!"

"I'm starved, actually."

Breakfast? Drew looks at his watch. It's a quarter of noon. But his family has always been a bunch of late sleepers.

"I could eat," he tells his mom.

"Good! I made eggs Benedict—well, not for Ed; he's having an egg-white vegetable omelet because of his cholesterol, but—Clara, are you all right?"

She swallows audibly, looking faintly green. Uh-oh.

"I'm fine."

"It's just that she's allergic to eggs, Mom," Drew speaks up quickly.

"*What?* How is it that I never knew that?"

"There are a lot of things you don't know about her," he tells his mother, draping one arm around her shoulder and the other around his wife's, winking at Clara as they make their way to the noisy kitchen.

There they all are:

Dad; Debbie and her husband Ken; Dani, who's married to Rick; Doreen and her husband Paul. His grandmother is there, too, and Aunt Stella, wearing her crash helmet. There are plenty of assorted kids and babies on laps, on scooters, on the floor in front of the open pots-and-pans cupboard.

After a flurry of hugs and kisses and rearranging of chairs, Drew and Clara squeeze in around the large oval table, along with Rick, who's finished loading the car. Drew's mother serves an egg-white omelet to his father, eggs Benedict to the rest of the family, and offers

Clara just about everything else in the fridge and pantry.

"Really, I'll just have a bowl of cereal," she insists, and his mother busies herself lining up an array of boxes on the countertop, reading all the ingredients to make sure that they don't contain eggs.

"You know, if this family grows any bigger, we're going to need to buy a new dining set," Drew's father announces from his perch at the head of the table.

"I hope it does grow bigger, Grandpa, because I want a sister," Drew's only niece, Katie, says wistfully.

Dani shakes her boyish haircut hard. "No more babies for me, honey. I've got my hands full with you and your brothers."

"Maybe you'll have a girl cousin someday," Debbie tells Katie.

"Yeah, Aunt Debbie will give you one," Doreen pipes up.

"No, no, no, I meant that Aunt Doreen would give you one."

Drew grins as his sisters, both the mothers of two boys, good-naturedly toss the responsibility back and forth, speaking to be heard above the pot-lid percussion ensemble on the floor.

Then his oldest—and loudest—nephew, Sean, announces, "Aunt Clara should have the new girl! She doesn't even have any kids yet."

"When are you going to have a baby, Aunt Clara?" Katie asks, lighting up.

"Oh ... someday." Cereal spoon poised in front of her mouth, Clara looks uncomfortable, and Drew knows it isn't just because the strong scents of eggs and coffee are wafting in the air.

"Hey, Dad"—he jumps in to quickly change the subject—"speaking of getting a new kitchen table ... what ever happened to that old one we used to have?"

"Which one?"

"You know ... the one that had the chrome trim around the sides and that aqua-colored Formica top?"

"I don't remember that table."

"That's because we didn't have one like that," his mother informs Drew, reaching past his shoulder to fill his coffee cup.

"Yes, we did. A long time ago, when I was really little, before you guys remodeled the kitchen. Right, Dad?"

"I don't think so. When we first moved in, we had a round oak table—"

"Oval," his mother corrects him.

"Oval?" He frowns.

"It was definitely oval, Dad." Debbie pats his shoulder.

"You know your father." Drew's mother affectionately ruffles what's left of her husband's hair. "Sometimes he remembers things all wrong."

"Hey! You don't remember the table Drew's talking about, either, Sandy."

"Well, you can't remember something that didn't even exist." She plucks an empty creamer pitcher from the center of the table.

"Sit down, Mom, I'll fill that," Drew's brother-in-law Ken offers.

"No, you all sit and eat your eggs before they get cold." She bustles away.

"You guys remember that old kitchen table, right?" Drew turns to his sisters.

"Definitely." Debbie nods. "Mom's right, it was oval."

"No, not that one! The aqua one with the chrome trim!"

They all shake their heads. All but Grandma, who looks uncertain, and Aunt Stella, whose expression is hidden behind her helmet.

Drew sees that Clara is looking at him wearing a strange expression. Her brows are knit and she's biting her lower lip as if pondering something.

"Sorry, Drew, but an aqua table sounds pretty hideous," Doreen comments.

"Maybe, but it must have been the style because the whole kitchen was aqua back then."

"Aqua was very popular," his grandmother announces, bobbing her white head. "Remember, Stella?"

"*Vrrrm, vrrrm,*" she says agreeably.

Drew looks around the modern kitchen, trying to remember it as it once was. Not easy, because the room in his memory bears little resemblance to this wide-open space with glass-fronted cherry cabinets, soapstone counters, vintage lighting fixtures, and a hardwood floor.

They must have knocked down a wall or two when they remodeled, Drew realizes, because the old kitchen was much smaller.

"Well, not everything was aqua," he recalls. "The cupboards were white—and metal, with long silver handles."

"The old cupboards weren't metal, they were wood," his father contradicts. "Dark wood."

"I'm pretty sure they were metal, and white, Dad. And the walls were white, too—white bead board. But the floor was this kind of speckled aqua linoleum."

"I don't remember that at all," Dani tells him.

"That's because you weren't a little kid, so I'm sure you didn't spend a lot of time crawling around down there like I did. I remember playing on it the way these guys are with the pots and pans. I had this game I used to dump out all over the floor—a bunch of metal rods and a magnet you used to pick them up, and Mom was always finding the rods all over the floor. Remember, Mom?"

Back from the fridge with a full pitcher of creamer, his mother shrugs. "I remember finding your matchbox cars all over the house, Drew—that must be what you're talking about. Little metal cars, not metal rods."

"I remember sticks!"

"Are you sure? Because you might have inherited Dad's lousy memory gene," Dani teases him.

Ignoring her, Drew says, "There were metal sticks and they were part of that game . . . and some of them had painted wooden knobs on the end."

He has a dim memory of playing it with one of his sisters, and it was probably Doris, who's closest to his own age.

Doris? You mean, Doreen!

Unsettled by yet another mental slip, Drew wonders if his mind is just playing tricks on him. Can he possibly be wrong about the game? And the aqua kitchen?

No. I can picture it all, clear as day.

He turns to his youngest sister. "I think you and I played that game together a few times. Don't you remember?"

"Hmm . . . what was it called?" Doreen asks, obviously clueless but hoping to jog her memory.

"I don't know."

"Well, we definitely never had an ugly aqua linoleum floor in here," Debbie says with maddening big-sister certainty. "Right, Mom?"

"Right."

"Yes, we did!" Talk about frustrating. "Come on, I can just see those metal sticks scattered all over it. I even remember the box the game came in—it was red and yellow, and it had a picture of an elf on it and I used to leave the cover off because he was creepy-looking and it scared me."

"Jack Straws!" Drew's grandmother blurts out, so unexpectedly that they all turn to look at her in surprise.

"Mom, are you okay?" his father asks, touching her wrinkled hand.

"Jack Straws!" she repeats, and Drew wonders if she's gone off the deep end like Aunt Stella. Or maybe senility has finally set in. Poor Grandma.

Then again, she is ninety-five years old. It's a wonder this didn't happen sooner.

"Who," Drew's mother gently asks her mother-in-law, "is Jack Straws?"

"Not *who*. *What!*"

"What?" Drew's parents exchange a glance.

"The game!" Grandma says impatiently. "The one Drew is talking about. Jack Straws."

"*See?*" Drew is triumphant. "Jack Straws. That's it."

Grandma to the rescue. He *knew* that game wasn't just a figment of his imagination.

"I had it, too, when I was a girl. Remember, Stella?"

Stella tilts her helmet thoughtfully.

Wearing a far-off expression, Grandma goes on, "Oh, yes, Santa Claus brought it to me the Christmas I turned five—you know, he only used to bring us one or two toys back then, not like the piles he brings all of you today."

Sean and Katie exchange a wide-eyed glance.

"One toy?" Katie asks sympathetically. "That's so sad."

"Were you a bad girl, Grandma?" Sean wants to know.

"Oh, bless you, no. I was always a good girl. Things were just different back then. We didn't have a lot, and we didn't need a lot, and we didn't want a lot."

"That's why they call them the 'Good Old Days,'" Rick says dryly, glancing at his wife and children.

"That game was brand-new that year," she reminisces on, "and all the kids wanted it, but I was the only one who got it. The metal rods with the wooden knobs, the magnets . . . there was an elf on the box, just like Drew said. Magnetic Jack Stra, it was actually called. Oh, we spent hours playing with that, just like Drew did."

As his grandmother smiles fondly, Drew wonders if he could possibly have been mistaken. Grandma was five years old in 1920. Was he really playing with the exact same game sixty years later?

He must have been, because he does remember it—and the aqua-colored linoleum.

Which his mother claims didn't even exist.

Puzzled, he turns to look at Clara and finds her gaping right back at him.

"What?" he asks, taken aback by the vivid alarm in her eyes.

"No, I just . . . I have to . . ." She jumps up and rushes from the table.

"Clara? Honey, where are you going?" Drew's mother asks as she races past.

"I just—I need to get some air."

Uh-oh. Obviously, the eggs and coffee finally got to her.

"She, uh, hasn't been feeling well today," he explains to his family, pushing his own chair back.

"There's a bug going around," his sister Doreen says.

"Terrific." Rick exchanges a worried look with Dani, obviously thinking of that eight-hour drive ahead.

"Is Aunt Clara going to hurl?" Kevin asks with interest as Drew hurries past him and his scooter toward the front door.

"No, no, she's fine. I'll be right back."

Drew steps into the damp, chilly air, closes

the door behind him, and looks around for Clara.

There she is, leaning against the porch railing, hugging herself.

"Are you okay?"

"I'm . . . not sure."

"Did you get sick?"

"No, it's not that." She seems to be avoiding his gaze.

"It's not?" Puzzled, he goes over to her. "What is it?"

She stares off into the distance, as if she's trying to make up her mind about something.

"Clara . . . what is it? What's up?"

She just shakes her head, clearly unwilling— or maybe unable?—to answer.

"Hey, you're kind of freaking me out. Talk to me."

Finally, she turns her head to look him directly in the eye, her face etched with grim determination that catches him off guard.

"There's something you should know, Drew. Something I should have told you a long time ago."

Chapter 18

Relieved to have left behind the postapocalyptic version of San Florentina, Clara steers the car up the winding road northeast of town.

"Arriving ... at ... destination ... on ... left," the GPS intones, and Clara slows the car to peer through the windshield.

Nine Sequoia Way is part of a new-looking townhouse complex nestled on the wooded hillside. The boxy two-story cookie-cutter units appear to be distinguishable only by the brass number affixed to the front doors.

This isn't the kind of place she and Drew would ever choose to live—not by a long shot. Not after their dream house.

Maybe something has gone horribly wrong with their finances, she finds herself thinking hopefully.

That would be much easier to swallow than

the alternative scenarios that keep trying to gnaw their way into her consciousness.

Dickens lets out a bark and she turns to see that he's up on all fours, panting, gazing out the window at the townhouses.

"Do you recognize this place, boy?" Clara asks him, turning off the ignition. "Are you home? Is that it? Is this where you live?"

Maybe he really is a stray.

A stray who looks like Dickens and acts like Dickens and answers to Dickens.

"I guess we'd better figure out what's going on. Come on." She opens the door and climbs out of the car with effort. It's kind of exhausting, lugging this big stomach around with her everywhere she goes.

The dog bounds out after her, making a beeline for unit number nine.

Clara follows slowly, taking in the neighboring townhouses. At first glance, they all looked alike, but now she recognizes subtle differences between them.

A tricycle and a plastic Little Tikes picnic table are visible in the yard next door to the right, and several cases of empty beer bottles sit beside the steps next door to the left. Starter homes for young families, transitional homes for singles . . .

Where do Drew and I fit in here? Clara wonders bleakly.

Dickens is eagerly parked on the doorstep of Unit 9, wagging his tail in anticipation. Clara reluctantly joins him and rings the bell, wondering what she'll say to whoever comes to the door.

But nobody does.

She rings again, waits again, knocks, knocks louder.

"Nobody home?" she asks Dickens.

Knowing it's nosy, but also perfectly appropriate under the circumstances, she leans toward the window in the door, cupping her hand over her eyes to peer inside.

A glance tells her the place is empty. Not as in nobody home—as in completely unoccupied. There's no furniture, no sign that anyone is living in the vacant rooms she can see through the door.

Not sure what to make of that, she looks at Dickens.

"Maybe we haven't moved in yet. Is that it?"

He trots down the steps and disappears around the corner of the townhouse in reply.

"Hey! Where are you going?"

She chases after him.

When she catches up, she finds him parked beside a pair of glass sliders on the back deck, clearly wanting—and expecting—to be let in.

Dickens is obviously right at home here. It's hard to believe he'd act this way if they haven't even moved in yet.

"Then again, you are a nutty kind of dog," she informs him.

Looking agreeable, he thumps his tail on the deck planks.

There's no sign of life back here, either, she notes. The deck is empty, while the neighboring ones have plastic chairs, an umbrella table, kids' outdoor toys. She wishes someone would come outside and perhaps recognize her—or Dickens, at least. She can't quite muster the nerve to knock on a door and ask if anyone knows her.

Oh, well.

"Come on, Dickens. Let's go."

He wags his tail, still looking at the door.

With a sigh, Clara reaches for his collar to drag him away.

Then something catches her attention out of the corner of her eye.

Turning her head, she sees that there is, indeed, a hummingbird feeder hanging from a hook beside the kitchen window.

Meaning . . . what?

Plenty of people like hummingbirds. Yes, Doris happens to be obsessed by them—but that doesn't mean she's responsible for this one.

Particularly since we haven't even moved in yet, Clara reminds herself.

Still, she looks back over her shoulder at it as she heads toward the car with Dickens in tow.

She can't help but feel like it's much more than a coincidence.

Her thoughts are scrambled as she drives back home through the fog with Dickens snoozing peacefully on the seat beside her.

Pulling into the driveway at home, she glances up at the house and through a veil of fog, is startled to see someone beside the front door.

"Drew!"

Hope soars into her heart.

Startled by her outburst, Dickens scrambles to life on the passenger's seat.

Then the mist thins and she realizes it isn't Drew after all, and the burst of hope nose-dives to her gut.

The figure belongs to a female. Whoever it is waves and comes eagerly toward the car.

Clara turns off the engine, puts the car into park, and tries to regain her composure.

The woman is a tall, blond, beautiful stranger.

But when Clara opens her car door and steps out, she finds herself caught in a fervent embrace.

"I'm so glad you're back!"

Caught off guard by the greeting, Clara replies, her voice muffled by her visitor's jacket, "I just . . . I just went to town for a little while."

With a laugh, the woman releases her. "You know that's not what I meant. Wow, look at your belly! You've gotten so big—I mean, in a good way," she adds hastily.

Getting a good look at her for the first time, Clara realizes she's not a woman after all. She's about college-age, and there's something vaguely familiar about her.

Having leaped out of the car, the dog hurtles himself at the girl and she welcomes him with open arms. "Hey, Dickens! It's so good to see you, buddy!"

Dickens.

So it is him.

Clara realizes she knew it all along, deep down inside. Of course it's Dickens. Crazy dog.

Crouching to rub Dickens's fur affectionately, the girl looks up at Clara. "Where's Drew?"

Good question.

And one she'd been praying the newcomer might answer. So much for that.

"He's not here—right now," she adds, her head spinning. Surely, if this girl knows her and Dickens and is asking about Drew, she'd been expecting to find him here.

That has to be a good sign, doesn't it?

"Awww . . . I wanted to tell him that on our last day I did a double black diamond chute in deep powder! He was so right."

"About what?"

"You know—when he told me that I'd be way more likely to regret it if I didn't try it than if I did. Last time we went I didn't do it, and I regretted it. So this time, even though I was scared out of my mind, I made myself try it. And I did it!"

"That's so great . . ."

"Yeah, and I would have done it again if we could have stayed another day. But my mom was ready to come back home first thing this morning. You know how she is—she just doesn't like to be in the house for Christmas—it's too hard. Anyway, she says maybe we can go back to Tahoe in January, so I'm definitely going to try it again."

Piecing together the fragments of conversational clues, Clara knows only that the girl has been away on a ski trip with her mother, who thinks Christmas at home is too hard.

Wondering who the heck she is, Clara looks around to see if her car offers a clue—and sees that there isn't one.

What, did she helicopter in?

"Well, I'd better get back home," she tells Clara, giving Dickens a final pat before standing again. "My mom wants me to watch my brothers while she goes out to get some groceries into the house. Don't tell Drew my news—I want to tell him myself. He's going to be really proud of me."

The girl starts away, toward the stand of trees alongside the driveway.

Ah—so she came on foot.

And all at once, Clara realizes who she is. She's a good head taller, but if you strip away the baby fat, the glasses, the braces, and . . .

"Amelia!"

Startled, the girl turns back. "Yeah?"

"Uh, tell your mom I said hello."

"Sure."

"And your dad, too," she adds as Amelia walks on.

The girl stops in her tracks. After a moment, she turns, and the look on her face makes Clara's blood run cold.

"Wh—what did you say?"

Oh no. God, no.

Something must have happened to Jeff Tucker. The pain in his daughter's eyes is as blatant as the freckles on her nose once were.

Three years is a long time. Freckles fade. Awkward little girls grow up to be beautiful young women. Loved ones are lost.

"I'm glad, too," Clara manages to say. "That's what I said. You know—about your black diamond run."

"Oh!" Amelia's expression relaxes. "I thought you said something else."

Clara shakes her head mutely.

"And it was *double* black diamond," Amelia amends with a smile, before starting toward home again.

"Double. Of course. Good going, sweetie."

Clara watches until the girl has disappeared between the trees.

Only then does she allow the thought that's been trying to break in from the moment Amelia asked about Drew.

She didn't ask about their child.

Nor did she glance into the backseat as though she were expecting to find someone small strapped into the car seat there—the car seat that doesn't exist.

Her heart aching anew, Clara unlocks the front door and steps over the threshold.

The house feels emptier than ever. She makes her way past the stacks of boxes to the kitchen, where she dumps some food into a bowl for Dickens. He dives noisily into the meal.

Realizing she's hungry, she looks around for something to eat. There isn't much. The fridge hasn't been replenished since yesterday, and the cupboards remain bare. Nancy Tucker isn't the only one who should be buying groceries.

But Clara is too exhausted to go out again. Maybe she can just order something. In town earlier, she'd noticed that Drew's favorite pizza place had reopened in a new location.

They had ordered so much takeout when they first moved into their house that Clara easily memorized the number. With any luck, they haven't changed it.

Picking up the telephone receiver to dial, she hears the static dial tone that indicates a waiting voice mail message.

Her heart skips a beat.

Quickly, she presses the incoming calls log, praying she'll see a familiar number.

There isn't one. There have been two calls since she left the house, and she doesn't recognize either of the numbers on caller ID.

Okay. That's okay.

Whoever called left messages, but she'll need a password to retrieve them. She hurriedly dials the message access code and that, at least, still works. She follows the automated prompts that lead to a request for her password. Then, holding her breath in anticipation, she enters the one she and Drew were using three years ago.

Please, let it work. Please, let it work.

"You have . . . one . . . new . . . message."

Yes! It works!

On the heels of that triumphant thought comes another: there's only one message. That means the other caller hung up without leaving one.

"First . . . new . . . message . . ." the robotic operator announces.

Please, let it be from Drew. Please, let it be from Drew.

Clara holds her breath.

"Clara, it's me," her mother's familiar voice

greets her. "I'm just checking in on you again. Where are you this early in the morning? Are you all right? Maybe you're asleep. Okay, call me as soon as you wake up so that I won't worry."

No chance of that. Some things never change.

But for once, Clara welcomes her mother's nagging questions. The knowledge that her mom is still out there somewhere, alive and well in 2012, is a tremendous comfort.

It would be even more comforting to discover the same thing about her husband.

Again, she checks the call log.

Who called and didn't leave a message?

Does it matter? It was probably a telemarketer, or someone taking a survey. They hang up on voice mail all the time.

Drew would have left a message.

Still, curiosity gets the better of her and she highlights the unfamiliar number, then presses redial.

Someone answers on the first ring—a familiar male voice saying a cheerful "hello."

"Drew!" she shrieks. "Oh my God, Drew! Where are you?"

But he's still talking.

"You've reached the voice mail of Drew Becker. Please leave a message, and I'll return your call as soon as possible."

Heart pounding, Clara waits impatiently through the drawn-out *beeeeeep* that indicates he's got numerous messages.

"Drew, it's me. Where are you? I missed your call, and I need you to call me back right away, please! Please, call me right back!"

Not wanting to break the connection, she presses the phone hard against her ear, trying to think of something else to say—something that won't strike him as odd.

Like, "I'm visiting you from the past and I'm clueless—where are you? Where's our child?"

In the end, she settles for a heartfelt "I love you," before hanging up the phone, tears running down her face.

Thank God.

Thank God he's out there somewhere.

But deep down, you knew he was really okay, didn't you? Just like you knew Dickens was really Dickens.

You didn't really believe something terrible had happened to Drew.

No. She didn't.

She only let herself wonder because nothing was making sense. She didn't understand why he wouldn't be here with her for Christmas, or why they'd be moving from their dream house, or where their child is.

She still doesn't get it, but there must be a logical answer to those questions. . . .

And to another one that's been nagging at her: why wouldn't Drew have left a message when he called? He's never done that before.

Things change, she reminds herself yet again. Maybe he was in a hurry.

Things change. . . .

What if it wasn't Drew who was calling her at all?

What if it was someone else, using his phone? Someone who'd found it, or stolen it . . . ?

Once again, her imagination takes flight, carrying her to the dark place where the only easy answers are the ones she can't bear to consider.

Chapter 19

Drew didn't miss the troubled shadows in Clara's green eyes when they faced each other on his parents' front porch earlier.

Before she could tell him what was wrong, half his family came running out to see whether she was okay, effectively curtailing their conversation.

The rest of the visit was strained. Watching her go through the motions with his family, Drew realized that she had been acting skittish all day—and last night, too, come to think of it. Something's been bothering her.

When was the last time she was her cheerful self?

Christmas morning, when she told him about the baby, and he gave her the puppy.

Then came the earthquake—and ever since, she's been oddly distant.

But there was no earthquake when they were sitting around his parents' table. What triggered her sudden departure?

He's been going over the nostalgia-laced conversation leading up to it, but he can't figure out what it might have been. One minute he and his family were talking about old times, and the next, his wife was fleeing the table in distress.

He'd assumed it was the sight and smell of eggs, making her sick. But maybe he was wrong about that. Maybe something else is going on.

Whatever it is, it isn't going to be good news—of that, he's certain.

As soon as they get into the car, he turns to her.

"Are you okay?"

She nods.

"No, you're not."

She pointed over her shoulder. "Someone's waiting for this parking spot."

"So? They can find another one."

She just looks at him.

He sighs, starts the engine, pulls away.

From here it's just a few blocks to the bridge. As soon as they're on the access highway, he says, "You have to tell me what's going on."

"I know. I will. But not here. Like this."

"Why not?"

"Because you're behind the wheel, and what I have to tell you might upset you."

That sends a sickening stab of fear through him. He gazes bleakly through the windshield at the red girders rising into the fog.

"Let's go somewhere to talk instead of driving all the way back home," he suggests. "We can stop in Sausalito and—"

"No, Drew, please. I don't want to tell you in public."

His mind teeming with horrible, intrusive thoughts, he navigates the bridge traffic, then the coastal highway toward San Florentina.

Was it just a few hours ago that they were heading in the opposite direction, talking about this being their lucky day?

Then again—that had been his take on it.

She hadn't seemed nearly as enthusiastic.

She yawns deeply as he speeds north, leaning her head back against the seat.

Is she leaving me?

The thought barges into his brain and his hands clench the wheel.

No. He can't fathom that. He knows his wife. She loves him. He loves her. Their marriage is solid. Of that, if nothing else, he's absolutely certain.

Then what else could be so difficult for her to say?

Is the cancer back?

Another cruel notion, storming in, demanding to be entertained.

She was just given a clean bill of health by her oncologist. She's pregnant. There's just no way.

But what else would upset her like this?

He glances over at her, certain she's fallen asleep. But her eyes are wide open, her jaw set grimly.

She's exhausted, yet obviously too disturbed by whatever is looming to sleep.

At last—or too soon?—they arrive home.

After pretty much speeding north over the bridge and up the coast highway, anxious to hear whatever it is Clara has to say to him, he does everything he can think of to delay the moment of truth.

He empties the car of a few months' worth of take-out napkins, straw wrappers, and empty water bottles. Then he goes into the house and lets the dog out. Upstairs, he changes out of the jeans and long-sleeved T-shirt he's wearing into another pair of jeans and another long-sleeved T-shirt. He lets the dog back in and feeds him.

Watching Dickens inhale a bowl of puppy chow on the kitchen floor, Drew knows he can't delay this any longer.

They've been home for almost fifteen minutes now. Time to go find out.

"Wish me luck," he tells Dickens, petting his soft black fur.

The puppy doesn't even glance up from his food bowl, probably holding a grudge for having spent much of the day in a crate.

He'll get over it.

Drew just hopes he himself will be able to get over whatever his wife is about to say.

In the living room, he finds Clara sitting on the couch, the room draped in winter shadows as the day wanes beyond the windows. The television is on, tuned to the Weather Channel.

For a moment, he thinks she didn't bother to change it. But then he realizes that she's watching avidly.

"What's the verdict?" he asks, and she looks up at him, startled.

"What?"

"The forecast—is it still going to be a beautiful day tomorrow?"

"Yes. And then it's going to start raining at night, and it's going to rain for a few days straight."

He shrugs. Typical weather in the Pacific Northwest.

He turns on a couple of lamps, plugs in the Christmas tree, the electric candles, the white twinkle lights. Now the room is bathed in a soft golden glow—the better to see the worried expression on his wife's face.

"There," he says, "that's better, don't you think?"

"Mmm-hmm."

"Do you want me to make us some tea or something?"

"No thanks."

Okay. Nothing left to do but sit beside her on the couch.

He does, and takes her hand. It's cold.

"Clara. Tell me."

She nods. "Okay."

He can tell she's uncertain where or how to begin—even though she's had a couple of hours now to try to figure it out.

But clearly, she's about to deliver a bombshell that deserves a real sit-down, face-to-face, private conversation. And now that the moment is here . . .

"I'm so afraid you're not going to believe me, Drew," she confesses.

"Why wouldn't I believe you?"

"Because if it hadn't happened to me, I wouldn't believe me, either."

Something happened to her.

Cancer?

No! Stop that!

"Look, just tell me, Clara. Whatever it is, if you say it's the truth, I'll believe you."

"That's easy for you to say now, but—"

"Tell me," he repeats, taking her other ice-cold hand in his as well and clasping them both.

She takes a deep breath. "Do you remember how you were talking about that game, Magnetic Jack Straws, back at your parents' house?"

Huh?

Whatever he'd been expecting her to say, this wasn't it.

He's so relieved that she didn't begin with "My oncologist called" that he merely nods, indicating that he does, indeed, remember.

"Remember how no one else in your family remembered your playing it, but Grandma said she had the same game?"

Another nod. Of course he remembers.

"Didn't you think that was kind of . . . unusual?"

What on earth is she talking about? Why this? Why now?

"Do you mean," he asks, trying to follow, "did I think it was unusual that my grandmother and I played the same game?"

"Growing up generations apart. Right."

"There are a lot of toys that have been around for years that are still being made today. I mean, I had Lincoln Logs when I was a kid and now my nephew—"

"No, Drew, that's not what I'm getting at. This is about your remembering something that

maybe didn't happen to you—not in this lifetime, anyway."

Not in this lifetime?

That's a bizarre thing for her to say.

This lifetime . . .

As if there were some other lifetime to com-
pare it to.

Something flits into the very edge of Drew's
consciousness, then back out again. He doesn't
chase after it. Maybe he's afraid to.

"So you're saying that maybe I never really
played with that game after all?" he asks slowly.

"Not in this lifetime," she repeats.

"Meaning . . . ?"

"Meaning maybe you played the game in
another lifetime. In a past life."

Whoa.

Is she talking about . . . ?

Obviously, she is.

"Reincarnation," he manages to say aloud, as
the dangerous thought teases his mind again.

"Reincarnation. Yes."

"I . . . I didn't know you believed in that
stuff."

"No. You wouldn't know, because I've always been careful never to bring it up to you."

"Why not?"

She just looks at him. "I don't even know
how to say this."

The thought that was dancing around the periphery of his brain is now demanding to be let in; he keeps it at bay.

"You know how my grandmother died young, and my grandfather never got over it?"

Drew nods.

"Well, I always liked to think that somehow, they got a second chance. That, you know, they were reborn as two different people who would find each other and fall in love all over again."

He smiles faintly. "That's pretty romantic."

"Do you think it could happen?"

"Let's put it this way . . . I guess stranger things could happen."

"I'm really glad you said that, because . . ." She hesitates. "There's just no easy way to say this."

Then don't say it, he wants to tell her.

Don't say it, because I'm afraid to hear it.

Let's just go back to living our ordinary, everyday life together.

This *life*.

"Drew, you know how you're always saying you and I were meant to be together? Well, I think you're right."

"Of course I'm right."

"No, I mean . . . I think you and I actually were together in another lifetime."

There it is.

And he knew it. He knew it was coming.

The whole thing is crazy, and yet . . .

Logical.

The way he felt like he knew Clara when he met her . . .

The way everything seemed to fall into place for them instantly, the way they both seemed to know they belonged together from the start . . .

Back then, he told himself that must be how it was when you met the right person and truly fell in love for the first time.

But it might not have been the first time.

"Do you think I'm crazy or hormonal?"

"No," he says quickly. "Not that at all."

"But you get what I'm telling you?"

"That you think we were reborn to find each other, just like your grandparents?"

"Well . . . *you* were. See, it didn't exactly happen the same way with us. I mean, you were someone else, in the past, and we were together, but—"

"When was this, exactly?" he cuts in as if that's even a reasonable question, as if it even matters at all.

Because really, there's nothing the least bit reasonable about what she's trying to tell him. And yet, he's buying it.

He's buying it because for the first time, a lot of things are starting to make sense.

"Do you mean when did you and I first fall in love?" she asks, and he nods. "It was back in the 1940s."

The 1940s.

World War II, and galoshes, and big band music . . .

"Oh my God," he whispers.

No wonder.

"You still don't think I'm crazy?" Clara asks.

"What? No! No, I always thought that maybe *I* was crazy."

"Why?"

"Because . . ." Does he dare tell her?

Looking into her eyes, he knows that he should. That he has to. That she'll believe him, just as he believes her. That they're in this together.

"Lately, I've had these flashes where I'd see something or hear something in my head, just like you do when you remember something from the past . . . only I knew that some of it had never happened to me, so I figured it was just my imagination or something. And apparently, some of the things I thought were actual memories never happened, either."

He shakes his head, remembering the earlier conversation with his family. He remembered that old kitchen table and the linoleum floor and the Jack Straws game so vividly. How was it, he'd wondered at the time, that no one else did?

No one but Grandma, who had grown up in another era.

"I've done a lot of reading about reincarnation," Clara tells him. "Sometimes, a person can have a flash of breakthrough memory that might really be a glimpse into their own past . . . as somebody else. Only they don't realize they're memories at all."

"So you think I really had that aqua table with the chrome trim and that magnet game in my other lifetime?"

"I *know* you did."

"How?"

"Because I saw them both. And the speckled aqua linoleum."

"What? Where did you see them? How?"

"I was there."

"In your past life?"

"No." She clears her throat. "In *yours*."

"But you just said you were there."

"I was. But not in my *past* life. In *this* one."

"You lost me. You just said we were reincarnated, and that—"

"No, Drew, I said *you* were reincarnated."

"But . . ." Confused, he tries to piece together what she's told him so far. He can't. His head is spinning. "I thought you said we were together in the past, and that we fell in love when we were other people."

"*You* were someone else. I was me."

"You were you. . . ."

"Right."

"You were Clara Becker, falling in love with some other guy in the 1940s, and—"

"I was actually Clara McCallum then," she cuts in. "It was three years ago. Right before you and I met."

"I thought you said it was the 1940s."

"It was. I mean, for you. And I . . . okay, this is going to sound absolutely out there, and even if you believe all this other stuff, you're never going to believe it. . . ."

"Try me."

"I time traveled."

"What?" He gapes at her.

Oh, hell. Just when he thought they were onto something . . .

Maybe she is all hormonal. Crazy, even.

He loves her anyway, but this is a little . . . *out there*.

She peers at his face and shakes her head. "You didn't believe me last time I tried to explain it, either—not at first. And I know I sound insane—"

"No, you don't." He pauses. "The thing is . . . there wasn't any 'last time,' Clara. You never said anything about time travel to me before. Trust me, if you had, I would have remembered, since remembering things—whether or not they happened—seems to be my forte," he adds wryly.

"I didn't say anything about it to *you*—not in

this lifetime. But when I was back in 1941, and you were Jed, I tried to tell you, and you—"

The name jumps out at him; he flinches as if he's been stung.

"Drew? What is it?"

He's silent for a long moment.

Realizing . . .

Remembering.

Riding down a vintage Main Street USA in an old-fashioned car with an *ah-ooh-gah* horn, a couple of unfamiliar boys in the front seat, a female voice calling to him from the sidewalk, and he turns to look . . .

"*Jed*," he says at last, aloud.

"Jed Landry," Clara says softly. "That was your name."

"That was my . . ." He struggles to wrap his head around the enormity of it.

"You were a soldier—"

"I was *him*. I was Jed. And that movie . . . the one you were making when we met . . ."

"That was based on his—your—life."

He leans back against the couch cushions and tilts his head to the ceiling, eyes closed, trying to absorb the shock.

Beside him, Clara emits a sound that might be a yawn, or perhaps a sigh of relief that it's all out there at last.

She waits for a few moments before speaking.

"When Denton sent that invitation to the premiere, and you insisted on going, I was scared that it might . . . I don't know, trigger something. Or maybe—maybe I wanted it to."

"It did." He opens his eyes and looks at her.

"What do you mean?"

"It was all so real. I tried to tell myself that's what a good movie is supposed to do, you know? It's supposed to put you in the moment, so that you can relate to the characters. But everything that was happening on the screen—it wasn't like I felt like it was happening to me right then and there. I felt like it had *already* happened to me."

"Why didn't you tell me that?"

"Are you kidding? I knew I was out of my element at a Hollywood premiere in the first place, and I was crazy about you. I wanted to fit into your life, I wanted you to fit into mine. . . . I wasn't about to say I was afraid I might have a few screws loose."

"I've thought the same thing about myself at times, and I never told you, either, so . . . I guess we're even." She yawns again, behind her hand, as if trying to suppress the exhaustion that's obviously overtaking her.

He holds out his arm and she gratefully snuggles beside him, her weary head on his shoulder. He tells her about the flashbacks he's been having since they met, with increasing frequency, about completely random things. Like fruitcake.

"I remember that. You said fruitcake reminded you of something but you didn't know what."

"Yeah." He shudders.

"But you did know."

He nods.

"Tell me," she says softly—sadly—as if she's already aware of it herself. "What did it remind you of?"

"I saw this old lady, lying in the snow, bleeding."

"Minnie Bouvier. She brought fruitcakes to your family every Christmas, and she was hit by a car that December that I was there."

Those last words jar him. "You were there?"

And all at once, in his mind's eye, he sees her, standing there with snow falling down all around her. Her hair is different, and her clothes are old-fashioned, and she's wearing dark red lipstick. . . .

But it's her. It's Clara. In the past. *His* past.

"I went back in time, Drew, like I said. I was with you. It was real."

"I don't know. . . . How can this be happening? Maybe it's just my imagination—our imagination."

She's shaking her head before he finishes. "I have proof. From Doris. I can show you."

Doris! Did you cut up my girdle to make a sling-shot?

"She was your sister, Drew," Clara is saying, and he's trying hard to focus.

She was my sister.

My sister . . .

"Penny." The name pops into his head out of nowhere and spills from his lips.

Clara looks startled. "I was talking about Doris, but Penny—she was your sister, too."

Doris and Penny.

Faces flash through his mind. Sisters. An aura of warmth and affection creeps over him.

"I think . . . I think Doris took Penny's girdle one time . . . and . . . I think she made it into a slingshot."

Clara smiles. "That sounds like her."

"So you . . . knew her?"

"I knew her in 1941—and I knew her recently, too. In New York, she found me, and—"

"Your Doris is . . . is *my* Doris?"

"That's one way to put it."

"You're talking about the hummingbird lady, right? The one you used to visit—that *One Life to Live* fan of yours—right?"

"Sort of. Only she didn't really find me just because I was on the soap."

"That's what you told me."

"I know, but . . . she found me because of Jed. Because she remembered me from her childhood, and she figured out that I was from the future, and she had been waiting to connect with me again for all those years."

Why this particular news, of everything she's revealed, should leave him flabbergasted, he has no idea. But for the moment, he's tongue-tied, imagining the kid sister in his mind's eye as an old woman with whom he, too, might actually have connected.

She should have told me, he finds himself thinking with some resentment—fairly or not. *It was my sister. I deserved to know.*

"Look, I know this is way too much coming at you all at once," she says quietly, "and this isn't how I ever wanted to tell you about any of it. But I guess there's really no good way to find out you've been reincarnated and your wife is a time traveler, is there?" She forces a little laugh.

He can't even muster a smile.

Clara touches his shoulder. "Are we . . . still okay?"

"We'll always be okay."

"You don't look convinced."

"I love you. I just need to get used to all of this."

"It's a lot. I know."

He can't hold back a sharp little noise that might have been intended as a laugh, but isn't.

"A lot. Yeah. It's definitely a lot," he tells Clara flatly.

"Are you mad at me?"

Yes.

All at once, he's furious.

"I have a sister."

"You have three."

"Doris. That's what I meant."

"I know what you meant." She looks down at her lap. "I'm sorry I didn't tell you, but you have to see it from my perspective. If I had told you, you would have—"

"Wanted to get to know her? Yeah. I probably would have."

"There's still—"

"Let's not do this now, okay?" He stands abruptly, not allowing himself to look at her face, knowing he'd see hurt there. But he's hurting, too. Because of her.

"Where are you going?" she asks quietly.

"Out . . . with the dog. I need to walk him, and . . . I just . . . I need to walk."

"Want some company?"

"No," he says sharply—and forgets to avoid her gaze.

There it is—the hurt in her eyes.

"Drew," she says quietly, "let me come with you."

"No, you're exhausted. You should take a nap."

"It's too late in the day. If I take a nap, I'll never be able to sleep later."

"You're sleeping for two," he reminds her. "I bet you will."

He leans over and plants a gentle kiss on her head.

Looking up at him, her eyes are still clouded. "Drew? There's one more thing I have to tell you about the time travel. . . ."

Dismay courses through him.

He can't. He just can't. He can't hear any more until he's had time to process all of this.

"Can it wait?"

She hesitates. "Sure. Of course it can wait. I love you."

"I love you, too."

And right about now, that's the only thing he knows for certain.

Chapter 20

"Come on, Drew. . . . Call me back! Please, please, please, call me back. . . ." Telephone receiver clasped in her hand, Clara paces around a stack of boxes in the living room.

Over three hours have passed since she figured out the hang-up call was from Drew's phone and left him a message in return. She's dialed the number several times since, getting his voice mail every time.

And she's left a message every time, trying not to sound frantic—nearly impossible when your heart is in your mouth.

Practically in tears when she left the last message, she was able to say little more than "It's me again. Please, call me."

So why hasn't he called?

It's a weekday. Drew is the kind of person

who checks his voice mail regularly even when he isn't at work.

Maybe something's wrong with the phone.

For whatever reason, he didn't get the messages, or he hasn't had a chance to call back yet . . . even though his wife is very pregnant and told him that it's urgent?

It makes no sense.

Oh God, what if—

The grim thought is curtailed by a sharp movement from deep inside her belly. She gently presses a hand over the spot, and it promptly happens again.

She smiles, realizing that a tiny foot has just given her a good, sharp kick.

"Thanks," she tells her unborn child. "I needed that."

Comforted by the reminder that she really isn't alone here after all, she paces on, negotiating the cluttered landscape of her home, stepping around Dickens, taking a nap in the middle of a doorway.

There are boxes everywhere. Maybe she should start opening them, looking for clues.

But what if a moving van shows up to take them all away? For all she knows, that could happen at any moment. Maybe Drew is at the new place even now, with their child, waiting for her.

9 Sequoia Way? Is that where they're going?

It isn't her dream house, but if they've fallen on rough times and that's where they're headed, then she'll make it a home for them.

It doesn't matter where they live, as long as they're together.

Drew, please, please, call me back.

Passing the spot where their Christmas tree stood just yesterday—three years ago—Clara can't help but wonder how on earth it came to this.

So they're moving. So what?

Couldn't they have postponed it until after the holidays? Or, at least, have gotten a small tree? Put up a string of twinkle lights?

She looks around the barren room. Christmas without a tree. No lights, no stockings, not a hint that it's the holiday season, even with a toddler in the house and a baby on the way . . .

Where is her other child?

Maybe Drew took him—her—away for a few days—skiing, or something, and I couldn't go because I'm pregnant. . . .

A two-year-old on a ski trip?

Over Christmas?

No. It would never happen in a million years. Not just the skiing, but a family—*this* family— spending the holidays apart. That only happens to other families. Families that are splintered, like her own family was, growing up; families with custody arrangements—

No! Not us!

To believe that's what's going on here would be to stop believing in her husband. In his love for her. In his promises that he'll be here for her, always.

I believe in Drew. He would never, ever leave me. Not willingly, not on Christmas, not with our child, not ever.

And so . . .

Even though Drew promised her that everything would be fine with the baby . . .

There isn't a child.

The terrible truth barges in on her so abruptly that she sinks into the nearest chair.

Before she can absorb the realization, the telephone in her hand rings, almost—like the baby's kick—on cue.

"Hello? Hello?"

"Clara! Are you all right?"

It's him.

He's alive.

Overpowered by a tide of emotion, she can't even speak.

"Clara? Are you—"

There's a burst of static on the other end.

Seized by panic, she recovers her voice. "Drew? Drew?"

No response.

She wails in disbelief and looks helplessly at the phone in her hand. Then, realizing he can't call her back unless the line is open, she hurriedly disconnects.

It rings again almost immediately.

"Drew! Where are you?"

Static. She can hear his voice, but it's garbled. That's okay. He's alive. He's out there somewhere.

Nothing else matters.

She wipes a sleeve at the tears streaming down her cheeks. "Drew, you're cutting in and out!"

". . . you okay?" she hears him ask. ". . . messages . . . happened?"

"I just needed to talk to you! I was worried and—"

"Are you okay?" he cuts in.

"I'm fine! I just didn't know where you were and why you weren't calling me back!"

". . . still in . . ."

"What? Drew, I can't tell what you're saying! This connection is really bad. Where are you?"

". . . Doris and I are—"

The line goes dead.

Again, she disconnects it hurriedly.

As she waits for him to call back, she goes over what he said.

Doris and I . . .

Is he with someone who happens to be named Doris?

Or is he with Clara's Doris? Jed's Doris?

But . . . he doesn't even know her.

Rather, he *didn't* know her, back in 2009. Maybe he met her after that. She is, after all, his sister. In a sense.

If that's the Doris he was talking about.

How many Dorises can there be in the world?

All right—there are plenty. But not in *their* world—hers and Drew's.

That call seemed to be coming across a great distance. The way it kept cutting in and out, the static, the poor connection . . . All of it would seem to indicate that Drew wasn't calling from around the corner.

He's far away. In New York?

Wherever he is, he's with Doris.

The knowledge should be comforting—and on some level, it is.

Unless . . .

What if Doris is another woman? His new girlfriend, or his new wife? Could Clara have been wrong about her marriage as well?

The thought makes her physically ill.

No. No way. I believe in Drew. No matter what.

I'm pregnant with Drew's baby, for God's sake.

But how can she know that for sure?

For one thing, hello—he's your husband!

Clara shakes her head. It's ridiculous to even imagine that Drew is no longer in her life— particularly by his own choice.

Anyway, Amelia from next door asked about him. She seemed to think he might be around.

Then again . . . didn't she give the impression that she hadn't seen Drew—or Clara, for that matter—for quite a while? What if something happened in the interim, something Amelia didn't even know about yet?

Clara tries to remember the driveway conversation, but her brain is swimming in fragmented details and emotion, and . . . and . . .

And the phone is still silent in her hand.

Maybe she didn't disconnect the call after all.

She presses the TALK button, lifts the receiver to her ear. There's a dial tone.

He could have gotten through, had he tried.

She hurriedly dials his number.

He'll pick up, and they'll have a better connection, and he'll explain where he is and why he's with Doris and everything will make sense at last.

"Hello. You've reached the voice mail of Drew Becker. Please leave a message, and I'll return your call as soon as possible."

She swallows hard.

"Drew, it's me. Please call me back."

Hanging up the phone with resignation, she knows there's nothing to do but wait.

Chapter 21

Clara awakens in darkness, instantly aware that she's in her own bed.

But in which year?

As her eyes adjust to the darkness, she's pretty sure that there are no stacks of boxes in the room. And there are candles in the windows.

She reaches down beneath the covers.

No tremendous belly.

It's 2009.

The digital clock glows on the bedside table; it's 4:40 a.m.

She hears a sound and realizes that Drew is snoring softly beside her.

Thank God.

She reaches out and rests a hand on his back. He doesn't stir. The warmth of his body and the rhythm of his even breathing soothe her.

With a yawn, she tries to think back to what happened yesterday. . . .

Drew called, and he said something about being away with Doris or someone named Doris, and then the phone went dead, and she waited and waited for him to call back, and she was exhausted so she must have dozed off—

Wait—that was 2012.

She remembers visiting her in-laws down in San Francisco, too, and the conversation at the kitchen table *about* the kitchen table, and spilling the whole long story to Drew when they got home. He left to take the dog for a walk; she fell asleep on the couch, utterly spent. . . .

Great. So you remember two different yesterdays. That's not the least bit confusing.

And apparently, you're capable of being in two places at once—here, in the present, and in the future, too. At least, your brain is.

It seems crazy—but when you get right down to it, what, about time travel, doesn't?

When she visited the past, though, it made more sense. Clara McCallum wasn't around in 1941, so she wasn't stepping into her own life. She was simply visiting a world she had never seen.

This time, she's visiting her own life; a world she will, indeed, see—three years from now.

But why, when she's in the future, doesn't she know what's going on around her? Why doesn't she remember anything about the three years between 2009 and 2012?

That doesn't seem fair.

It seems that although she's in her own future body—and a very pregnant one, at that—she still has her 2009 brain. Apparently, she—2009 Clara—is capable of slipping forward in time and glimpsing the future—*her* future—but she hasn't yet lived the years in between.

Terrific. That's some feat.

For my next trick, I'll walk the high wire without a net.

Oh, wait—that's what I've been doing all along.

That's what it feels like, anyway, to pop up in 2012 without Drew there to catch her if she falls.

Drew. Where, oh where, is Drew in 2012?

Clara sighs, and the sigh turns into a yawn.

She rolls over again, plumps the pillow, tells herself to go back to sleep. She needs it. The baby needs it.

Sleep. Come on, sleep.

Instead of drifting off, she finds herself thinking about the mysterious Doris. Misgiving slithers through her and she's wide awake, thinking about the future.

Gradually, she becomes aware of a slight ache in her stomach. Not nausea, for a change, but . . . pain.

According to the book, she's going to be feeling all kinds of unusual aches and pains as the pregnancy progresses. And she did already experience firsthand the heartburn and lower back pain that comes with the third trimester. Maybe abdominal pain goes along with the morning sickness and aching breasts of the first trimester.

I'll have to call the doctor. Or at least find that book and check out the normal symptoms again.

She presses a hand against her stomach, wishing the baby would kick in response. But of course, that can't happen just yet. Not for at least another few weeks.

The life inside of her is still in the embryonic stage, just a few millimeters long and not yet a fetus.

Maybe that's why she doesn't feel the same reassuring sense of connection to this pregnancy that she does three years from now. She can't see the evidence that the baby is in there, and she can't feel movement . . .

It's just too early for kicking. Too early to be showing.

Too early, too, to put aside the nagging worry that something might go wrong.

What was that statistic she had read? At least twenty percent of pregnancies are lost in the first trimester.

Once it's over, she'll breathe more easily.

But what if this pain means—

Stop that! she tells herself sharply.

Drew was right. What-ifs *are* toxic.

Focus on what happened yesterday—the real yesterday. Then you can figure out what you're going to do today. The real today.

She vaguely remembers Drew's return from his walk. She was dozing on the couch, and he told her to go up to bed.

But it was too early for bed, and she couldn't have gone if she wanted to; her body seemed incapable of moving.

Now she knows where the term *bone-tired* came from. Whoever coined it must have been pregnant.

So Drew covered her with a blanket; later he asked her if she wanted some soup.

She didn't. She wanted only to sleep.

She vaguely recalls waking up sometime in the evening to make her way up to the bedroom. Drew was already there, asleep. Rather than lying awake, as she had feared, she drifted off again, swaddled in dreamless slumber.

If only she could go back there right now, so she wouldn't have to think about any of this.

But she's wide awake.

Wide awake, and sick, or starved, or both.

She sits up and her stomach roils.

Food. She needs food. *Now.*

She gets out of bed, grabs her robe, and hurries down the hallway to the stairs. As she descends, she hears movement in the kitchen and stops dead in her tracks.

Then she hears a whimper. Oh! The dog. Dickens. She'd forgotten all about him. By the time she's reached the kitchen, he's barking and, quite literally, rattling his cage.

She flips on a light and is promptly taken aback at the miniature version of the dog who made Gerald and his owner run for his life just yesterday.

"Dickens, shhh! You'll wake up Drew!"

She heads for the fridge, but the puppy barks even louder. With a sigh, she does an about-face back to the cage.

"You're not going to let me get something to eat before I let you out, are you?"

The dog pants eagerly and wags his tail.

Clara hurriedly opens his crate. "You'd better just hope I don't barf on you," she advises him as he scampers past her legs.

She opens the refrigerator and is greeted by a blast of cold air—and a distinct aroma. Dairy, produce, leftover Thai . . . all of it mingles to create the most nauseating smell ever.

Gagging, she slams the door closed and leans against the counter, swallowing hard.

After a minute or two, the nausea subsides just enough for her to make it to the cupboard. Grabbing the first box of cereal she sees, she shoves a handful into her mouth, mechanically chewing and swallowing. Another handful. Another.

Oh, ick. She doesn't even like Cap'n Crunch on a good day. But somehow, the sickly sweet corn cereal does the trick and after a minute or two, she feels—well, not good, but definitely better.

She returns to the cupboard, finds a loaf of bread, and puts two slices into the toaster. Starting to put the cereal box back on the shelf, she thinks better of it and takes another handful.

Hearing a whimper, she looks down to see Dickens at her feet, in a classic sit-up-and-beg pose.

"Hey, I thought you weren't trained."

He glances at the cereal box in her hand. So does she.

"Can dogs eat Cap'n Crunch?" she asks him, and he seems to nod eagerly. "Oh, what do you know? You ate someone's coat. For all I know, you want to eat the box. You like paper, right? Probably cardboard, too."

He seems to nod.

"Sorry, pal. I don't think that's very good for you."

She fixes him a bowl of puppy chow, then sits on a stool, watching him eat it and thinking back to yesterday's conversation with Drew.

How many times, over the years, had she imagined telling him the truth? How many times had she rehearsed the scenario in her head?

How many times had she searched Drew's brown eyes for some sign that he might already know?

Once or twice, she thought she saw a flicker of awareness—but she could never be sure.

Then yesterday, he had mistakenly referred to his sister as Doris. . . .

Doris.

Doreen.

She wondered, standing there in his parents' foyer, if he somehow knew, somewhere deep in his subconscious mind. Wondered whether that slip of the tongue was evidence that memories of his other lifetime might be poking through.

Then, mere minutes later, Drew mentioned that aqua table with the chrome trim and the speckled aqua linoleum—things he remembered so clearly from his childhood, and no one else in his family even recognized.

Jed Landry's house had an identical aqua table with chrome trim, and identical speckled aqua linoleum.

Even more telling: tucked among the Landry family's discarded odds and ends in the loft over the garage, Clara had seen a game called Magnetic Jack Straws, stacked on a shelf with Tiddlywinks and Monopoly.

Jed had mentioned that it had been his favorite when he was a child.

Had he lived, Jed would have been around the same age as Grandma Becker is now.

Clara knew, then and there, that none of it was a coincidence.

She knew it was time to tell him the truth. The whole truth.

But they never got to finish their conversation yesterday.

She still needs to tell him about traveling to 2012, and about the earthquake. The Big One.

Today is the day.

She'd realized that the moment she'd seen yesterday's weather forecast.

This is going to be the only sunny day of the week. Tonight, the rain sets in, and it doesn't let up until after New Year's.

She glances at the bank of windows above the sink and sees only her own reflection. But out there, beyond her troubled face and the glare of kitchen light, she knows the sky is still pitch-black.

For the time being, they're safe.

But it's coming.

How can she just sit here, knowing what she knows, and let the town be demolished?

I can't.

The toast pops up abruptly.

She stands, retrieves it, butters it, eats it.

But she doesn't even taste it and her morning sickness is all but forgotten. By the time she's brushing the last crumbs from her fingers, she's got a plan. Not a great one, but at least it's something. Even if it doesn't work, at least she'll have tried. At least she'll be able to live with herself . . . afterward.

She returns Dickens to his crate and shakes her head at his reproachful look. "I'm sorry, puppy, but it's only for a little while longer. It's almost morning, and I'll probably be back before Drew even wakes up and if I'm not, he'll let you out. Okay?"

Clearly not okay.

Feeling guilty, she turns off the kitchen light and returns upstairs. Five minutes in the bathroom, two more to get dressed, and another to scrawl a quick note to Drew in case he wakes up before she gets back.

> *Had a craving. Went to the store. Be back soon. Love, Y.W.*

Y.W. means *your wife.*

Y.H. means your *husband.*

She and Drew always sign notes and e-mails to each other that way. It's just one of countless, comforting married rituals they share. Without them—without him—she'd be lost.

For a moment, she stands, dressed, at the foot of the bed, watching him sleep.

She could wake him up right now and tell him the rest of the story—about the earthquake that's coming.

But no need to do that right now. If today is the day, then it's going to be a while before Drew—or anyone else in San Florentina—sleeps so peacefully again.

Chapter 22

The woods are blanketed in snow, and he can see his breath in the air as he stands by, waiting for Doris to make the final verdict on the tree.

"But I really love that one," she says plaintively, and he looks up at the towering pine in amusement.

"Let it go."

"But it's so beautiful. Come on, Jed, let's get it."

"Maybe if I were Paul Bunyan."

"Please?"

"Even if I could cut it down and drag it to the DeSoto and somehow get it all the way home, there's no way we'd ever get it into the house. Hurry up and choose one, Toots. It's freezing out here."

"But I don't want a dinky little tree. I want a big one!"

"How about this one? The shape is perfect, and it's not dinky," comes the voice of reason. Clara, in a red coat and hat and mittens, looks like a beautiful cardinal perched against the monochromatic backdrop.

"It's not big, either."

"It'll look plenty big when we get it into the house," he promises his kid sister, who grudgingly agrees at last.

He picks up the ax and begins to swing the blade against the evergreen's trunk. With every *thwack*, the rich scent of pine further saturates the air. Beside him, Clara and Doris are singing, "Oh, Christmas Tree."

Thwack . . .

Thwack . . .

Thwack . . .

And then another sound, distant, out of place.

Startled from the dream, Drew sits up in the predawn darkness, instantly alert. "What was that? Clara? Did you hear that?"

When his wife doesn't stir, he turns to look at the bed beside him. Even in the dim light, he can see that it's empty.

Somewhere outside, a car engine turns over.

"Clara?" he calls out, seeing the arc of headlights swing across the bedroom ceiling through the window. She can't be out there, driving away in the middle of the night . . . can she?

She doesn't reply. Downstairs, the dog is barking.

Drew gets out of bed, concerned. A glance out the window at the driveway below tells him that her car is indeed missing. And in the bathroom, he finds a note on a yellow Post-it stuck to the mirror.

A craving?

He can't help but smile as he returns to the bedroom and crawls back between the sheets. Closing his eyes and hoping to slip effortlessly back to sleep again, he opens them immediately when he remembers the dream he was having.

He and Clara were in the woods chopping down a Christmas tree with his sister . . . *Doris?*

Everything Clara told him yesterday roars back into his mind like a tsunami, sweeping away any chance of returning to slumber. Wide awake, he again tries to grasp the incredible tale his wife told him.

It isn't that he doesn't believe it.

Or even that he doesn't want to believe it.

So many things would make sense if it were true.

Of course it's true. Clara would never lie.

She did lie, though. About how she knew Doris. She told Jed that the woman was a soap opera fan who had become a friend, and Jed believed her.

Why wouldn't he? He'd had no reason to

question his wife's relationship with a little old lady; truth be told, he'd barely given Doris a second thought.

Now he finds out she's his sister?

He supposes it's going to take some getting used to—the idea that he lived another life, decades ago. That he existed as a total stranger, as someone other than Drew Becker. Someone who had a kid sister named Doris—

"Come on, Jed . . ."

"Maybe if I were Paul Bunyan . . ."

But he wasn't. He was Jed. Jed Landry.

And the dream from which he'd awakened just now hadn't really been a dream. Maybe none of his dreams have been.

He sits up again, staring into the darkness, wishing he could accept all of this and move on without this feeling of . . .

Betrayal.

Admit it.

Yes, that's what it is—this sick feeling in his gut that had begun gnawing at him yesterday when Clara told him. He had gone for a walk, hoping to get rid of it somehow, as if he could somehow sweat or breathe it all out and come back without the burden.

With Dickens on a leash he had walked down to the road and then made his way down the rocky coast and along the beach, deserted in the

December dusk. Ordinarily he would have relished the solitude, the sight of fat seals on the rocks, the chance to let the dog run free to chase after gulls and waves.

But the whole time, all he could think was, *She didn't tell me. How could she not have told me?*

No, she would never lie. But for all those years, Clara had kept the truth to herself. Isn't that the same thing?

Of course it isn't. You know it isn't.

And yet . . .

He had been glad she was asleep when he returned. He hadn't been ready to talk about it again.

He still isn't.

He glances at the clock, then gets out of bed abruptly.

Technically, it's not time yet for him to get up and head for the office. But he can't sleep anymore, and it's never too early to hit the desk when you're new on the job, and . . .

Come on, who are you kidding? You know why you want to go early today.

As he turns the shower tap, he wonders how soon Clara will get back—and whether it's wrong of him not to want to be here when she does.

Of course it's wrong.

It's running away—and he's never been one to avoid conflict.

I just need a little more time, a little more space, he tells himself, staring at the water rushing from the tap. *I need to feel like myself again.*

He hopes a few hours is all it will take— because a few hours is all he really has.

Chapter 23

The road to town is pitch-black and fog-shrouded at this hour of the morning, and Clara wonders whether she's made a huge mistake. Maybe she should have waited until daybreak, at least.

But daybreak means the sun will be up, and the sun was shining when the Big One struck.

She forges ahead, trying to ignore the dull ache in her stomach. Nerves. It must be. This is a life-and-death mission, and there's no time to waste.

She'd had the foresight to bring along the notes from her conversation with her old physics teacher, and she'd been planning to rehearse what she's going to do and say during the drive. But as she creeps the car along the treacherous curves high above the Pacific, it's all she can do to focus on getting there in one piece.

She'll just have to play it by ear when she does.

At last, she reaches town.

Even through the veil of gray, she can see that everything looks as it should.

There are no unexpected traffic lights or detours, no heaps of rubble or construction sites.

Swept by nostalgia for what hasn't yet been lost yet, Clara knows she's experienced the sensation before.

This is what it felt like, back in December 1941. This is how she felt, knowing the world around her was about to be hit hard, out of nowhere, and nothing would ever be the same again. Utterly helpless, she could do nothing about it.

She couldn't stop the attack.

And she can't stop the earthquake.

But there is something she can do this time. Something she considered—and dismissed—back in 1941.

San Florentina police headquarters are housed in a Spanish mission-style stucco building a block from the town green. All is quiet at this hour—but then, all is usually quiet here.

Not for long.

I have to warn them.

Clara parks in the nearly empty lot, reaches into her pocket, and unfolds the page of notes. Laying it against the steering wheel and cracking the door open so that the overhead light will go on, she reads down the page.

Fault lines and foreshocks fresh in her mind—and a sense of urgency greater than ever—she marches from the car to the double glass doors.

The lone uniformed cop at the desk looks up as she enters.

She recognizes him the moment she sees the blond stubble on his head, the mustache, the round face.

"Bobby!" She rushes toward him. "I'm so glad you're the one who's here."

For a split second, he seems taken aback—then, quite obviously, he's wary, standing. "Ma'am, how can I help you?"

She glances down at the desk, where a placard reads OFFICER ON DUTY: ROBERT SHELTON.

Not Bobby.

Oops. She was so happy to see him that she'd momentarily forgotten what year it is. They might be on a palsy-walsy first-name basis in 2012, but right now it's 2009 and they have yet to even meet.

Talk about starting off on the wrong foot.

Then again, when you're the prophet of doom, is there really a right foot?

"I, uh—I have some information that I need to share."

"About a crime?" He reaches for a clipboard.

"No," she says quickly, "not a crime. About a catastrophic event."

"*Excuse* me?"

"I know this might sound crazy, but you need to evacuate San Florentina right away . . ."

Seeing his expression, she amends, "Okay, I know it sounds crazy. But I promise you, I'm not."

Even though I'm a total stranger who burst in here in the middle of the night and called you Bobby and ran at you like a long lost friend.

"Ma'am, I'm not sure what you're—"

"Please, Officer—just listen to me . . ." She trails off, feeling a sharp pain in her abdomen. Nerves?

Of course. Hurry up and get this over with.

"There's going to be a major earthquake today," she blurts, and sees the lines instantly deepen between the cop's sandy brows.

"And you know this . . . how?"

"I'm a scientist. Physics," she adds. "Earthquake physics, to be specific. I study . . . paleoseismology."

Is that even a word?

It wasn't in her notes but she seems to recall that Mr. Kershaw used it. Or something like it.

Whatever. It sounds good, and now Bobby the cop is looking at her with more interest than suspicion.

"What's your name?" he asks.

She hesitates only slightly. "Clara Becker."

She'd considered saying *Doctor* Clara Becker to sound more official, but you don't lie to a cop about something like that.

No, only about the rest of it.

Ignoring a flicker of guilt, she hurries on, channeling Mr. Kershaw, "According to an August 1984 report in the *Bulletin of the Seismological Society of America*, forty-four percent of the—the, uh, strike-slip earthquakes in the San Andreas system were preceded by immediate foreshocks defined as having occurred within three days and ten kilometers of the main shock."

He frowns. "But that doesn't mean—"

"Following the Bayer theorem—" Which might very well have been the Bayes' theorem; she couldn't read her handwriting there—"the conditional probability that the Christmas Day quake was merely a foreshock to a catastrophic quake is very high."

"How high?"

"Very high," she repeats.

She can tell he isn't sure whether to be dubious or concerned.

Feeling desperate, she forges ahead. "Officer, I've been studying the activity along the fault for the past few days using my official uh, paleoseis—mologic"—*Paleoseismologic? Paleoseismic?*—"equipment, and I'm telling you, an earthquake is imminent."

He shakes his head.

Maybe it was paleoseismic.

But how the heck would he know?

"Look, I'm sure the work you're doing is groundbreaking—" He breaks off to grin delightedly. "Ha. Groundbreaking. Get it?"

She gets it.

And obviously, he doesn't get it at all.

"Please, Officer Shelton, you have to evacuate the town. If I'm wrong, then I'm wrong. But if I'm right, then . . ."

"Then you can tell me I told you so," he says, setting the clipboard aside, its page still blank. "How's that?"

"That's not good. That's terrible!" Tears spring to her eyes. "You're joking around and thinking I'm crazy and I'm telling you—"

"Listen, Ms.—Becker is it?" At her nod, he continues, "Believe me, I don't think you're crazy, and I don't take earthquakes lightly. But no one knows how to predict them—that's in the news all the time. I just saw it in the paper yesterday, after that last quake—an article about how scientists are looking for a breakthrough, and they need more funding, and yada yada yada."

"But—I am a scientist, and I made a breakthrough, and we're all in danger right here, right now. Today."

He's silent for a long moment, looking at her. Then, steepling his hands in front of his mouth, he says, "You're talking about a large-scale evacuation. Do you know how complicated that is? I can't just decide to do it—it's not even up to me."

"But can't you talk to whoever does decide, and tell them they have to evacuate—"

"For no apparent reason. Look, you don't go up and down the streets with a bullhorn saying, 'Something might happen, so everyone leave.'"

"Something is *going* to happen."

He shrugs. "I used to work down in Florida, before I moved here. We'd get hurricane warnings. Not watches. Warnings. Based on the kind of science that's actually proven."

"But this is proven, too. I told you, according to that article published in—"

"Look, that doesn't even matter. I'd still have to get an official evacuation order from the local government. That's how it works. That's how it worked down in Florida, too. And when they finally told us to order people to evacuate, believe me, that didn't happen instantaneously. Sometimes, it didn't happen at all."

"What do you mean?"

"We'd tell people to go, and they'd refuse. They didn't believe the forecast, or they didn't want to be bothered, whatever. So they'd stay to ride out the storm."

"But this isn't a storm."

"I know. Look, I'm sorry. I hope you're wrong

about a quake. I really do. But my hands are tied."

She stares bleakly at him for a long moment.

"All right. I understand," she tells him heavily. "But if you can't evacuate the town, you can at least make sure that your own family gets out of here. Please."

He opens his mouth, closes it, opens it again. "I don't . . . I don't know what to say about that."

"Say 'I'll do it.' And then someday, say, 'thank you, Clara, for saving their lives.'"

Without another word, she turns and walks out.

In the east, the miasma of gray mist is just barely tinted with a glow of pinkish-orange.

The fog will lift soon, and the sun will be up, and the sky will turn blue.

Any other day, the forecast would bring promise. Today, it brings only a devastating threat.

Clara gets into the car, starts the engine.

As she drives the deserted streets through lamplit mist, she takes one last look at San Fernandina, wanting to remember it the way it is.

Nothing will ever be the same here.

But nothing ever stays the same anywhere, does it? Regardless of war, or acts of God.

The New York City and Glenhaven Park she visited in 1941 bore little resemblance to their present-day counterparts. Time marches on. The landscape is little more than an ever-changing backdrop for the real drama. People are born, they live their lives, they die.

And everything changes, yet nothing ever does.

Wiping tears from her eyes, Clara heads toward home, fighting the urge to take one last look over her shoulder.

It's time to move on.

Time to tell Drew the rest of the story.

He'll believe her now, after everything else.

The two of them will leave right away, and go someplace where it's safe.

Someplace where they can ride out the storm.

The sky is just getting light when she reaches her own driveway—light enough for her to see that the spot where Drew's car was parked is empty.

Dread overtakes her.

She bolts for the front door, finds it locked, realizes she left the keys in the car and the car running.

Hurriedly, she turns it off, returns to the door, unlocks it, and bursts into the house.

"Drew? Drew! Where are you?"

No answer from her husband, but somewhere in the back of the house, Dickens barks.

Still calling for Drew, she rushes to the kitchen to see that the puppy is in his crate.

"Where did he go?"

Dickens just looks at her helplessly through the wire.

"Okay, okay, come on out of there." She opens the cage for him and he trots out.

Turning away, she spots a note on the counter. Snatching it up, she reads:

> *Good morning. I hope you satisfied that craving. I woke up when you left, couldn't go back to sleep, so I went to the office. I'll call you later. Have a great day.*
>
> Love, Y.H.

A great day.

Oh, Drew.

She grabs the phone, dials his cell.

Half-expecting it to go into voice mail, she's surprised when he picks up on the first ring.

"Hey, there you are. So was it pickles and ice cream, or something more—"

"Drew, listen to me. You have to come home right now."

"What's wrong? Are you cramping or bleeding or—"

"No!" So much for the man who promised her everything will be fine.

He's as worried as I am, she realizes. *He just won't admit it. He thinks he always has to be the strong one.*

And her stomach—it really is hurting. She's

certain the anxiety isn't helping, but—what if it's not just that?

She forces the thought from her mind. *One thing at a time.* "Drew, listen to me. When we were talking yesterday, I said there was something else I had to tell you. I—"

"Clara, you said yesterday that this is not the kind of thing we should be talking about with me behind the wheel. I shouldn't even be on the phone. There's a lot of fog, and—"

"I know, be careful. Just turn around and come home. I'll be waiting for you."

"I know you have more to say, and of course I want to hear it, but right now, I just have to get myself to work and get through the day without thinking about any of that."

Work.

In San Francisco.

Suddenly it dawns on her: he'll be safe down there.

There's no need for her to worry about him for the time being. She already knows he's going to survive.

And so am I. Dickens, too. And the house.

Everything is going to be okay. Drew was right.

"You're right—I shouldn't be bothering you with this now. You go ahead to work."

"Okay. We'll talk tonight."

Tonight. Yes. The quake will be behind them.

"I love you," he says.

Her own voice thick with emotion, she says, "I love you, too."

She hangs up the phone, takes a deep breath to compose herself, and nods, her mind made up.

She's got to get out of here, right away.

She'll take the dog, and she'll go . . .

Where?

San Francisco, maybe. She can go to her mother-in-law's, or Drew's office, or . . . wherever. It doesn't matter, as long as she's far from here when the quake hits.

A glance at the window confirms that daybreak has arrived. There's not a moment to lose.

"Come on, Dickens," she calls, her thoughts on what she'll need to take with her. It might be a while before they can get back to the house with all the damage to the surrounding area.

Her gut twists at the thought of it, but she can't let herself get distracted now. The immediate future is about self-preservation. It has to be.

"Dickens!" she calls again, stripping off the jacket she threw on earlier to go down to the police station. She'd better bring a warm coat instead, and gloves—for herself and for Drew. A couple of changes of clothing would be a good idea.

She'd better go up and pack a bag.

She's halfway to the stairs when she spots the front door standing wide open, keys in the lock.

What the . . . ?

Remembering the way she'd left the car running when she'd first arrived, she realizes she must not have bothered to close the door behind her, either.

As she reaches for the knob, she flashes back—forward—to Christmas morning 2012, when a big black dog cannonballed from the shrub border and into the house.

To think she wasn't even sure whether it was him.

What other dog would—

Oh no.

Hand poised on the doorknob, it occurs to her that if he could run into the house through an open door—then he could just as easily run out. Especially as a frisky new puppy who's been locked in a crate for hours.

"Dickens?" she calls again, her heart sinking. "Dickens, come back here right now!"

The world beyond her doorstep is still. And beyond the tree line, through the lingering mist, the sun is rising.

Chapter 24

She should have told me.

She should have told me.

Drew presses his foot harder on the gas pedal, as if speed will somehow allow him to escape the refrain that's haunted his every waking hour since yesterday. It was all he could do not to blurt it into the phone when she called him just now. Somehow he held his tongue. Now is not the time or place to get into all that with her. Now is not the time for her to tell him whatever else she has to say about the crazy situation when she managed to keep it to herself for all these years.

She should have told me.

But she did, he reminds himself. *She told you yesterday.*

Well, she could have—she *should* have—done it sooner.

Three years. For three years, she kept it from him. How could she?

I'm so afraid you're not going to believe me, Drew. . . .

Everyone has secrets. Secrets they're afraid to reveal—even to their spouse.

Especially to their spouse.

Who are you to question her? You have secrets of your own. You were afraid to tell her about the visions, and the voices. You were afraid she'd think you were going crazy. You were afraid . . . just like Clara.

Okay. So maybe he shouldn't have left in such a hurry this morning. Maybe he shouldn't have been so short with her on the phone just now. What if she thinks he's . . .

Running away?

He shakes his head, disgusted with himself.

Coward.

After all they've been through together, he can't deal with this?

Of course you can deal, he reminds himself defensively. *It's not like you're leaving. You're just going to work. You just need some space.*

It's fine.

She asked him to come home, though. She wanted to discuss it further.

He refused. He said he has to get to work.

Well, he does. She probably won't think anything of it.

But *he'll* know. He'll always know that there was more to it than that.

And maybe she will, too, later. Later, when he comes home and tries to pretend, same as always, that he can handle everything without missing a beat. That he's strong enough to take anything life throws at him without flinching.

Isn't that what marriage means, though? Dealing with whatever comes your way, good or bad, believing in happily ever after no matter what?

Yes. For better and for worse.

When it comes to worse, he and Clara have certainly been there and back more times than he cares to remember. Cancer, unemployment, a move, unemployment again, financial struggles . . .

So a little thing like finding out that you knew your wife in another lifetime—to which she time traveled—is the thing that's going to push you over the edge? After cancer, for God's sake?

Come on, Drew. Buck up, man.

All right—so maybe he should call her right now and tell her . . . what? That he loves her?

She knows that. He just said it.

He can say that he's sorry he made himself scarce in the aftermath of her revelation. He can say that they'll talk more about it later, tonight.

He starts to reach for his cell phone, then

glances at the dashboard clock, hesitating. It's still early.

She wants to talk to him. See him.

And she will . . . tonight.

Right now, you need to get into the work mode.

But the truth is, he doesn't have to be at the office just yet. There's time, if he hurries, to go back home to San Florentina and see Clara. Hear the rest of the story. Maybe even admit that he's shaken up by all of this—and really, who wouldn't be?

Yet . . .

In the grand scheme of better and worse . . . who's to say this new development won't fall into the better category?

After all, he knows now that he and Clara were meant to be together no matter what. Soul mates. Nothing ever came between them—not even death. And nothing ever will.

Drew makes a U-turn, heading back home.

Chapter 25

"Dickens!" Clara shouts, carefully picking her way over the steep terrain of the hillside alongside their house, the ache in her stomach growing worse. "Dickens, where are you?"

She's been outside searching for a good fifteen minutes, around the house, down by the road, and now up here. There's been no sign of the dog.

How can she leave without him?

How can she not?

The day has grown brighter by the minute, the sun burning through the last film of fog.

She already knows that Dickens is going to survive, no matter what. Maybe he's better off out here. Maybe his animal instincts made him seek out a safe place and she should just leave him be.

"Clara!"

Hearing a shout, she turns to spot Jeff Tucker on the hillside. He's wearing boots, jeans, a thick canvas jacket. Swap out the Oakland A's cap for a cowboy hat and he could've stepped off the set of a Western.

He looks so rugged and vibrant, standing there in a patch of sun streaming down through the trees. With a stab of sorrow, Clara wants to warn him to be careful.

She doesn't know what's going to happen to him, or when or where it's going to happen, but she remembers the look in his daughter's eyes when she thought Clara had asked about him. She remembers Amelia saying that her mom couldn't bear to spend Christmas day in their house.

"You're looking for the puppy, right?" Jeff asks.

She nods, dragging her thoughts back to the present. "He ran out the door when I wasn't looking. Have you seen him?"

"Nope—are you okay?" he asks, seeing her wince and touch her stomach.

"I'm fine, just—" Pregnant. But he doesn't know that. "I don't know, maybe it's something I ate."

"Listen, I can help you look for the dog for a few minutes, but we're getting ready to hit the road."

"Where are you going?"

"Tahoe."

"That's nice," she says in relief. So he's getting out of town. Maybe she was wrong about something happening to him—in the quake, anyway.

"Nice?" he snorts. "This is Nancy's idea, not mine. I'd just as soon stay home. Lugging three kids and carload of stuff up into the mountains in the snow isn't my idea of a great way to spend vacation. I don't even ski. But my wife does and, anyway, I'm not the boss."

Caught off guard by his candid admission, Clara doesn't know what to say.

Before she can think of something, a female shout echoes over the hillside.

"That's Nancy."

"Go ahead. I know you have to go."

"I can help you for a bit."

"No, really—I'm fine. Just go ahead, get on the road." *And hurry!*

"I guess I'd better." He turns back toward his property.

"Have a good trip."

"I'll try," he says glumly, and heads off through the trees.

Clara watches, wondering whether she's ever going to see him again.

Should she chase after him and warn him about the earthquake?

Remembering Bobby—Officer Shelton's—

reaction, she decides against it. Maybe if the Tuckers weren't about to leave town, anyway. But they, like Drew, will be out of harm's way today.

I'm the one who needs to get moving.

And her stomach is really hurting now. Somewhere in the back of her mind, she wonders if she should be concerned. But there's only so much she can worry about at one time, and right now, she has to focus on finding the dog and getting the hell out of here.

"Dickens!" she shouts again. "Dickens!"

She listens, one last time, for the telltale sound of an animal scampering through the underbrush.

Nothing.

He's going to be okay, she tells herself. *But you can't wait any longer.*

She heads back down the hillside toward the house, again going over what she needs to bring with her. Toiletries, her cell phone, the checkbook . . .

Rounding the corner of the house to the driveway, she looks up and gasps.

"You little . . . Dickens!"

There he is, sitting on the front doormat, waiting for her.

"Where have you been? Didn't you hear me calling you?" She bends over and scoops the puppy into her arms.

He laps her face with his tongue. His dog breath makes her stomach turn, but she doesn't mind. Much.

She'd better pack some snacks, too. Or maybe even fix herself something to eat before she gets on the road. All at once, she's feeling queasy in addition to the dull ache in her gut.

In the house, she hurriedly makes herself a peanut butter sandwich and eats it while she throws everything she can think of into the new Filson bag she got Drew for Christmas.

That seems like a lifetime ago. In a way, it was.

She gathers some clothes—her own and Drew's, whatever is on the top of the piles in their drawers. Toiletries. Her phone and charger. Oh, and the checkbook and credit cards. The laptop! What else? Their framed wedding photo from the dresser, her new slippers, her pillow, his pillow . . .

Downstairs in the kitchen, she loads a bag with boxes of cereal and crackers, some fruit from the basket on the counter, the jar of peanut butter. She wouldn't mind grabbing a couple of cold bottles of water, but she doesn't dare open the fridge again.

She'd read somewhere that a woman's sense of smell becomes more acute with pregnancy. Boy, is that ever true.

She herds Dickens out the door to the car

and into the front seat, then loads the bags, one at a time, into the back. They're pretty heavy. Her stomach is hurting worse.

You probably could have left a lot of it behind, she thinks, as she returns to the house for one last look. It's not like they don't have toothpaste or apples in San Francisco.

She goes into the kitchen to make sure the coffee pot and toaster are unplugged—they are—and spots movement in the window above the sink.

Startled, she sees that there's a hummingbird fluttering around the feeder hanging outside the glass.

That's strange. She could have sworn Doris once mentioned that it's rare to see them at this time of year. And she hasn't even filled the feeder yet with nectar.

She takes a few steps closer, frowning.

That's a hummingbird, all right.

Maybe it's some sort of sign.

About to turn away, she sees Drew's orange medicine bottle on the windowsill.

She hastens over to grab it.

If it hadn't been for the hummingbird, she never would have remembered it.

Maybe most people would chalk that up to coincidence. But in her world, everything happens for a reason. In her world, there's magic.

Smiling for the first time today, she hurries back out to the car.

"Okay, we're good to go," she tells Dickens, who is wide awake and glancing anxiously out the window.

He snoozed all the way to town the last time she drove him someplace—but then, that was three years from now. He's still a puppy, probably not yet used to being in a car.

Or maybe he senses that this isn't an ordinary joyride.

Taking a long, last look at the house, she reminds herself that it will still be standing when she comes back. Of course it will. There isn't a doubt in her mind.

Still, she feels a twinge of trepidation as she drives away. There's bound to be damage, inside and out.

She heads south on the winding coastal highway, mindful of Dickens still sitting up straight and alert, as if he's aware of the steep drop-off just beyond his window. There's no shoulder here; just a few inches separate the car and the sparkling blue Pacific far below.

Clara should probably be glad it's not a foggy day, because there are plenty of accidents out here when visibility is reduced. But then if it were foggy, she wouldn't be out here in the first place.

Her stomach—it's really hurting now. This isn't good.

But you can't do anything about it. Just keep on driving. Don't think about it.

She turns her thoughts to the coming quake—yeah, there's a brighter subject—going over again what happened back home during the Christmas Day foreshock.

Maybe she should have spent less time just now packing belongings that can easily be replaced and more time gathering—or at least securing—all the precious things that can't.

Photos, papers—she had considered, and then discarded, the idea of taking them with her. It's not as if there's going to be a fire or flood in the house.

Rounding a curve, she adjusts the visor against the bright morning sun and wishes she'd thought to grab her sunglasses.

No, violent tremors can't really damage photos or papers.

Glass—that's a different story.

Another stomach pain.

Another curve ahead. Squinting, she readjusts the visor and is glad to note that the road straightens out a bit beyond.

She remembers all the broken glass crunching under her feet that day, when she and Drew were trying to clean up after the quake. Shards of glasses and plates, lightbulbs, a couple of tree ornaments—

"Oh no!"

The snow globe.

Clara slams on the brakes involuntarily, then belatedly glances into the rearview mirror to make sure no one is right behind her.

She has to go back.

How could she have forgotten the most sentimental possession she owns? The best gift ever, from Drew on their first Christmas together.

And it's made of glass.

About to make a U-turn, she feels a tremendous jolt, and the car sways oddly. Before she can react, the tires seem to vibrate. Dickens leaps off the seat and lets out a yelp.

This is it.

Dear God.

Instinctively, she clings hard to the wheel, frantic with fear as the world shakes violently around the car, and the puppy cowers on the floor beneath the passenger seat.

She had almost gotten away in time.

If she hadn't stopped to pack . . .

Looking longingly through the windshield at the distant highway she'd been about to travel, she sees it buckle and roll like a length of billowing fabric. And then, right before her eyes, the unimaginable happens: a huge section of the road ahead gives way and tumbles into the sea.

One moment, the terrain is there; the next, it's gone.

Clara gasps in horror.

She hadn't almost gotten away.

She had almost been killed.

If she hadn't stopped to go back, she'd have been on that stretch of highway. She wouldn't have, couldn't have survived.

Everything happens for a reason.

But it's not over yet.

The landscape continues to quake around her, jarring the car. Crippling pain sears her midsection. Dickens cowers on the floor. Beyond the window, mere inches of road separate the tires from the sheer drop-off.

Clara closes her eyes, and there's nothing to do but ride it out.

Chapter 26

Heading back north on the two-lane coastal highway toward home, listening to an old Van Morrison CD meant to take his mind off his troubles, Drew is surprised at the traffic at this time of day. The cars in front of him have slowed to a crawl, and he's beginning to wonder whether he's actually going to be able to make it all the way home and then back to the office again in time for work.

He should probably just forget about connecting with his wife this morning. It's probably stupid to risk being late for a new job that was so hard to come by in this economy. The logical thing to do would be to turn around and head south again, to the city.

But for some reason, he's not in the mood for logic this morning.

And he doesn't just want to see Clara—he

needs to see her. He doesn't understand why, but he's feeling an increasing sense of urgency about it.

Maybe because he's so frustrated by the string of brake lights through the windshield.

Or maybe because she was so insistent when she called. At first, anyway. Before he said no, and she dropped it, as if she realized it was a lost cause.

It isn't like her to back down so easily.

What was it that she had to tell him, and why—

Hearing sirens, he glances into the rearview mirror and spots flashing red lights coming up behind him. Cars are doing their best to get out of its way, but there aren't many options.

Good thing he's not on the southbound side of the road alongside the steep drop-off to the sea. There's no shoulder on the northbound side, either, but at least he's not teetering on a precipice as he moves right as far as he can to let the emergency vehicle pass.

Must have been an accident up ahead somewhere, because now another vehicle is coming up behind him, heading in the same direction.

An anxious twinge darts through Drew. He does his best to dismiss it, reminding himself that he's not exactly feeling logical this morning. If he were, he wouldn't be worrying that there's some connection between the sirens and his wife. He wouldn't be feeling so uneasy about her without any apparent reason.

Clara was safely back home again after her run to the store. He talked to her. He knows that. And anyway, San Florentina is still miles away from here.

With its hairpin turns, this road is notorious for accidents. Someone—some poor stranger—probably went off the road up ahead. Tragic—but it's not his tragedy.

He just needs to get home, or turn around and get to work. One or the other. And he can't sit here all day to figure it out.

He turns on the radio to see what's going on up ahead. It's rush hour. There should be traffic reports all over the dial. Prepared to search for one, he's glad to hear an announcer's voice as soon as the audio comes up.

". . . on the coastal highway, and authorities are asking residents of areas surrounding San Florentina, where the quake was centered, to please stay off the roads so that emergency vehicles can get through."

Quake?

But . . . that was the other day.

Why are they talking about it now, as if it just—

"Again, if you're just tuning in, a major

earthquake has struck the coastal region north of the Bay area."

Drew must have been too far away to feel the tremors, but Clara . . . she would have been right there. Right in San Florentina.

His blood runs cold.

Chapter 27

Time has passed since the terrifying pitching and rolling came to an end.

How much time, Clara, drifting in and out of consciousness, doesn't know.

Interminable time.

Maybe five minutes, maybe an hour.

Huddled on the seat of the car with Dickens beside her, she knows only that the quake is over, and that she survived . . .

And that something is terribly, terribly wrong.

Dickens peers at her, making the sorrowful squeaking sound that's become a refrain punctuated by screaming sirens in the distance and the crashing Pacific far below.

Clara wonders whether he sees the blood, or smells it.

It's hard to miss, soaking her clothes from the waist down and smeared all over her hands.

At first, she tried to stanch the flow as if that could save the baby, though she knew, somewhere in the back of her mind, that it was already too late.

The agony gripping her body, though, has yet to subside. If anything, it's getting worse. So bad she's afraid it's going to kill her. Unless it already has.

Maybe she didn't pass out earlier. Maybe she died, right here, on a cliff high above the ocean, so close to home.

And now she's . . . a spirit?

But if that's the case, she'd be floating somewhere above her body, wouldn't she? That's what she's read. There would be no more pain.

Amid the fog of pain, she has reminded herself that she can't be dead, because she lives to see the future. She's still going to be around three years from now.

Unless she was wrong about that. Maybe she was—is—a ghost. A Ghost of Christmas Yet to Come, haunting her own future.

Dickens nuzzles her face with his wet nose, and whimpers.

Maybe she really is dead, lying here in the car, covered in blood.

But if she's dead, she'd be cold, and right now, she feels as though she's burning up.

She needs fresh air.

Mustering all her strength, she reaches over

to pull the handle. It takes a few tries. She's so weak.

At last, she feels it give.

She pushes the door with the last of her strength, and it opens just a crack.

Not enough, though.

Air. She needs air.

Realizing one of her feet is pressed against the door, she thrusts with all her might. It seems to weigh a ton, but at last, it swings open and a salt breeze fills the car.

She inhales gratefully.

She's alive. Definitely. Alive, and it hurts to breathe, but breathe she must. In, out, in, out, pain slicing her midsection, a heavy shroud of darkness stealing over her once again.

Beside her, the puppy barks excitedly.

Too late, she realizes her mistake.

"No, Dickens!" she screams—or at least, tries to scream—as the dog leaps over her body toward the escape.

But her voice comes out a faint croak, drowned out by the sickening sound of squealing brakes.

Chapter 28

Hearing a bark and a far-off knocking sound, Clara opens her eyes.

Sun is streaming through the bedroom window. Not the thin, pale blush of early morning, but the unmistakable bright light of midafternoon.

Groggy, she looks around to get her bearings. She isn't beneath the covers; she's lying on top of the quilt, fully clothed—a nap? The clock reads 1:47.

She glances around, noting her belly, the boxes . . .

Welcome back to 2012.

"Drew?" she calls hopefully.

No reply, but Dickens is barking and again, she hears a knocking coming from downstairs. Someone is at the door.

Please, let it be him.

But why would he knock?

Maybe he locked himself out, forgot his keys. . . .

Please, please, let it be him.

She hurriedly stands, briefly grasping the headboard to steady herself before heading for the stairs.

Dickens meets her at the bottom, still barking anxiously at the door. Through the window, she can see a man on the doorstep. Of course, it isn't Drew.

Her heart sinks.

Drawing closer, she can see that he's holding a clipboard. There's a large truck parked on the driveway with the back doors open, and a second man is setting up a ramp there.

The movers, obviously.

Still, bred on street smarts, Clara stops at the door, calling, "Yes?" through the glass.

"Delivery for Becker," the man calls back over Dickens's incessant barking.

"Delivery?" she echoes, shrugging to show him that she must have misunderstood.

He motions for her to open the door.

Hesitating, she weighs the odds that he and his accomplice are going to throw her into the back of the truck.

Deciding to take a chance, she reaches for the knob and opens the door a crack, holding Dickens back by the collar.

"We have your crib and changing table," the man informs her promptly—and impatiently.

"Excuse me?"

"Crib."

"Crib?"

"And changing table."

"For me? Are you sure?"

He glances pointedly at her hugely pregnant stomach, then consults the clipboard. "Got it right here. Drew Becker. That you? You ordered a crib and changing table on December nineteenth from the Lullaby Lounge in San Francisco?"

"That's my husband." Heart racing, she tightens her grip on the dog and opens the door wider. "Are you sure this is where you're supposed to deliver it?"

He looks at the address on the form. "Yup."

Why not the new house? she wonders, puzzled. *Did we change our minds about moving?*

The deliveryman checks his watch.

"Um, that's fine," she tells him. "Bring it in."

"Where do you want it?"

"Upstairs," she decides quickly.

Yes. In the room with the yellow walls.

"And you want the crib assembled."

It isn't a question, but given his expectant expression, he wants an answer.

Yes?

No?

She settles on, "I don't think so."

"It says here it should be assembled."

Then why are you asking me? she wants to retort, suddenly weary. Not physically— emotionally. Weary of wondering what's going on in her life, of never knowing whether she's going to wake up three years from now or three years ago or . . .

"You paid for the assembly," the delivery-man informs her, after flipping through his in-voice. "If you don't want it, I'm going to have to call my boss." He reaches for his phone.

"Wait—just let me figure this out for a sec-ond. I'm trying to figure out what my husband was thinking when he ordered it."

"He was probably thinking he didn't want to put together a crib and changing table."

"No, I mean . . . we're in the middle of a move."

He shrugs. "One less thing to unpack and put back together."

"Out. We're moving out."

"Yeah? Why?"

Your guess is as good as mine.

"We just need a change of scenery, I guess," she says lamely.

"How long have you been here?"

"A couple of mon—*years*." Yes, years. Just over three, to be exact.

"Yeah? So you were here for the quake?"

She nods.

Yes, she was there for the quake. In her car, on the coastal highway, scared out of her mind, her stomach hurting like crazy, bleeding, and Dickens jumped out of the car, and—

And that's the last thing she remembers.

No. There were squealing brakes, too. A car . . .

"How much damage?"

She blinks. "Excuse me?"

"How much damage did you get here in the quake?"

"You know . . . quite a bit." She shifts her weight, wishing the deliveryman would just get down to business.

"You're lucky the house is still standing. Most of them around here aren't."

"No, I know. We're really lucky."

"So, you want us to assemble, or not?"

Why would Drew have paid for assembly if they're just going to move everything right back out again?

Wondering how complicated it will be to take apart a crib that wasn't supposed to have been put together yet, she makes a decision. "Yes. Assembled. Thanks."

As the deliveryman returns to the truck, she closes Dickens into the utility room off the kitchen.

"Shush, it's only for a few minutes," she calls over his barking protest.

Back in the front hall, she finds the men already rolling a dolly bearing an enormous crate toward the house.

After pointing them in the direction of the empty nursery, she tells them she'll be in the living room if they need her. There, she sinks onto the couch.

Back to 2009—in her thoughts, anyway. The earthquake.

She shudders, recalling how close she'd come to being hurtled into the Pacific when the highway collapsed. If she hadn't thought of the snow globe and headed back here . . .

Her eyes automatically go to the mantel, to the familiar spot where it once sat.

Of course it's empty. The mantel has been cleared of any decor. Everything that once sat upon it is packed away for the move.

Given her conversation just now with the deliveryman, it's hard to imagine that the fragile antique snow globe could have survived the violent quake. It probably shattered into a million pieces on the hearth.

Hearing a thump and voices overhead, she again wonders about the new nursery furniture Drew ordered. The delivery company probably made a mistake. It must have been designated for the new place.

When Drew shows up, he's going to ask her why she didn't tell them.

And she's going to say . . . ?

Because I didn't know.

I didn't know where we were going or why you weren't here or when you were coming back. . . .

All I knew was that it was going to be all right, because you promised me three years ago that it would be.

She sits staring into space for a long time, thinking about Drew and the little family they had planned. About this house, and happily ever after . . .

As her weary eyes droop closed, tears escape to roll down her cheeks.

Chapter 29

The sound of barking reaches Clara's ears, and she's back—back from the dark, quiet place where there is no pain.

Back . . . where?

The car?

The earthquake!

Dickens!

Somewhere outside, a car door slams. She hears a male voice. More barking, urgent now, and much closer to where she is, lying helplessly on the seat.

"You shouldn't go running out in front of cars, you know that, fella?" says the voice, and she's heard it before.

Clara hears a jangling of dog tags, and then Dickens is beside her again, licking her face and barking. Footsteps sound on gravel. Human footsteps.

"It's all right, boy, calm down. What are you doing in there?"

Then Clara hears a gasp.

She opens her eyes to see a familiar face looking down at her, eyes wide with concern.

"Thank goodness." Officer Robert Shelton smiles faintly, but his eyes are worried. "I was just about to take your pulse. You don't look so good."

"I don't . . . feel . . . so good," Clara manages.

"It'll be okay."

"My baby . . ."

"Shhh, try to stay still."

"Please . . ."

"I'll take good care of you. One good turn deserves another, as they say."

Clara closes her eyes, opens them again. He's nodding at her.

"I took your advice."

What is he talking about? Clara struggles to find her voice, but darkness is closing in, sweeping her away from the fear and the pain at last.

The last thing Clara hears before she blacks out are Bobby's heartfelt words: "Thank you, Clara, for saving my family."

Chapter 30

A loud ringing sound startles Clara awake.

She opens her eyes and slowly gets her bearings. She's in her living room. In 2012.

Another shrill ring, and her heart skips a beat when she realizes it's the telephone on the bedside table.

Grabbing the receiver, she blurts a breathless, "Hello?"

"Clara. It's Nancy."

For a moment, she's so bitterly disappointed that it isn't Drew that she has no clue who Nancy might be—nor does she care. Then she remembers—her next-door neighbor. Amelia's mom.

"Nancy. How are you?"

"I could be better. Christmas was hard. Jeff tried to change the custody order and keep me from taking the kids up to Tahoe, but that didn't happen, thanks to Amelia. You know how she is about him."

Her words fire at Clara like a round of pellets. Jeff? Custody?

Nancy sighs on the other end of the line. "It breaks my heart when I think of what a daddy's girl she was when she was younger. Sometimes I think she felt even more betrayed when he left than I did."

Clara doesn't know whether to be jubilant that her neighbor is alive after all, or disturbed that he and his wife are so obviously divorced.

"It's hard on children," she murmurs, knowing firsthand.

"Harder on Amelia than on the boys, I think. Maybe they're too young to remember what it was like when our family was intact. Josh doesn't even remember the earthquake, if you can believe it. He was four."

"Maybe he blocked it out."

"Maybe." Nancy pauses. "Anyway, I wanted to say that we've missed you, and see if you wanted to get together for lunch since—"

"Mrs. Becker?" the delivery man calls, and Clara hears footsteps on the stairs.

"Oh, Nancy—can I call you back in a little bit? I've got someone here right now."

"Sure. I'm going out to run some errands but I'll be back in about an hour."

Hanging up, Clara hoists herself to her feet

and rests a hand on her aching lower back as she makes her way back to the hall.

The moving man with the clipboard is waiting; through the door, she can see that his partner has already headed back out to the truck with the packing materials.

"You're all set."

She signs the paperwork and tips him with a couple of bills from her wallet.

"Have a great day." On his way out the door, he calls back, "Hey, good luck with the baby and everything."

Trying to sound as casual as he does, she returns, "Thanks."

I'm going to need all the luck I can get.

She locks the door behind the deliverymen.

Maybe she should call Nancy back right away, try to catch her before she goes out. She seems to be a good friend—she must be if she missed Clara over the holidays, like she said. Maybe she can shed some light on Drew's whereabouts.

But remembering her neighbor's brittle tone, Clara decides that the return call can wait a little while. She isn't in the mood right now to hear about a divorce or heartbroken children.

Instead, she heads upstairs to see the nursery.

She's done her best to ignore the room since the first time she opened the door and found it empty.

Now, the door is ajar.

Riddled with trepidation, she hesitates in front of it for a minute, then turns away.

No. I don't want to see.

Why should she? They're moving away. The nursery she imagined won't belong to this baby.

She continues down the hall to the sun-splashed master bedroom she and Drew share—shared?—*share*, she thinks firmly. Eyeing the stacks of boxes, she notes that most of them are labeled CLOTHES or BEDROOM.

One, however, reads simply CLARA. It sits on top of two others, at about her chin level, all of them stacked against the wall. She reaches out and gives the top box a cautious tug.

It feels heavy . . . but not *that* heavy.

And this stack, unlike the other, is braced against the wall.

She looks around the room and spots the bench Drew sits on every weekday morning to put on his shoes after getting dressed in his suit. A fierce pang of longing sweeps through her and she would give anything—*anything*—if she could blink and find him sitting there again, bent over a pair of wingtips with a shoehorn.

Stranger things have happened.

She closes her eyes for a moment, and a couple of hot teardrops manage to squeeze through her lashes. Wiping at them with her sleeve, she swallows hard, then opens her eyes again.

No Drew.

But the bench is still there, looking pretty solid. Solid enough to hold her, even at this weight.

Right. She's pregnant. She can almost hear her mother's voice, nagging, worried about her, and the baby—worried about everything, as usual.

You shouldn't be climbing, Clara.

But it isn't that high, and I'll be careful.

She drags the bench over to the boxes, right up against the bottom two, then pushes it a little to see if it wobbles.

Not at all.

Still . . . this probably isn't the best idea she's ever had.

She looks down at her belly, up at the boxes.

CLARA

What's in that one?

She has a pretty good idea—and right now, she really, really could use a look at the letter that reached her across more than six decades and gave her hope.

Right now, she could really, really use some hope.

Mind made up, she climbs—oh, so cautiously— up onto the stool. For a moment, she just stands there, braced against the boxes, making sure she has her balance.

Yes. You're okay. You're fine.

Just . . . do something. Fast. Before you . . . get dizzy and fall or something.

Nudging the top box, she notes that it's heavy enough to contain a suitcase filled with clothes. And heavy enough to make lifting it a risk.

Lifting . . . but not opening.

She slides a fingernail beneath the edge of the packing tape stuck to the side of the box and pulls it loose. It comes up easily. In a matter of seconds, she has the box flaps open and stands on her tiptoes to peek inside.

There it is—the suitcase.

Relief coursing through her, she runs her fingertips over the reassuringly familiar marbled surface. Then, arms stretched above her head, she flips the latches and opens the lid carefully, propping it against the wall behind it.

Even on her tiptoes, she realizes she can't quite reach the opening in the lining. Frustrated, she strains, her arms beginning to ache from the effort, to no avail.

Anyway, who's to say the letter is still hidden in the lining? Drew knows now. Maybe she keeps it somewhere else. Maybe even tucked it in among the layers of clothing. She doubts it, but still . . .

Her fingertips encounter neatly folded garments, and then . . .

Something else.

Not a letter. It feels like a ball of tissue paper, but when she lifts it, it has some weight. It's something *wrapped* in tissue paper—and she has a good idea what it might be.

As she lifts it out, the bench beneath her wobbles slightly. It's enough to throw her off balance. She teeters, grabs blindly for something to hold on to, and the tissue-wrapped object flies from her hands.

It hits the hardwood floor and rolls under the bed as Clara cries out in dismay. After quickly regaining her balance, she climbs down from the stool, shaken and angry with herself.

That was stupid.

She could have fallen and hurt herself—hurt the baby.

And why? Because she needed to see a letter as proof that Drew is out there somewhere? To be reminded that he'll find his way back to her again?

She kneels beside the bed and feels gingerly around underneath it, not wanting to cut her hand on the broken glass.

But when her fingertips encounter the tissue paper, it's still wrapped around the fragile object it was meant to protect.

Pulling it out, Clara gently peels away the layers, and there it is: somehow intact.

The dark-haired angel with the broken wing smiles up at her through a watery glass dome swirling with flakes of white.

Slowly, clutching the snow globe in her trembling hand, she gets to her feet and makes her way back into the hall.

This time, reaching the nursery, she pushes the door open and peeks inside.

Aglow with sunlight, the room seems to radiate promise even before she allows herself to look directly at the new furniture.

Both the crib and changing table are white and crafted in vintage style, just as she always pictured. Clara swallows hard and looks down at the rounded swell of her stomach, imagining the sweet baby nestled there.

"I so wanted to be a mommy in this room," she whispers, her throat aching.

Somewhere deep in her womb, the baby moves.

"What? Are you trying to tell me something? What is it, little one?"

But she already knows. Knows that it's not about the room. It's not about the house, or the snow globe, or the letter. . . .

It's about something that can't be shattered in an earthquake.

Love.

As Clara's left hand—the one that wears her wedding band—rests against her stomach, her child's tiny hand nudges her as if to say, *Good. You get it now. Don't ever forget it.*

From somewhere outside, she hears the distant rumble of an engine.

It must be the delivery truck leaving, she thinks vaguely—then realizes it's been quite a while since she locked the door after them.

And the noise is getting louder, not fading away.

She goes over to the window and looks out.

An unfamiliar dark sedan is pulling in, parking.

From up here, she can't see who's behind the wheel. Can it be . . . ?

It is. I can feel it. It's him.

Pulse racing, she goes for the stairs, carefully holding the snow globe in her right hand, tightly grasping the banister with her left, and forcing herself to descend carefully when she wants to jump down them two or three at a time.

Reaching the front door, she stops short, reminding herself that it might not be Drew, no matter what her heart is telling her.

Just don't get your hopes up.

She throws open the door, steeling herself for disappointment but certain, somewhere in the back of her mind, that it isn't going to come. That her husband is home at last.

The sun glares on the windshield, making it impossible to see inside the car.

But the driver's side door is open.

A man is getting out, and . . .

He isn't Drew.

Chapter 31

In the aftermath of perhaps the worst earthquake the region has ever seen, the streets surrounding the nearest hospital—twenty miles away
from San Florentina—are jammed.

Realizing he'll never get close to the parking
lot, Drew leaves his car in a no-parking zone on
a side street and runs the rest of the way. The
hospital itself is in chaos: shell-shocked victims,
frantic loved ones, scurrying personnel, media,
law enforcement, clergy.

With growing trepidation, Drew all but pushes
his way through the throng in the lobby. At a
security desk near the elevators, a guard stops
him with a stern, "Sir!"

"My wife—she's here. She's hurt. The quake—
I got a phone call on my cell phone from someone here. They said she was in surgery, and—"

"Okay, okay—hang in there, buddy." The

guard swivels his chair toward the computer screen. "What's her name?"

"Clara Becker." As he watches the guard search the files, he braces himself for the worst.

"She's on three. Take this and go on up." The guard thrusts a pass into his hand.

She's on three. She's on three. Thank God, she's on three.

It doesn't mean she's okay. It might not mean anything at all. If something had gone terribly wrong, they wouldn't let the security guard break the news to her next of kin right here in the lobby.

Next of kin.

The phrase sends a chill through him now, just as it did when he first heard it almost an hour ago.

He was still in the car at the time, still trying to fight his way home through the traffic, desperate to find Clara. He couldn't reach her at home or on her cell phone; he couldn't reach the Tuckers, couldn't reach anyone who could tell him that she was okay.

All he knew was that there had been a catastrophic earthquake in San Florentina. As the radio announcers reported the breaking news, it sounded more and more grim.

When his phone rang, he was so sure it would be Clara.

It was a nurse, asking whether he was Clara's next of kin, telling him that she had been taken from her car out on the highway south of town and was in the hospital.

His momentary elation that she was alive gave way to immediate panic. "Why couldn't she call me herself?"

"She was taken right into surgery."

The nurse, sounding harried, had then given him directions on where to find his wife, refusing to elaborate on her injuries.

She'd been in the car. Did she lose control and go off the road? Did she have an accident? Did something hit her?

All sorts of possibilities—some more grim than others—have whirled through his brain since he found out.

Then he steps out of the elevator on the third floor and sees the directory sign on the wall: Obstetrics and Neonatology.

Consulting the number on the pass in his hand, he double-checks the directory. There must have been a mistake.

"Can I help you?" a woman in pink scrubs stops to ask on her way to the elevator bank.

He wordlessly shows her the pass.

"It's right down that way." She points to a corridor and hurries on.

Thoughts flying faster than his feet, Drew

rushes down the hall to a reception desk and blurts, "I'm Clara Becker's husband, Drew. She was hurt in the quake. I was told she's here."

The middle-aged man behind the desk turns slowly to his computer screen and reaches for the mouse with maddening care. "Becker . . . Becker . . . ah, Becker. You can go right down that way to 344. It's on the right."

Drew is sprinting in that direction before the man stops speaking, desperate to get to her, every prayer he ever learned jumbling in his head.

He stops short in the doorway of the room, seeing a brunette in a white lab coat standing over a patient.

Clara.

Relief courses through him and he stands frozen, taking in the doctor's somber demeanor, the IV, the tears streaming down his wife's cheeks, her face etched in pain. Physical? Emotional?

The doctor catches sight of him, and Clara follows her gaze.

"Drew!" she cries out as he rushes to her side.

Before he can take her into his arms, the other woman stops him with a firm hand on his arm. Her gray eyes are kind, but stern. "Please be careful, Mr. Becker. I know you're happy to see her—"

Happy to see her?

Happy?

You have no idea, lady, so step aside.

"—but she's very fragile right now."

His animosity toward the doctor disintegrates in a heartbeat; dread creeps back in. "What . . . what happened?"

"Prudence Connor."

Drew sees that the doctor has moved her hand from his arm and is holding it out toward him. What is she doing? What is she talking about?

"Prudence Connor," she repeats. "I'm an obstetrician here."

Oh. Realizing that she's introducing herself, he shakes her hand quickly, then looks again at his wife's distraught face.

"Were you in an accident, Clara?"

"No," she tells him, her voice frighteningly weak. "Nothing like that. I was driving, and . . . the quake happened, and I turned around and started to drive back home, but I was having this terrible pain . . ."

"What kind of pain?"

Clara's eyes flood, and he knows. He knows before he hears the words.

"The baby."

"You lost it?" he manages to choke out.

"It's more serious than that, Mr. Becker," Dr. Prudence Connor tells him. "Your wife has suffered an ectopic pregnancy—meaning the embryo developed in her fallopian tube rather than the uterus. The tube ruptured and she hemorrhaged. It was extremely dangerous, but fortunately your wife had the presence of mind to flag down a passing police officer who got her to the hospital."

"Bobby," Clara murmurs, and he looks at her, confused.

"She's heavily medicated," the doctor explains, and he nods.

"No," Clara protests. "It was Bobby. The officer who helped me. But I didn't flag him down. Dickens ran out, and he slammed on the brakes, and Dickens led him over to the car, and he saw the blood . . ."

Sickened at the thought of his wife, alone and bleeding on the side of the road—after an earthquake, for God's sake—Drew struggles to find his voice.

Clara touches his arm. "Drew—we might not be able to have any more babies."

"There was significant damage to her right fallopian tube and we had to remove it," the doctor tells him. "In the future, it might be very difficult to conceive and carry a child to term."

Drew's eyes are locked on Clara's. For once, he can't find the words to reassure her.

But this time, he doesn't have to.

It's Clara who lifts her chin stubbornly; Clara who says, "It's going to be okay. We believe in magic; don't we, Drew?"

He nods, squeezing her hand in his. "Yes. We do. We absolutely believe in magic."

Chapter 32

Standing on the doorstep, staring at the stranger climbing out of the black sedan on her driveway, Clara feels as though her heart has made a screeching crash into a stone wall.

He's wearing a dark suit, sunglasses. Who is he?

Does it really matter?

He isn't Drew.

I told you not to get your hopes up.

Yes, but she listened to her instincts, anyway, and her instincts had told her that it was going to be him.

Her instincts, intuition, sixth sense . . .

Maybe there's no such thing. Maybe she's been caught up in an illusion of hope all along, believing in something—someone—because she so desperately needs to.

Because someone once said to her, a long,

long time ago, *"Look for me, Clara . . . because I'm going to find you. I promise."*

Someone she loved—and lost. But not really.

What if . . .

What if she imagined that, too? What if Jed was simply Jed, and Drew is simply Drew? What if there's no such thing as magic after all?

She can't bear to look at the stranger on her driveway, so she looks down—and there it is, right in her hand.

Hope.

Proof.

Magic.

The snow globe.

He's going to come home to you. Maybe not now, but he will. You have to believe that.

You have to believe in magic.

"Clara!"

Out of nowhere, the sound of his voice jolts her to the core and she's certain she must have imagined it—until she hears it again.

"Clara!"

Slowly, she looks up to see Drew climbing out of the sedan's backseat as the other man, the driver, stands with his hand still on the back door handle.

"Drew!"

Arms outstretched, heart soaring, she runs toward him, laughing—or perhaps crying—with relief.

"Hey, careful!" Grinning, he meets her halfway, sweeping her into his arms. He hugs her, then reaches for her wrist. "What's this? The snow globe?"

Too overwhelmed to speak, she nods.

He takes it from her and carefully tucks it into the deep pocket of his jacket. "This has been through a lot. We don't want to break it now."

She buries her face in his shoulder, breathing him in as he holds her tight again.

"Drew, where have you been?" she manages to say when she finds her voice at last.

"The flight was late."

Flight? She glances over to see the driver unloading luggage from the open trunk, carrying it back and forth to the house.

"I would've called when we landed," Drew goes on, "but she had a hard time on the plane—the flight was endless—and she fell asleep as soon as we got into the car. I was afraid to wake her up with my voice."

"Her?" Clara echoes. "She?" Utterly confused, she looks from the mounting pile of luggage in the foyer back to Drew.

Then she follows his gaze to the backseat—and sees, for the first time, that it isn't empty.

Chapter 33

Struggling against yet another wave of drowsiness, Clara clings to Drew's hand as he sits beside her hospital bed.

"I need to tell you something," she says. "Alone."

Standing next to Drew, Dr. Connor laughs good-naturedly. "Oh, hey, I can take a hint."

"Sorry," Clara tells her, wishing it didn't hurt to smile.

"Don't be. I get it. I have a husband, too. And believe me, if I didn't know for sure that right this very minute Harry is safe and sound, I wouldn't be hanging around here in the first place. But I'll leave you two alone for a bit."

"Thanks, Doctor," Drew murmurs, his eyes fixated on Clara.

"I have to warn you, Mr. Becker—the medication will probably knock her out pretty quickly. Actually, I'm surprised it hasn't already."

"No, it can't. I need to talk to Drew," Clara tells her—tells both of them. "It's important."

"Obviously." The doctor smiles again, then turns back to Drew. "Just know that the drugs she's on can cause various side effects. Do you understand what I'm saying, Mr. Becker?'

"I understand."

So does Clara. The doctor is telling him that Clara might talk nonsense, or hallucinate.

"No," Clara protests, but either the word isn't loud enough for them to hear her, or it doesn't make it past her lips at all.

They're looking at each other, not at her. And the look that's passing between them fills Clara with despair, as does the doctor's final warning to Drew.

"One last thing—between the medication and the trauma, your wife might not remember any of this later. She's been through hell."

"I know she has," Drew says grimly.

"She seems to have blocked out certain details entirely. And that might be a blessing."

With that, the doctor discreetly disappears.

Drew is closer now, looking down at her, his eyes suspiciously shiny. "Hey," he whispers.

Clara closes her eyes briefly, gathering her strength, unwilling to waste what little she has on telling him that the doctor was wrong about the medication. She can do that later.

"Drew. Listen."

"You sound so weak," Drew tells her softly, squeezing her fingers. "It can wait. Whatever it is."

"No, it can't. Please. I need you to help me."

"I'm here. We'll get through this together."

"No, Drew . . . I've been visiting the future. Our future. And you're not there. You're somewhere—you're alive—but you're not with me. You call me and tell me that you're with Doris, but Doris is dead, and I'm so scared . . ."

"Shh, it's the medication," Drew tells her. "Strong stuff. Just—"

"No! This is real!"

"Okay . . ."

"I've been going back and forth to the future, and it's Christmas, and I'm pregnant again."

A shadow crosses his face. He opens his mouth, and she knows he's going to tell her that there's a good chance she'll never be pregnant again.

"She's wrong, Drew."

"Who is?"

"The doctor—Prudence. She's going to be a friend of mine, actually, in the future, and she's going to have a baby and name it Prudence because I told her to."

"What are you talking about?"

"Just listen to what I'm telling you," she says, and she can tell that he's trying; he really is. And she doesn't blame him for being confused.

But there's no time to explain every detail; she's fading fast, and she has to get it all out.

"I'm going to be pregnant again. Three years from now. Christmas 2012."

A tear escapes to slip down his cheek, and he shakes his head sorrowfully. "I don't want you to get your hopes—"

"I know, but it's going to happen. It's not impossible, Drew. I've been to the future. Do you understand what I'm telling you?"

"I do," he says, but he doesn't. She can see by the look in his eyes that he's chalking it all up to medication or trauma or hallucination.

He doesn't believe her.

"Please, Drew. Please . . ."

"It's going to be okay. You just need to worry about yourself right now. Just get better, so you can come home."

"I will. I've been there. I've seen it all."

"What—?"

"The future," she reminds him, frustrated. Exhausted. Why won't he just listen?

"Clara—"

"Stop. You don't have to say anything else. You don't have to even believe me right now. I don't care. I just need you to do something for me. "

"Anything. But we'll talk about it later," he says anxiously. "You can barely stay awake, and you need your strength to get better."

"Drew . . . three years from now, you're not going to be with me for Christmas, for whatever reason. I'll be in our house—our house is going to have to be rebuilt, Drew. I'll be there, but you won't. Please . . . don't let me be alone there, waiting and worrying and wondering where you are. Please find me and let me know. Even if you don't want to. Even if you don't love me anymore."

"Oh, Clara, that's insane. I love you. I always have and I always will. Nothing is going to change that. Do you believe me?"

"I do," she tells him, "if you believe me."

For a long time, he just looks at her. Then he nods. "I do. Now close your eyes. Sleep."

And she does.

Chapter 34

"Poor thing, she was fussy the whole trip," Drew is saying as Clara's head spins.

What is he talking about?

Who is he talking about?

Someone is in the backseat of the car. Her heart pounds.

"I'm glad she got some rest on the way back from the airport, at least," he goes on, "because I didn't want her to be cranky when she met her mom for the first time."

"Mom?" Clara echoes faintly, certain she's never been more confused in her life.

Or maybe she has.

Hell, yes. Lately, it seems she's been nothing *but* confused.

But Drew is with her now, and everything is going to be okay.

Dazed, she feels Drew take her hand and finds herself being led over to the car.

There's a car seat buckled in the back.

Fast asleep in the seat is the most precious baby Clara has ever seen.

"Are you ready to meet your daughter?" Drew is asking.

Dressed all in pink, with a pile of soft black hair and skin the same warm color of Drew's eyes, the baby can't be more than six months old, if that.

Speechless, Clara looks up at her husband.

"I know. She's amazing, isn't she?"

Amazing doesn't begin to cover it.

"She's . . . my . . . daughter?"

"Our daughter," he amends with a grin, and glances down at Clara's swollen middle. "I told her she's going to be a big sister in a few weeks, and she seemed pretty happy about it. She seems pretty happy about everything, actually—except flying."

Still trying to comprehend, Clara watches him reach into the backseat and gently unstrap the baby from the car seat. She stirs slightly as he lifts her, but doesn't wake up.

"Here you go, Mom."

As Drew hands over the baby, her lashes flutter and she stares solemnly up at Clara with a pair of piercing blue eyes.

Shocked, Clara looks over at Drew. "Her eyes—"

"I know. Unusual coloring, isn't it, for where she came from? Most newborns lose the blue eyes eventually, but I think hers are here to stay, aren't they, Doris?"

"Doris," she echoes softly, staring at her daughter.

"You know, I wasn't sure that was the greatest name for a child, no matter who she's named after." Drew tells her. "But you were right. It's perfect. It's unique, just like our baby girl."

Our baby girl.

Our daughter.

"All set, Mr. Becker?" the driver asks, closing the trunk.

"Yes, thanks for getting us home, Jerry."

"My pleasure. Congratulations, Mrs. Becker."

"Oh . . . thank you." She glances up only briefly before turning her attention back to the baby cradled in her arms.

"Home at last." Standing behind her, Drew encircles her with his arms and rests his chin on her shoulder. She realizes the car has driven away.

"If I never go back to Ethiopia, it'll be too soon."

Ethiopia?

Another piece of the puzzle falls into place. Ethiopia. No wonder.

"It was brutal being away from you for Christmas," he tells Clara, pulling back to look at her, "but it's a good thing the doctor forbade you to travel, because it would have been too hard on you. Things are rough over there."

"I'm sure it was hard on you, too."

"I survived."

"So did I."

He pulls back, and seems to be searching her face for . . . something.

"Clara—"

At that moment, the baby opens her mouth and makes a sound. Not her first word, exactly . . . but a sweet, soft coo.

"Drew, did you hear that?"

"I did."

"What do you think she said?"

"Probably 'thanks, Mom and Dad.'" He strokes the baby's cheek with his fingertip. "Thank God she's too little to remember the orphanage. This will be the only home she'll ever know—until she grows up and goes away to college, anyway."

Clara sees that he's gazing up at the house.

But . . . what about the move?

Before she can ask, he goes on, "You know, I felt completely overwhelmed when everything happened all at once last summer—the adoption coming through two days before you found out you could get pregnant again after all—I mean, that you *were* pregnant. And then the contractor told us the rebuild wasn't going as smoothly as he'd been hoping and we wouldn't be able to get back into the house by fall after all. . . ."

Clara's eyes widen as she comprehends at last.

They aren't moving *out* of their dream house.

They're moving back *in*.

The baby in her stomach seems to punctuate the realization with a joyful kick.

"I never told you this," Drew goes on, "but I wondered how we were going to deal with everything, and I thought maybe we shouldn't go through with the adoption. But you kept saying that the moment you saw her picture, you knew she was meant to be ours, and . . . you were right. It took me a little longer to figure it out, but she's as much ours as the new baby will be. In the grand scheme of things, it doesn't matter how she came to us. All that matters is that she's here."

The words strike a chord with Clara.

She's always thought the same thing about Drew. Or Jed. Or whoever he is—this man who promised to be with her always.

"Clara . . ."

She finds him watching her closely again, wearing that same, strange expression.

"Is that . . . you?"

Her heart is pounding, but she doesn't dare let on, just in case. . . .

"Of course it's me!" she tells her husband. "Are you feeling all right?"

"No, I know it's *you*, but . . ."

Say it, Drew. Say you know all about what happened, because I told you that day in the hospital. Say that you believed me, and that's why you're asking me this now.

"Did you get my note?" he asks cryptically.

"What note?"

"I left it, just in case . . . in case you woke up on Christmas morning and you didn't know where I had gone."

A smile plays at the corners of her mouth. He does know. He did believe her.

"Where did you leave the note?"

"Right in the middle of the kitchen counter."

The kitchen? But she's spent so much time there, ever since Christmas morning when she awakened to find herself in a familiar house without Drew, but with an unfamiliar, huge dog who—

"Dickens!"

"What?"

Clara shakes her head. "He was eating paper that first day. It must have been your note."

"Oh, for the love of . . ." Drew rolls his eyes. "Crazy dog. I suppose you spent the last few days thinking I had fallen out of love with you and gone off someplace without you."

"No," Clara tells him, "I didn't think that. Well, not for more than a few seconds, anyway. I knew you were out there somewhere, and I knew you'd find your way back. We belong together . . . remember?"

"I do. I just wasn't sure you would," he tells her with a sad, enigmatic smile.

"What do you mean?"

"Memory is a strange thing, isn't it?" Drew kisses her gently on the forehead, then touches the baby's tiny hand, wrapped around Clara's finger. "Come on, let's take her inside. I have some belated Christmas presents to give you."

"But this time," Clara tells him softly, gazing down at their new daughter, "you didn't save the best gift for last."

Chapter 35

"Happy New Year!"

Clara looks up to see Dr. Connor in the doorway of her hospital room, stethoscope around her neck and clipboard in one hand—a potted white poinsettia in the other.

"Ready to go home?"

Drew, sitting beside her bed as he has been for the past several days—most of which she's spent sleeping—answers for her.

"She sure is. Right, Clara?"

She nods and forces a smile. Home? Yes, she's ready to go home.

If only she could.

But their dream house, hers and Drew's, has been demolished.

Drew didn't exactly put it that way when he reported that a massive earthquake—the one that had struck San Florentina a few days after Christmas—had caused serious damage to their home.

"It's just . . . uninhabitable," is what he said, and she knew he was trying to spare her the gory details.

"I want to see it. No matter how bad it is."

But Drew shook his head. "Don't put yourself through that," he said. "Not after . . . everything else."

Everything else. Their dream house isn't the only thing they've lost.

Their dream of parenthood, too, has been destroyed. There will be no baby this summer.

Maybe one day, Doctor Connor told them. Because miracles are possible. But Clara doesn't expect one.

How can she, when she's already had more than her share?

She escaped death twice on that awful day— the day she doesn't even remember.

According to Officer Shelton, her car tires were inches from the edge of the drop-off on the coastal highway when she was found.

And according to Doctor Connor, she'd very likely have bled to death if he hadn't gotten to her when he did.

Clara is glad she has no recollection of what happened to her there, in the car. Or during the quake.

Or, for that matter, for a few days before that.

The last clear memory she has is of being in the kitchen with Drew on Christmas morning. He was making her French toast, and they had a new puppy and a baby on the way.

After that . . . a blur.

Dissociative amnesia, Doctor Connor called her condition. She said Clara's brain is suppressing traumatic memories as a sort of defense mechanism.

"Will she ever remember what happened?" Drew asked worriedly, and Clara wasn't sure whether he was hoping she would, or wouldn't.

"Possibly," Doctor Connor said gently. "But probably not. Maybe it's for the best."

She sets the poinsettia on the table beside Clara's bed.

"This is for you and Drew—to brighten your new place."

The new place is down in San Francisco, an apartment in a Victorian home not far from his parents. They'll be staying there only until they can find something temporary back in San Florentina, though that, Drew warned her, might take a while.

She knows. When she hasn't been asleep, she's been watching the television news. Their beautiful little town was reduced to rubble in the quake.

"Maybe we should make a fresh start somewhere else," Drew told Clara yesterday, but she shook her head vehemently.

"No. We're going home."

San Florentina is where they're supposed to be. On a hillside south of town, in a dream house with glass walls. A house—a home—they're going to rebuild, no matter how long it takes.

"I'll be calling to check up on you, Clara. I have all your contact information, and we have an office visit scheduled for next week, remember?"

She nods. Yes. That, she remembers.

"Thank you for everything," Clara tells the doctor whose kind gray eyes have brightened these bleak hospital days. "I'm going to miss you."

"Oh, we'll see each other again. I live in San Florentina, too, you know."

"Actually, I didn't."

Drew and Dr. Connor exchange a glance, and Clara realizes that this is just one more thing she must have known at one point, and forgotten.

"I've been meaning to ask you—how badly was your house damaged in the quake?" Drew asks Dr. Connor, who shrugs.

"It could be worse. Harry and I are both all right. Nothing else really matters, does it?"

"No," Drew agrees, looking at Clara. "Nothing else really does."

What about our baby? Clara wants to protest. *Our baby matters.*

But she doesn't say it. She doesn't want to talk about it because she'll cry, and she's cried so much these past few days that her eyes feel sandblasted and her throat has been clenched in a permanent ache.

Dr. Connor spends a few more minutes chatting with them, examines Clara one last time, and declares her good to go.

"See you in San Florentina," she says with a wave from the doorway.

"See you there," Clara returns with a smile—this time, one that's genuine.

After Dr. Connor has gone, Drew comments, "Looks like you've made a new friend."

"What?"

"Prudence."

"Who's Prudence?"

"Dr. Connor."

"Her name is Prudence? How do you know that?"

"She told me. And so did you."

"I did?" Clara falters, but only for a moment. She might as well get used to this feeling that she's missing something. "But Drew, she's not my friend, she's my doctor."

Something flickers in his eyes. "I have the feeling she might become a friend, too."

"Really?" It seems like such an odd thing for him to say, and the way he's watching her . . .

"Oh, ish kabibble!"

The familiar voice, loud and clear, reaches their ears from the corridor outside the room.

Clara's eyes widen and she props herself up in bed.

"I'm no visitor," the voice goes on. "I'm family!"

A split second later, a familiar figure appears in the doorway, accompanied by a nurse who hardly looks thrilled.

"I'm sorry, Mrs. Becker, she barged right up here and we couldn't—"

"Doris!" Clara cries out, arms open wide. "What are you doing here?"

"I told you a late Christmas present would be popping up on your doorstep. I would have, but your doorstep isn't there anymore." Doris is right there, hugging her hard. "And then *she*"— she gestures darkly at the nurse—"tried to stop me when I finally figured out that this is where to look for you. Your neighbor Amelia told me where you were. Cute kid. Just like I used to be."

"But . . . you're here. In California!"

"Not really. Well, I am now, but I moved in with my daughter over in Reno."

"Reno?"

"Reno." Doris looks quite pleased with herself.

Clara is incredulous. "I thought you said you would never do that."

"Oh, Clara . . . didn't you learn anything from me? Never say never. That's what I always say."

Clara laughs.

For the first time in what feels like years.

Laughs so hard her stitches hurt, but she doesn't care, because it feels good.

When she stops laughing, Doris pats her hand. "I'm glad you're so amused."

"I just can't believe you're living in Reno. It's just a few hours away from here."

"Yes, and they have casinos, you know. You should come visit. We'll go play the slots."

"Ma'am," the nurse begins again, but Drew cuts her off.

"It's all right, she's family," he says firmly, "and we haven't seen her in years."

Family. She certainly is—to Clara, anyway. And to Drew, too—literally. But he has no clue about that, and he's never met Doris at all, so why would he say he hasn't seen her in years?

It's almost as if . . .

Nah.

He can't possibly suspect that the little old lady was once, in another lifetime, his kid sister.

"Drew," Clara says belatedly, "I'd like you to meet a very good friend of mine. This is Doris."

Doris turns to her husband and stretches a blue-veined hand toward him, blue eyes twinkling. She knows . . . even if Drew doesn't.

"It's about time I got to meet you," she tells him. "Although, I do feel like I already know you. Thanks to Clara, of course," she tags on hastily.

"I feel the same way."

He *does*?

He's obviously just humoring Doris—and Clara, for that matter. He doesn't know Doris from the next dotty old lady.

But Drew goes on, incredibly, "I feel like I know you so well that a hug is more appropriate than a handshake at this point, don't you?"

Doris looks delighted. "Oh, I never turn down a hug from a handsome fellow."

Watching the two embrace, Clara swallows a lump in her throat.

Maybe she *should* tell Drew the incredible truth.

Something tells her he might just understand.

But not now—someday. In the future.

As Drew always says, they have all the time in the world.

Epilogue

Ninety degrees in the shade doesn't happen often around here, even in the dog days of summer.

"It's like being back in Manhattan again," Clara tells Drew, pushing a sweat-dampened clump of hair back from her forehead as they stroll along the sidewalk in the midday sun.

"At least it's not humid here."

"True. But ninety degrees is hot, humidity or not."

"Just be glad you're not wearing fur."

They both look at poor Dickens, whose tongue is hanging out as he walks sedately at the end of the leash in Drew's hand. If it weren't for the heat, chances are he'd be pulling them along the sidewalk as always. Their dog has always had a mind of his own, and advancing age has done little to temper that.

Then again, willfulness tends to run in the family.

"No way!" Doris shouts at her sister. "Get your own if you want them!"

"Shh!" Angelina steals a glance over her shoulder at Clara and Drew, and flashes them a casual smile that's obviously meant to assure them that she's not instigating any kind of trouble.

It's a look they've seen often—and one that's hardly reassuring.

Funny, that a baby so beatific they impulsively named her after the precious little figurine who brought them together has turned out to be anything but angelic.

But then, the snow globe angel wasn't perfect, either. She had a broken wing.

And Clara wouldn't trade her—or Angelina, or Doris—for perfection.

"What's going on, girls?" Drew sternly asks his daughters.

"Angelina wants me to get a cherry on my ice cream sundae so that she can have it."

"Two cherries. Mr. Martino always gives double if you ask."

"She wants me to get *two* cherries," Doris

amends. "And I don't want to get any. I hate cherries."

"But I love them."

"So?"

"Doris, we don't say 'so,'" Drew reminds her—household rule number nine hundred and ninety nine.

"Please, Doris," Angelina cajoles.

"Get your own cherries."

"I can't!"

"Girls," Clara interjects, "stop—"

Dickens erupts into a barking frenzy as a pair of teenage boys roll by on skateboards, eating slices of pizza.

"Easy, boy." Drew strains to hold the leash. "You can't eat pizza."

"Or skateboards," Clara adds, and her husband flashes her a grin. Even at his age, Dickens is always up to his old tricks. Just the other day, he ingested one of poor little Prudence Connor's Barbie dolls while she was having a playdate with the girls.

Luckily, both little Prudence and her mom—also Prudence—seemed to understand. They know Dickens, of course. But Doris and Angelina were mortified, as was Clara.

Still, she wouldn't trade the crazy mutt for a perfect dog who only eats things that are meant to be eaten.

"Why can't you get your own cherries?" Doris demands of her sister.

"I told you, I'm not getting a sundae," Angelina explains impatiently, "I'm getting a root beer float. You don't put cherries in a root beer float. That would be disgusting."

"Well, cherry juice all over my whipped cream is even more disgusting, so—"

"Girls!" Clara cuts in, as they round the corner to see the familiar green awning that marks Scoops Ice-Cream Parlor. "No more!"

"If you don't stop this instant," Drew adds, "only Mommy and I are getting ice cream."

"But I didn't even do anything," Doris protests.

"I didn't even do anything, either," Angelina echoes.

"What?! You started the whole thing by—" Seeing the look on her father's face, Doris clamps her mouth shut.

Drew and Clara exchange a weary glance.

"Whose idea was this, anyway?" he asks as Dickens barks maniacally at the long line of customers stretching out the door of Scoops.

"Coming into town to get ice cream with the kids and the dog on a blazing hot Saturday? Yours."

"I meant having two kids and a dog in the first place."

"Yours again."

"I beg to differ. I didn't—"

"Okay, I'll take half the blame for the kids, but the dog is all your fault, and so is this little ice-cream adventure."

"I must have been delirious from all the heat."

"Or all this happiness," she says dryly, and links her arm through his, leaning her head on his shoulder.

Fifteen minutes—and an ongoing cherries/no cherries argument—later, they at last arrive at the front of the line.

"If it isn't the Becker family!" Paolo announces, wearing his usual jovial smile and ice-cream smeared white apron. "How are you all today?"

"We're just peachy," Clara tells him, before the girls can relaunch their complaints. "How's your family, Paolo?"

"Couldn't be better. I just found out I've got my fourth grandchild on the way."

"Four? Congratulations!" Clara tells him.

"Thank you. I can't believe it. It wasn't so long ago that my kids were babies themselves. You think you have all the time in the world, but before you know it, these two"—he points at Doris and Angelina—"are going to be all grown up. And you two"—he points at Clara and Drew—"are going to ask yourselves where the years went. Trust me. I'm always right."

Drew grins. "I have to admit—you always are."

"Aha! See?" Paolo gives a satisfied nod. Then he asks, "But how do you know that?"

"A long time ago, when Clara and I were first married, you said that if a man can wake up every morning and look at the same woman, and say he's happy, he'll be happy forever, because it gets better and better."

"And . . . ?" Paolo prompts.

"And it's gotten better and better," Drew tells him, and puts an arm around Clara. "We're happy. Right, hon?"

"Deliriously," she agrees. "And sometimes, we're just delirious."

Drew sighs and shakes his head.

But, really, it *has* gotten better and better. They have everything they've ever wanted—two beautiful children, their health, a dream house, a career, a dog . . .

Things are pretty much . . . well, not perfect. But, as Doris always liked to say—among other things—perfect is boring.

"Mr. Martino, can you please put extra cherries on my sister's sundae?" Angelina asks.

"No! I don't want cherries!" Doris explodes.

Maybe someday they'll get along, Clara thinks optimistically. Maybe, when they're all grown up, they'll be the best of friends. Wouldn't that be nice?

It would.

But you can't control what might happen in the future any more than you can change what happened in the past.

"*All you can do is live,*" Doris told her once, a long time ago. "*Live for today, live for each other, live for yourself.*"

Oh, and one more thing . . .

"*I believe in magic, and so do you. Don't ever forget it.*"

"*I won't,*" Clara promised her old friend, the last time she ever saw her—in this lifetime, anyway. "*I won't ever forget.*"

And she never has.

Turn the page for an excerpt
from Wendy Markham's

If Only in My Dreams

Available now from www.penguin.com

In the heart of formerly-countryside, now-suburban Glenhaven Park is a town green that looks like something out of *It's a Wonderful Life*. Especially today, thanks to the Oscar-winning art director's holiday magic.

Store windows are artificially frosted and some, like the five-and-dime, display packets of holiday cards, compartmentalized boxes of metallic ornaments, and bags filled with fancy ribbon candy. Every lamppost is wrapped in shiny silver garland. Nostalgic strings of wide-spaced, bright-colored bulbs line the gingerbread eaves above most front porches; flocked trees decked with bubble lights and tinsel stand in picture windows; door wreaths abound.

As long as you don't look at the vast condo community sprawled on a hillside above the Congregational church, overlooking the town, you might actually believe you've stepped back in time.

A wide, grassy strip runs the length of the town, encompassing three blocks. A brick path meanders among trees and shrubs, wrought-iron benches and tall posts that appear to hold gaslights.

On either side of the green, Victorian-era homes and businesses that line the sidewalks have been stripped of anything post-WWII. Flags with fifty stars have been replaced with flags bearing forty-eight. In place of SUVs and foreign sports cars are vintage roadsters parked in driveways and diagonally along the curbs. The Internet café has been transformed into a five-and-dime; the trendy clothing boutique now advertises STYLISH WOMEN'S HATS and MODERN SLACKS.

A half mile up the commuter railroad tracks, an authentic diesel locomotive—painted a cheery red—has been positioned. It's ready to steam into town towing old-fashioned domed, corrugated railroad cars, and dispatch Clara and several extras on the platform to block the first scene.

Clad in platform shoes with high wedge heels, a trim-fitting gray wool skirt suit, black wool coat, and brimmed black velvet hat, Clara boards the train with a crowd of period-costumed extras.

She's struck, as she was during rehearsals, by the dated rotating mohair seats and ornate lighting fixtures. What a far cry from the modern commuter railroad she takes out to her father's place in Jersey.

"It smells like smoke in here," one of the extras comments, fanning the stale air.

It *does* smell like smoke.

Repulsed, Clara clasps her wrist against her nostrils to inhale instead the potent fragrance of the essential oil she dabbed all over herself this morning. A blend of lavender and geranium, the concoction is, quite suitably, called Calming.

God knows Clara can use as much of that as she can get these days.

"Do you think this was once a smoking car?" one of the extras asks.

"They were all once smoking cars, dude," somebody replies.

Cigarettes. Why did you have to smoke all those cigarettes when you were younger?

Cancer. You have cancer.

Her thoughts catapulted back to her diagnosis, Clara can't help but wonder if things might be different now if she hadn't.

You can't second-guess everything you ever did, she reminds herself. *What good is that now?*

What is, is.

Nothing to do but accept this. Accept it and fight it.

"Clara?" someone prods impatiently, and she realizes that nearly everyone is in their places now.

Everyone but the bit actor playing the conductor, and the leading lady.

Fighting the overwhelming urge to scratch the itchy spot where the rough woolen collar brushes her bare neck, Clara takes her designated spot standing beside the door. She's supposed to be the first passenger off the train.

Her character, a disillusioned office worker, is eager to reach her small-town destination and begin her new elementary school teaching position at the redbrick schoolhouse.

Little does Violet know that she's about to be swept off her feet by the so-called swooniest fella in town.

"Here you go, Clara." With a grunt, Lisa, the prop mistress, sets an authentic 1941 Samsonite Streamlite suitcase on the floor at her feet.

"It looks heavy. It *is* heavy," Clara exclaims, lifting it slightly to test the weight. "What's in this thing? Sandbags?"

"I stuck a bunch of outfits from wardrobe inside. Stuff we decided not to use. You can go through it after the shoot and keep what you want."

"Are you kidding? I can't wait to get back into real clothes when this shoot is over. I don't know how women back then dealt with being this dressed up every day—and can I ask why this suit doesn't have more than one pocket?"

"For what? Your iPod?"

"Nope, it won't fit. I keep that right here. She grins and lifts her jacket, showing Lisa the slim device tucked into her waistband. The skirt fits loosely, and she can't seem to get used to the fact that it's a size twelve—which, as the wardrobe mistress has repeatedly reminded her, is the equivalent to a modern four, her usual size.

"Hey!" Lisa protests. "You can't carry one of those in the scene. This is supposed to be 1941, remember?"

"Shh! Nobody knows it's here. And I'll take it out when we shoot later. It comes in handy in this endless blocking. Nobody will ever know it's there."

"*You* will. It might interfere with your authenticity."

"Nah, I'm a pro, and anyway, we're not shooting yet." Clara sighs and scratches the back of her neck again. "God, I would kill to be wearing a sweatshirt and jeans."

"And here I thought you were a glamour queen actress," Lisa says dryly. "So much for the Hollywood illusion."

"Yeah, but I look like one today, right?" Clara asks with a grin, reaching up to pat her head beneath the trim hat. The hairstylist tamed her brunette mane into a controlled pompadour high above her forehead, with sleek waves falling to her shoulders.

Her smile fades as she remembers that it won't be long before her hair is falling to the ground in clumps.

"Places, everyone!"

At last the train is ready to steam toward Glenhaven Park for the first run-through.

Clara clutches her purse in one hand and grabs a pole with the other in anticipation of the train's movement. Time to conjure an expectant, exhilarated feeling.

You're going off to start a new life. . . .

The train starts chugging. It quickly picks up speed.

"How can you ride facing backward?" asks an extra seated nearby. "Doesn't it make you feel sick?"

Clara merely shakes her head, trying to focus on her character's motivation.

It's 1941 . . . you're Violet . . . off to start a new life. . . .

Nearly losing her balance as the train rounds a bend, she holds the pole more tightly, wondering if they should be going this fast. Positioning her too-tight vintage platform shoes farther apart to keep her balance, she glances at the landscape flying past the window.

Get into character. Come on. You're an actress.

Yes, an actress with a hell of a lot more on

her mind this morning than work. But there will be plenty of time to brood later.

The train hurtles forward toward Glenhaven Park; she stares at the back wall of the car, convincing herself that she's Violet. Violet, living her uncomplicated 1941 life, embarking on a new adventure in a brand-new place.

Any second now, you're going to meet the man of your dreams. . . .

Yes, and he's going to go off to war and die.

But Violet doesn't know that now.

Violet is all hope and anticipation.

Lucky, lucky Violet. Healthy. Happy. About to make a fresh start.

What I wouldn't give to be in her shoes for real, Clara thinks wistfully. *Not forever.*

Just for now.

Just for the happy stuff . . . like not having cancer and falling in love with Jed Landry.

The whistle blows.

Shouldn't the train be slowing down by now? Clara wonders, suddenly on edge. She doesn't know why, but her body feels almost as though it's been zapped with a surge of electricity, every nerve ending tingling with . . .

Apprehension?

A bit of fear?

They're going so fast . . . they might overshoot the station if they don't slow down.

Clara bends her head to peek out the window and gauge how close they are to town. She catches a fleeting glimpse of the low stone wall. Then she sees the back of the wooden WELCOME TO GLENHAVEN PARK signpost.

The train slows abruptly with a deafening, high-pitched squeal of brakes as it rounds a curve.

Clara is thrown off her feet, toward the back of the car, slamming her head against the hard edge of the nearest seat.

"Ow!"

Her hand flies up to rub her temple. The pain is so stunning that for a moment she sees nothing but a blinding glare.

Then it subsides just a bit and she's left with a dull ache.

Terrific.

Just what she needs in the midst of filming.

A lovely bump above her eye.

A bump to match my lump, she thinks grimly.

Cancer. I have cancer.

She shakes her head.

I'm Violet. Violet doesn't have cancer.

Violet is happy, giddy, naive—about to fall in love.

At last, the train is slowing down. Turning to face forward, she looks out the window and sees a vintage Packard tooling along the road beside the tracks. In the front seat is a young extra dressed in a military uniform.

And . . . that's funny. The ground is dusted with snow.

She doesn't remember seeing snow when she left her trailer a little while ago.

Some snowflakes must have fallen while they were setting up the scene back there. A lot of snowflakes. Enough to cover the ground and rooftops.

How the heck did I miss it? she wonders, and decides it must be fake snow, part of the set decoration.

Then she catches a whiff of cigarette smoke.

Glancing around, she sees that two of the female extras have swiveled their seats to face each other and are puffing away.

She wrinkles her nose in disgust. Period authenticity is one thing; a public health hazard is another.

She opens her mouth to object when the conductor appears in the aisle. "Station stop is Glenhaven Park. Glenhaven Park. Next stop, Brewster. Please exit to the rear of the car."

Clara gapes at him, wondering why he seems different. For some reason, she thought the conductor was a much older, rotund character actor type.

He isn't. He's a skinny beanpole of a guy,

with pockmarked cheeks and an overbite. She can't help but feel as though she's never before laid eyes on him in her life.

Good Lord, am I becoming so much of a diva that I'm no longer noticing the little people?

Pushing aside the troubling question, she bends to lift the suitcase Lisa stuffed with clothes.

I'm Violet. Expectant. Exhilarated. New life.

The train chugs to a halt.

She gazes out at the platform, wondering why the crew isn't in place.

The door opens and she steps out into the brisk December chill, purse tucked under her arm, suitcase in hand. *Brrr.* Is it her imagination, or has the temperature dropped a good thirty degrees in the last ten minutes?

She descends from the train, trying not to wobble in her narrow 1940s' heels. The wooden platform is caked with snow and ice—which *must* be real, because it's pretty darned frigid out here.

Hmm, she could have sworn the platform was made of concrete . . . and shouldn't the crew have salted it?

Oh, wait. They probably left it genuinely slippery for authenticity.

You take three steps, and then you slip, she reminds herself, moving forward, lugging the suitcase with her.

Yes, she slips, and Michael catches her.

So where is he?

And where are the other actors who are supposed to follow her off the train, chatting?

She doesn't want to blatantly turn her head to look, but she seems to be the only one who got off the train, and Michael doesn't seem to be on his mark. *Oh, well.* He must be there. And the cameras and lighting, too. They're just more unobtrusive than she would expect.

Start walking.

One step . . .

Two . . .

Three.

"Oh." Clara cries out, slipping on cue . . .

And falling to the hard planks with an excruciating thud as the train chugs off into the distance.

Dazed, she looks around the empty platform.

Empty?

Wait a minute.

Where are the other extras who were supposed to disembark with her?

Where's Michael?

Where's Denton?

And where are the damned cameras, and the lighting crew, and . . . ?

Clara frowns.

What the . . . ?

I'm alone out here.

She slowly gets to her feet and brushes the

powdery snow off her skirt. Her breath puffs white in the wintry air.

Shivering in the wind, she looks around, bewildered.

Glenhaven Park looks just as it should: flags flying, vintage automobiles parked along the green—now blanketed in white.

She can see costumed extras bustling along the sidewalks. Swing music even plays faintly from a distant radio.

The crew has thought of everything.

Everything but me, Clara thinks ruefully, uncertain what to do next.

Maybe Denton called a meeting in one of the trailers. Maybe he's going to adjust the blocking schedule because of the snow.

It doesn't make sense—none of this makes sense—but it's the only explanation Clara can come up with.

She looks in the direction where the location trailers were parked in an A&P supermarket lot down the street.

That spot is occupied by a large Victorian mansion with a mansard roof.

Huh?

Where's the supermarket?

She squints, blinks.

No trailers.

No parking lot.

No A&P.

Maybe she's mistaken.

Maybe the trailers were on the opposite end of town.

She turns her head—still throbbing from the bump on the train—to took the other way.

No trailers.

No parking lot.

No supermarket.

All she can see, beyond the white steeple of the Congregational church, is the tree-lined hillside overlooking the town.

Her heart pounds so violently, her knees weaken so abruptly, that it's all she can do to remain on her feet.

Just the hillside.

Nothing *on* the hillside but trees.

Nothing.

Somehow, an entire condominium complex has vanished into thin air, along with the rest of Clara's world.

At the sound of a car horn honking in the street, Jed looks up to see wiry, bespectacled Arnold Wilkens, a childhood friend, passing by the five-and-dime in a new blue Packard. Arnold waves at him, and Jed waves back, wondering whether Arnold's wife Maisie has had their first baby yet.

About to return his attention to the store, Jed notices big fat flakes in the air—drifting lazily, almost horizontally in the air as opposed to falling furiously as they did early this morning.

He turns away from the window—then back, realizing that he just glimpsed a familiar figure coming down the block.

As he trains his eyes on this woman, he's so caught up in admiring her shapely legs—even as he notes that she appears to be wearing stockings, and wonders where she managed to find them—that he momentarily forgets to look up to see who she is.

When he manages to tear himself away from those glorious gams, he realizes that he doesn't know her after all.

Or does he?

He takes in the well-made hat and coat, the waves of chestnut hair curled fashionably above her shoulders. . . .

Even from here, he can see that she's a real dish.

He can also see that she's hauling a large suitcase. Is she coming or going?

Coming. Definitely. Because she seems lost. He can tell by the way she's looking around, as though she's searching for something.

She must have just stepped off the train from Manhattan. In fact, everything about her says Glamour Puss.

Still, there's something familiar about her. . . .

Jed is almost one hundred percent positive that he's seen her someplace before.

So certain is he that he raps on the plate glass window to catch her attention.

She looks up, startled.

Her smile is at once tentative, relieved, and laced with recognition.

So I must know her, Jed realizes, watching her approach the store. *And obviously, she knows me.*

It's about time, Clara thinks, waving at the guy in the window of the old-fashioned five-and-dime. At last, a temporary haven from the icy wind, and a familiar face.

Not nearly as familiar—or as welcome—as, say, Michael's would be. Or Denton's.

But this costumed bit player—whom she must have met in passing on the set at some point—is better than a total stranger.

She just can't help wondering why she didn't recognize any of the other vintage-fashion-clad extras she glimpsed hurrying along the sidewalks as she walked over from the train station. Maybe she was just too busy trying to figure out what on earth was going on with the set . . . and the scene she's supposed to be blocking.

She supposes something could have come up and caused the camera crew, Denton, and Michael to beat a hasty retreat.

Maybe Michael's contagious stomach bug has infected the whole production.

Or maybe there was a problem with the filming permit. The town's administration is a stickler for rules.

It just would have been nice if somebody had mentioned the abrupt change in the schedule to the cast and crew on board the train.

Yet a communication breakdown doesn't explain the vanishing condo complex on the hill. A cluster of buildings can't just walk away.

Then again, Hollywood magic can make anything possible. Clara has seen, at the hands of capable set designers, the southwestern desert become a tropical island beach, a wall of white Styrofoam blocks transformed into an ancient Roman villa.

All right. Maybe they've created some kind of optical illusion to camouflage the condos.

It would have been nice if somebody had mentioned that, too.

And what about the enormous bronze statue on the green—the one that depicts the eleven lost soldiers of Glenhaven Park? Obviously, it's been removed for the duration of filming. Yet she could have sworn the set designer tried—and failed—to have the statue relocated. The town refused to allow it to budge an inch. Yes, and Denton had to alter a number of long establishing shots as a result.

Clara glances again at the spot where the statue should be. Nothing there now but a towering maple tree. The kind of tree that can't be plunked down by a set designer to hide an unsightly bare spot. The kind of tree that takes centuries to grow . . . and wasn't there last week. Or yesterday.

But that's crazy. You must be imagining things.

And no wonder. It's so cold, and her head hurts, and this suitcase weighs a ton. Is it so surprising that she can't think straight at the moment?

Noticing that the actor in the store is now out beneath the striped awning, holding the door open for her, Clara covers the last stretch of icy sidewalk quickly, and gratefully.

"Come on in . . . chilly out today, isn't it?" he asks pleasantly as she steps over the threshold and deposits her suitcase on the worn wooden floor with a thud.

"That's the understatement of the year." Her teeth are chattering as he closes the door behind her.

"Have we met?" he asks, and she turns to find him looking curiously at her.

"I don't know. . . . I'm Clara," she says politely.

"I'm—" Instead of introducing himself, he frowns, peering into her face. "I thought you looked familiar, but I didn't realize . . ."

You were the star.

How often has she heard that? People are always saying she comes across as a regular gal because she doesn't put on airs like some actresses.

". . . I was wrong," he concludes the sentence unexpectedly.

He was wrong?

She looks into his eyes and sees that he doesn't seem to have a clue who she is. Either that, or he's a terrific actor.

He smiles pleasantly, revealing teeth so white she wants to ask who did them and how much he paid. She's had her own professionally whitened twice in the last year by two different oral health care experts, with less than perfect results.

She wonders why this guy's dentist didn't repair the slight gap between his front two teeth while he was at it. Then again, if it weren't for that barely visible flaw, he would be almost too handsome.

He's clean-shaven with angular features, a full mouth, and a deep cleft in his chin. His hair, so dark it's almost black, is neatly trimmed over his ears without a trace of sideburn. It's so short it spikes up on top with the help of some gel, as though he combed it straight up from his forehead with his fingers. His eyes, wide set beneath straight, sooty slashes of brow, are the striking blue of the sky on a clear winter day.

Clara is so busy noticing his good looks that it takes her a moment to confirm that the lack of recognition is mutual. She's never seen this guy before. He must be a local. She thought he looked familiar when she spotted him from afar. But up close and personal like this, he's as much a stranger as anyone else in this town.

Disconcerted by his expectant blue gaze, she looks away and is startled to find that the dime store's interior now matches the forties' facade. It isn't just the pressed tin ceiling, exposed pipes, soda fountain, or antique register . . .

The set dresser went to a lot of trouble to track down authentic-looking merchandise, too. Everything on the shelves and in the bins— from Christmas decorations to clothing to penny candy—is either an incredibly realistic reproduction, or in terrific condition for being at least sixty-five years old.

Just last week, this was an Internet café. She checked her e-mail on a computer right over in that corner, now occupied by a display table holding a pile of bright blue boxes and a sign that reads PARAMOUNT STAR-LITES.

"Are we shooting interior scenes here?" she asks, wondering why anyone would bother to go to these lengths if they're not—and she could have sworn they aren't.

About to lift her suitcase and move it away from the door, he looks up and frowns as though he doesn't comprehend.

He must not speak English, she realizes in the

split second before she recalls that he did, indeed, speak English when he greeted her.

"Shooting?" he asks blankly without a trace of an accent.

"I thought this place was just for exterior shots," she clarifies, and is met with an even more puzzled expression.

Oh. Maybe he's a little slow, like Eddie, the bag boy at Gistede's near her apartment. That would explain, too, why he was knocking on the window and waving at her as though she's a long-lost friend. He probably knocks and waves at everybody.

"Never mind," she says sympathetically. Marlene, the casting assistant, must have hired him for his looks. He can't possibly have a speaking part.

"Say, what's in this thing?" he asks, grunting as he moves her suitcase. "Rocks?"

"I thought sandbags," she tells him, surprised that he manages to sound so . . . well, fluent. "But Lisa said it's just vintage clothes."

"Vintage?"

"You know Lisa. She lives her art, and she wants the cast to live it, too." She glances out the window as a huge black vintage automobile rumbles by, a horizontal evergreen tied to the roof. Very charming, very realistic. "I've got to keep an eye out for the crew and find out what happened to my scene."

He seems as though he's about to ask a question, but thinks better of it. Instead, he asks, "Can I help you find something?"

"Definitely. Denton would be a great place to start."

"Denton?" he echoes, then nods as though a lightbulb went on. "Oh! Right this way."

He ushers her past a display of ladies' hats and retro cosmetics to a row of shelves. Gesturing at a small stack of pastel clothing of some sort, he asks, "What size?"

"Excuse me?"

"Sizes three and up come with a roll collar now. See?" He lifts a folded garment and unfurls it to reveal a child's one-piece footed pajamas with a trap door in back.

Clara just stares.

"Too big?" he asks. "Or too small?"

"What are you doing?"

He looks taken aback. "Showing you the Dr. Denton's. You asked for them, didn't you?"

She can't help but laugh. Uneasily. And notice that he speaks with the distinct vintage speech pattern she's been working to learn. He must have a speaking part; maybe they even share the same voice coach. But this bit actor manages to make the dialect sound far more natural than she's been able to manage so far.

"No, I meant . . . I was looking for *Denton.*"

"What's that?"

What's that, he asks. Not *who's* that.

Not that *who's that* would be any more acceptable a question, under the circumstances. He should know.

Unless . . .

Unless she's mistaken about this guy being part of the cast.

Because anybody remotely involved with the movie would know who Denton is. In fact, anybody with the slightest knowledge of pop culture for the past three decades would know who Denton is. When it comes to Hollywood directors, he's like Woody, or Spike, or Ang. No last name needed.

Right. So maybe this guy is just some freak who wandered onto the set.

Or maybe . . .

"Am I being punked?" she asks, looking around for a camera crew and a bunch of practical joker colleagues.

"Pardon?" Again, he looks utterly clueless.

Okay, so he's just some random freak. Hopefully not a dangerous one. Clara checks to see how many steps it would take her to get to the door and away from him.

"Are you all right?" the freak asks politely.

"I'm fine."

"You're shivering."

No, I'm shuddering. Big difference.

"Why don't you sit down? Can I get you a cup of hot coffee?" He nods at the glass percolator, then at the row of stools along the soda fountain.

She hesitates. She'd be tempted to sit and feed her caffeine addiction even without too-tight dress shoes and an unshakable chill from the subzero temperatures.

But shouldn't she be . . .

Where?

Shooting a scene?

She can't exactly do that single-handedly, so . . .

"I'd love a cup of coffee," she informs the dimwit heartthrob, setting her purse on the counter. "I don't suppose you have any fat-free hazelnut creamer in here, do you? That would be heaven."

He hesitates. "I'm afraid not."

Figures. So much for her vow to avoid artificial sweeteners from now on—not that the fat-free creamer would have been much healthier.

But she'll have to worry about chemicals and cancer later. Right now, she just needs coffee and a reality check.

"What about Splenda?"

"Splendid?" he echoes—sort of. "What is?"

"What?"

"You said something is splendid?"

"No . . . never mind," Clara says with a sigh,

settling on a stool beside a *Life* magazine display featuring a cover close-up of a Boeing B-17 above the ten-cent price tag.

"I'll just take black coffee," she decides. "And your cell phone, if I can borrow it." Too bad she didn't stick hers into the antique purse. A lot of good the iPod does her now.

"My what?"

"Your . . . cell . . . phone," she articulates, and wonders why she's bothering. Obviously, this guy is clueless. About everything.

"Phone?" He gestures at an old-fashioned black one at the far end of the counter. "Go ahead."

"That works?"

"Why wouldn't it?"

"I thought it might be just for show." She shrugs, lifts the heavy receiver, and waits for a dial tone.

Instead, she hears a woman's voice.

"Somebody's on the line," she informs the guy behind the counter, who's watching her with an expression of . . . concern.

Almost as though *she's* the crazy one. *Yeah, right.*

"It's the switchboard operator," he says with a slow, troubled nod.

"The operator? But . . ."

She trails off, her head swimming in confusion, and hangs up the receiver.

"What about your phone call?"

"It can wait," she says, sinking onto a vinyl-topped stool. "I just need that coffee. Please," she remembers to add, realizing that her tone is bordering on hysteria.

"Coming right up, Clara."

"Thank you. . . ." She interlaces her icy, trembling fingers on the marble counter. "What did you say your name was?"

"I didn't," he says with a smile, extending his hand to shake hers. "But it's Jed. Jed Landry."

Jed Landry.

The name slams into her like a two-by-four, taking her breath away.

That's when she realizes why he looks so familiar—and that he isn't crazy after all.

She is.

She must be, because she recognizes not just his name—Jed Landry is the character Michael is playing in the film—but also his face.

She saw it just a few weeks ago in a black-and-white photo in the Glenhaven Park archives—the hero soldier who's been dead for more than six decades.

Also Available from
WENDY MARKHAM

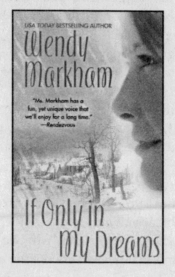

After stepping off an old-fashioned train on a movie set, Clara McCallum finds herself whisked back in time to 1941 and into the arms of Jed Landry, a man whom she has read about and knows will die a hero at Normandy three years later—or is it 62 years ago?

Clara's convinced it's some sort of hallucination, but before long she finds herself swept away by the handsome soldier, and wondering if her plunge into the past could change the course of the future—and turn out to be the best Christmas present ever.

Available wherever books are sold or at
penguin.com